Carla

THE
VIA
DOLOROSA

Michael Gryboski

Jan-Carol
Publishing, Inc
"every story needs a book"

Carla: The Via Dolorosa
Michael Gryboski
Published September 2024
Little Creek Books
Imprint of Jan-Carol Publishing, Inc.
All rights reserved
Copyright © 2024 Michael Gryboski
Front Cover Design: Tara Sizemore
Front Cover Photograph: © Jonathan Stutz/Adobe Stock

ISBN: 978-1-962561-42-6
Library of Congress Control Number: 2024947943

You may contact the publisher:
Jan-Carol Publishing, Inc.
PO Box 701
Johnson City, TN 37605
publisher@jancarolpublishing.com
www.jancarolpublishing.com

For God, Family, Country

ALSO BY MICHAEL GRYBOSKI:

CARLA

CARLA: THE ANTITHESIS KILLER

CARLA: THE END OF REASON

CARLA: THE CHERUB OF DEATH

CARLA: A DEATH IN PARIS

CARLA: THE DARK CYCLE

Table of Contents

I.

Alba Delacruz was a self-made woman. Born to a poor family living in a shantytown, Alba dreamed of more. Her first memories were of a crowded apartment complex, in which she shared a two-bedroom unit with five siblings and two working parents. Many times, they went without electricity or running water due to failures to raise enough money to pay the bills. Christmas involved simple gifts, like cheap dolls or finger-painted pictures. They always had food, at least to her memory. Perchance, being the youngest, she always got a share of what little was around, and thus did not recall any deprivations on that front. Alba remembered the more desperate times passing once her oldest siblings became old enough to join the workforce and contribute income.

Alba was a hard worker. She always said yes when her boss asked if she was able to stay late, and often worked double shifts at her various sources of employ. Many times, she came back to the apartment, drained and thoroughly sore. Blue collar work was her lot, given the lack of professional connections and her parents being unable to send any of their children to college. During the winter months, as the window for sunlight narrowed, Alba would go days at a time without ever seeing sunlight. The moon would be out when she entered the store, and the moon would be out when she exited. She rarely took vacations, again credited to the economic stresses of her upbringing. Her parents had encouraged all of their children to use the holidays as opportunities for shift work.

Alba had come a long way from that upbringing. It began when she had a boss who moonlighted as an arms dealer. Her work ethic won him over,

1

and so he brought her into his more shadowy enterprises. There was no hesitation on her part, neither was there much soul-searching as she delved ever deeper into the violent profession. For her, giving her siblings and parents nice gifts and being increasingly capable of paying their bills made up for any blood spilt. Before she had taken on increasing responsibilities for the illegal dealings of her jefe, Alba and her family simply survived. By the time she took his place in the syndicate, most of the Delacruz clan lived in houses.

Alba did not play favorites. Her business serviced groups regardless of creed, politic, or race. There were gangs that exchanged fire, and the guns pointed at each other all came from her. No faction felt particularly offended when learning of her wide range of clientele. She was the best at procuring arms, transporting drugs, and, as her financial standing only grew, providing loans. Although well-respected in the Latin American underworld, there was still some death threats, competitors, or outright nefarious rivals. A fair amount of her expenses came from providing security for both herself and her growing extended family. These efforts even included a personal food taster.

Alba was not alone that evening. She sat in a comfortable booth in the backroom of a popular restaurant, located within miles of the Rio Grande. A substantial part of her wealth had come from border crossings, both legitimate and otherwise. This led her to publicly identify as an "importer/ exporter" whenever polite society queried about her labors. Alba had been to the dining facility before, always on business. She trusted the cooks and the owner, who often catered meals at her palatial home. The food taster preferred the place, as he knew that his odds of being poisoned there were low.

The meeting was an amicable one. She wore her favorite red cocktail dress, with matching red heels that gave her an extra three inches of height. She carried a small black purse, which had in its pouch a photo identification card, a mirror, a tube of lipstick, and a miniature revolver. She had bright red lipstick on, with a touch of color added to her cheeks, and deep thin lines along her eyes. Alba had never learned to drive, but the issue was moot given her security. She had yet to kill someone personally yet was ready to do so if necessary. She had never married, though she often flirted with potential male clients.

The man for which she was negotiating business with that evening was yet another to receive the occasional light affection. Technically, he was more powerful. He oversaw a cartel whose soldiers outnumbered her security force by four to one. When not dealing with external setbacks, the combined output of the plantations and businesses under his domain churned out more product than everything belonging to Alba. He was similarly self-made, having gradually risen through the ranks of the cartel, eventually becoming its leader when his predecessor had been assassinated.

He was a lover of the late twentieth century films that featured Latin American cartel villains. While these figures were not meant by their creators to be glorified, he had taken a different route. He had modeled his own look after those cinematic idols, growing his jet-black hair into a short ponytail, and frequently wearing black shirts with a rolled-up bright jacket. He was known to wear a fair amount of gold jewelry, just to cap off the appearance. He fancied himself a powerful figure, with his large cartel army, strong array of armed backup, and gigantic hacienda.

Raul Torquemada was not bargaining from a position of power, however. Alba was cognizant of this, and the underlying issues had been a source of tenuous conversation as soon as they sat down at the private booth. There was no shouting, no signs of overt incivility. And yet, Torquemada and Dela-cruz were struggling to make terms on the details of their business exchange. He wanted more, she questioned why. She wanted a certain percentage, he argued that it should be lower. Their words went unheard by most everyone else in the facility, as the booths on either side of theirs remained empty. Only two security men, one provided by Alba and the other by Torquemada, were nearby. Also, there was the food taster, who readied for the next assignment as the waitress came.

At that point, there were a few things on the tabletop. This included two cylindrical glasses containing water and ice, as well as two wine glasses containing red fermented liquid. They had clear stems and a wide bulb shape, which helped to allow the aroma to reach the nostrils before the first sip was taken. There were also two small plates, each five inches in diameter, which had had salads on them. Delacruz and Torquemada had picked clean the appetizers, putting the plates and salad forks to the side as they continued to speak to one another, sometimes amiably, sometimes not.

Alba saw the young woman arrive, causing the dialogue to die down. As with her coworkers, the waitress wore a white button-up shirt with red ascot, black slacks, and black shoes with flat heels. Compared to the petite Alba, she was rather tall. Nevertheless, she was shorter than Torquemada when he stood straight. She had skin as pale as Alba, but also had puffy blonde hair that seemed fake, and a pair of thick-rimmed black glasses on her face. She stood at the edge of the booth between the two figures of power, balancing the silver platter that had the warm ordered meals on top. As she bent forward to put the plates in front of the two guests, Alba noticed a faint scar along the side of her face. The thin line went from her forehead down to the space between the corner of her eye and her ear. The thickness of the blonde curls nearly obscured the scar, but failed.

Alba had ordered three chicken quesadillas, with the peppers and spices removed per her request. This was done for two reasons. The first was for security purposes, as it reduced the number of ingredients that could be used to poison her. The second was preference, as Alba defied the stereotype and actually hated spicy foods. She attributed this to her upbringing, as her parents often skirted on spices for baked meals for financial reasons. Torquemada ordered a well-done steak, with potatoes and a second helping of salad. Both were given a new set of utensils for their meals, with a fork, knife, and spoon wrap in a textured napkin. Each was carefully put alongside the respective dish.

As the waitress began putting things onto the booth table, she was careful to mind a small tablet hidden behind one of the plates on her platter. As she picked up one plate, she took control of the capsule by pinching it between her pinky and her ring finger on her right hand. After placing the plate down on the table, she retracted her arm a little. As she made this fleeting motion, Alba and the food taster were looking at her sumptuous-looking meal, while Torquemada was looking at Alba. The two security guards were looking around the large dining room. As a result, none of them saw the waitress drop the tablet into the wine glass of Alba, where it quickly dissolved.

"Buen provecho," the waitress stated as a formality before leaving the booth.

"Ven aquí," Alba ordered the food taster.

He was happy to do so, as quesadillas were a personal favorite. With a knife and a fork of his own, he cut into each triangular crust, taking a piece and putting it in his mouth. While he never viewed himself in a chivalrous light, Torquemada patiently waited before beginning to eat his food. He was not inclined to take such precautions, despite his company insisting in earlier correspondence that he should. Torquemada looked down for a moment, trying to mask the feeling that such precautions were unnecessary, especially for a woman like Alba. The food taster stood there for a few moments, still and unharmed. He smiled, having never really doubted his chances of survival, and took a few steps back.

Torquemada took this as the cue that he was allowed to begin eating. Included on his platter was a small cup of sauce, which he immediately poured upon the long frame of the cooked meat. He then punctured the steak with a pointed knife and the prongs of his fork, hearing a slight squeak as the blade made it all the way down to the ceramic surface of the plate. Yet, as he looked up, he saw Alba crossing herself. He had heard no words and did not see her lips move or even her eyes close, but he did see the religious motion and a judgmental look from the businesswoman.

"What is it?" he asked, their conversation being in Spanish.

"You do not pray before eating?" she inquired.

"No."

"You should," she said, in a motherly tone. "I am not a religious woman, but I want as much protection as possible before putting something in my body."

"I understand."

"I recommend it," Alba stated. "It might even save your life."

"I will think about it," said the cartel leader, trying to be more accommodating.

"Muy bien," she said between bites. "Are you able to think of my offer, also?"

"Is it final?" asked Torquemada, who was less than thrilled by her most recent proposal regarding the loan and its interest.

"Definitely," she said.

Torquemada went over the details in his mind. He took advantage of the presence of food to fill his mouth with pieces of steak. As he chewed, he saw his company sitting confident. She knew that he would have to say yes, eventually. Torquemada was trying to force himself to accept the terms. While the interest rate was high and the price of the shipping considerable, he had few alternative options. As he was willing himself to accept, Alba swallowed a little more than she had planned of one of the quesadillas. Rather than go for the glass of water, she reached for the wine glass. The crimson liquid helped to push the food down, with her finishing off all but the dregs.

"I admit, it is a better offer than I thought," said the cartel leader. "Your business is very strong, and my expenses will be smaller than my long-term gains."

"Verdad," said Alba, her confidence growing.

As he was about to further cushion the blow of accepting a deal that was not fully to his liking, Alba felt a little off. At first, it was a sudden need to take a deep breath, and that breath not being enough. Her head began to hurt, especially around the temples. Then, her breathing gradually grew more intense, as though she was walking instead of sitting down. Pain started to introduce itself to her left side. Initially, she thought it was her arm falling asleep, or just a minor bit of pain that comes with living. Yet the sensation became worse, and then it spread to her left arm. It was becoming horrific enough that she was unable to suppress the misery and began to massage her arm.

"Alba," said her company. "Esta bien?"

The pain sharpened; her breaths became gasps as though she were drowning. She began to flail on her side of the booth, her body knocking over the glass of water, its clear liquid and chilled cubes splashing onto the tabletop. The food taster and the security rushed to her as she fell on to the cushioned seating, her face looking upward in her struggle for life. Demands were shouted for an ambulance, to which a few patrons took out their phones and called for one. Torquemada stood up from his seat, staring at Alba as her eyes closed, but the heavy breathing and the anguish continued.

* * *

"Buen provecho," Carla al-Hassan Sharp said to the two guests.

The two patrons barely gave her much attention as the food taster came in from her right in order to confirm that the meal was not poisoned. Carla then turned around, continuously telling herself to not walk too fast, lest the security detail for the cartel leader and the arms dealer become suspicious of her. She knew that the capsule would act quickly; however, she did not know when the target was going to drink the wine again. Before that evening, Carla had practiced the delicate handling of the capsule while also putting the plate down, with her failing most of the time. It was all one careful, fragile, yet hopefully successful operation to snuff out a malicious entity.

Carla became less tense as the distance grew between her and the booth. The guards were not running after her, no one was calling for her, either by her real name or her fake one that she gave to the restaurant when applying for work weeks earlier. The capsule drop was not the first poisoning in the operation, as she had had to make sure that the waitress scheduled to cover that part of the restaurant became violently ill before her shift began. Carla achieved this through lacing her packed food with a nonlethal substance. Within the next 24 to 48 hours, the waitress would make a full recovery.

Carla did not look back, tempted as she was to do so. Peering over her shoulder presented a risk of discovery. Neither did she stop walking once she got out of the range of vision for the security. She had no idea how long it was until the tablet was consumed. Indeed, she was not even sure if the tablet was going to be consumed. Carla and her handler knew that it was very likely that the target might not drink from the glass again; although, research into her life had indicated that she always finished her wine at a meal. As such, putting the pill in the wine rather than the water increased their odds.

Carla kept going. She went back into the kitchen, camouflaged by the hectic atmosphere of the dinner hour. Cooks were busy baking, waiters and waitresses darted to and fro, taking up individual dishes with each hand, or undertaking a platter with the orders placed upon them. Washers cleaned the dishes, either using machines or sponges. A pair of cleaners made sure to go about the room, between the machines and the people, replacing trash bags, picking up discarded ingredients and other items. Everyone was doing something that compelled them to ignore one lone waitress.

After getting by the rest of the staff sans problem, Carla entered the women's locker room in the back. Most of the female staff came to the restaurant in their street clothes, changed in the locker room before their shift, and then returned to change back before leaving. The walls had dark blue lockers all along them, with a row of them in the middle of the room. A gray topless trashcan with a black bag and an opening that was two feet wide was stationed near the door. The implication was that waitresses would toss anything unacceptable for their shift last minute before entering the restaurant proper.

Carla removed the wig, her black hair cut short and flattened by a net, and threw it into the can. The thick-rimmed spectacles went as well, their frames being only glass. She removed the buttoned-up shirt next, revealing a sleeveless white undershirt. Normally, Carla did not prefer to wear such revealing tops. However, a concern over perspiring during the operation led her to wear the less modest option. Everything had to appear normal, up until the moment that the target drank the wine. From there, she went to her locker, quickly did the combination, took out a brown jacket, and closed it for the last time. There was only one other woman in the room, but she was on the other side of the median of lockers, and thus did not notice Carla. Waitresses so often came and went into the facility that few who had worked there long gave much attention to the sounds of others.

Carla went toward the door at the back of the locker room. It was the entrance that employees were supposed to use when coming in for shifts and leaving after clocking out. Carla did not clock out that night, nor would she ever return to do so. Even as the door between the kitchen and the locker room opened, she stayed focused on the exit. She pursed her lips together and kept her stride, deciding that she would not turn around, even if the people behind her were the security detail itself. Again, she was spared a confrontation, as whomever entered the locker room made no effort to get her attention. Most likely, it was a coworker or two either taking a break or leaving for the night.

Upon departing the building, Carla got a faint gust of cool wind when entering the outside. The restaurant and the town for which it was based were in the desert. As such, nightfall made for chilly air. Before her was an alleyway, which was used by the local trash pickup when they made runs along the strip of restaurants and businesses planted on that part of the town. Her eventide walk was not going to last, as a black SUV was parked several feet away from the employee entrance. Its lights were on, facing down the way, and its muffler gave off a small plume of smoke.

She recognized the driver as she neared the vehicle. He was a tan-skinned Latino with well-combed black hair who, when standing, was the same height as Carla. He grinned as he saw her approaching his car. She did not reciprocate the gesture, though she was relieved to see him rather than a cartel soldier or another potential hostile party. From her vantage point, she saw the driver pressing something. A moment later, she heard the door unlock. Carla grabbed the handle, pulled open the passenger door behind the driver, and hopped into the SUV. No sooner did she slam the door than Alfredo Hernandez put the vehicle in drive and went off. The radio was off as Carla buckled her seatbelt.

"You dropped it in, I assume?" he asked.

"Yes."

"Here's hoping that she drinks it," said Hernandez, who turned left to get out of the alleyway and onto a proper street. "Señorita Delacruz was known to love her wines."

"Verdad."

"Muy bien," said Hernandez.

Before the driver was able to make another comment, possibly another query into the implementation of the plan, both he and Carla heard the noise. It was faint at first, barely registering over the sounds of other engines. A vague hounding, a sound of panic. As it got closer, the flashing lights were visible, then the vehicle itself. The cubic emergency transport rushed past stopped cars and through traffic signals with impunity. Driver and passenger beheld the ambulance as it sped toward the restaurant, slowing down as it got to the front of the establishment.

"I guess it worked," Hernandez commented, shrugging his shoulders.

9

"Yeah," said Carla, looking down. "It did."

* * *

Speeding through the traffic, sirens blaring and horns sounding, the ambulance was as a mechanical lightning bolt darting through the streets. Within the back of the vehicle, paramedics tried their best to keep the woman alive. An oxygen mask covered her nose and mouth, and a defibrillator was charged and used multiple times. For a moment, it seemed as though she had been brought back. The beeping of the vital signs was weak, but consistent. And yet, as the ambulance neared the hospital, she again went into death throes, the medical professionals fighting a losing battle. Again, the line was straight; again, the long note announcing a dead body sounded in the vehicle.

Torquemada had been with her in the ambulance. He had entered the moving room along with two security guards and the food taster, who was unharmed. Once the vehicle came to a full stop, the back swung open with the paramedics taking the dying patient with them, rolling the gurney down the incline and then onto the pavement of the lot in front of the hospital. They rushed into the entrance, a wide space opened up by automatic doors which parted to allow them entry. Torquemada and the others tried to keep pace, jogging along with the fast-moving personnel and their gurney. Efforts continued to try and revive her, then efforts moved toward putting her on life support.

In the minutes that passed, others joined the nefarious people who knew her. They included a pair of cartel people who answered to Torquemada. One of them was a young man named Pedro Aguilares. Nearly six feet tall, muscular, and sporting a stubby black beard, he was occasionally mistaken as a hired gun rather than an increasingly prominent member of the cartel. He had an inherent respect for Torquemada, which was reciprocated. All of them continued to wait, having been ordered to remain outside of the emergency wing of the facility. A couple of those under the employ of the dying patient had spoken of forcing their way into the area where their boss was suffering, but they were overruled. The food taster was the most visibly distraught, having cried much of the time.

Finally, a woman wearing light blue scrubs went through the doors between the emergency room and the waiting area. She recognized the people who had been with the paramedics when they first arrived. She approached with caution and dourness, likely fearing the backlash she would receive once she gave the news. Although neither Torquemada nor any of the others had informed the staff of their identities, there was something about them that betrayed their underworld affiliations. Nevertheless, she walked up to them, with Torquemada meeting her halfway.

"Well?" he asked.

"Unfortunately," she began, the food taster crying once again at the utterance of the one word, "she did not survive." The doctor shifted in her posture, a moment of silence so that the men gathered in the waiting room could absorb the news. "It appears that she had a massive heart attack. She just was not strong enough to endure the trauma."

"I see," Torquemada said calmly, understanding that his very presence wrought trepidation. He pointed at the food taster and the two security guards with him. "They will want the body. Talk with them."

"Claro, señor," she replied, and then walked over to discuss the details with those who were once employed by the late Alba Delacruz.

"Este es muy mal, mi jefe, muy mal," Pedro whispered to him.

"Yo sé," said Torquemada, hands on his hips and head bowed.

"We needed that deal," Pedro continued. "This is the third person we have tried to do business with this year who has ended up dying suddenly."

"Then you agree with me," said Torquemada. "This was not a natural death. Muy obvioso, no?"

"Sí, mi jefe."

"We are being starved to death."

"I agree," said Pedro. "With respect, what can we do about it?"

"I will think of something."

"The other lieutenants will not be happy," said Pedro. "They expected better results with this one. You told them that this one was guaranteed."

"Yo sé, Pedro, yo sé," said Torquemada, visibly annoyed. "I am still the head of the cartel. I am still unchallenged. The lieutenants are permitted to grumble as they please. Not one of them has the power to take me on."

"Punto bueno, mi jefe."

"Ultimately, they will fall in line, as they always do," Torquemada assured Pedro. "They know that no one else has the drive or the will or the ability to run the cartel. I know you will not join their efforts."

"Claro, no."

"Muy bien," said Torquemada. "Therefore, they have no one. There is no one they can rally behind. At least, no one who is still alive."

"Yes, I remember Señor Brennenberg," said Pedro, identifying the very figure that his superior was alluding to. "He was as competent as he was frightening."

"I admit to you alone that I had fear of him, too," said Torquemada, who began to slowly walk away from the waiting room, with Pedro and the other cartel figures following suit. "His sadism was disturbing, even by our standards. A part of me is glad that someone shot him dead during our last effort in the United States."

"Tambien."

"Well," said Torquemada. "We must get back to the hacienda. We will continue to talk with whomever takes over Señorita Delacruz's business. It is possible that they will want to do business with us regardless."

"Yes, it is possible."

"Doubtful," admitted the cartel leader. "But, still, it is possible."

* * *

It was the darkest of night at the airstrip. A dearth of city lights made many a constellation visible to the souls below. Vacant space was found on all sides. A line of mountains was off in the distance. Sometimes, a desert creature lumbered about or glided in its crawl. Yet, they stayed far away from the little oasis of civilization, which included three dark gray buildings, a large hangar of the same shade, and a long-paved road used by the flying mechanical beasts. At that hour, few were around the small landing spot. This was intentional, for common traffic was not permitted.

Carla and Hernandez were there, with the latter having parked the black SUV in a small lot beside one of the gray buildings. They were joined by Marisol Contreras, the fiancée of Hernandez. She was a young woman who, against the advice of her love, joined them at the border area for the operation. The only one of the three who was still in their twenties, Marisol bore a faint resemblance to Carla in that she had black hair and pale skin. However, she was a few inches shorter and lacked any scars. Marisol still struggled with English, so the three kept to Español for their conversations.

For the time, though, they were not speaking. Instead, they were gathered at a recreation room located in one of the buildings. The room occupied the whole of the first floor of the two-story structure, and included two pool tables, four vending machines, a flat screen television with cable that was hooked up in the corner, and three pinball machines lined up, side-by-side. There were two couches that formed a right angle that were facing the television, as well as three other couches lines along the walls. On one end of the room were three card tables with metal folding chairs, along with a dresser drawer full of various board games, dice, poker chips, and decks of cards, with various designs.

Carla, Alfredo, and Marisol were seated at one of the round tables, using one of the available decks. They had gotten sodas from one of the vending machines, which they periodically drank from while concentrating on the game. In the middle of the table was a growing pile of cards that were face down. The game was commonly called BS by the two Americans, their Central American friend being unfamiliar with it. Each player had to put down the next number or coat in the proper sequence, even if they did not have the correct card. At some point, everyone had to bluff. As the pile grew, the three players listened to a news report on Hernandez's smart phone.

"The woman was then rushed to the hospital, having suffered an apparent heart attack," explained the newscaster. "We have just gotten word that she has passed away. At present, her identity is being kept confidential until her next of kin can be notified..."

"Pero, we know her name," said Hernandez with a smile, dropping two cards onto the pile and then stating what he claimed the facedown cards were: "Two sixes."

"Yes," said Carla, adding to the pile. "One seven."

Hernandez gritted his teeth.

"If you want to say it, say it," Carla challenged him.

Hernandez waved it off.

"Your turn, Marisol," Carla said.

"Did you BS us?" asked Hernandez while his fiancée put down one eight with honesty.

"It was a two," she admitted.

Hernandez growled in feigned anger. "Next time I think you are lying, I am calling you out." The handler put down two more cards. "Two nines."

"Can we listen to music, please?" Marisol asked. "We already know she is dead."

"Very well," said Hernandez, who picked up his smart phone and exited out of the livestreamed newscast. He then selected a playlist with some modern R&B, which he knew Marisol liked and that Carla was able to tolerate. "My turn?"

"Sí, señor," Carla replied. "You need to have one queen. Una regina."

"And I have one," Hernandez countered, the number of cards in his hand becoming quite small. The case was similar to Carla, while Marisol had the most. "Una regina."

Carla stared at her handler, hesitating to take her turn.

"Adelante, Carla. If you think I am lying, say so."

Carla was still silent. She thought about it.

"It is your turn, Carla."

"I am calling it," she said, still looking at Alfredo. "BS!"

Hernandez grinned a sadistic grin. Carla was already doubting her decision, yet she was unable to take it back. Alfredo maintained his smile, even as he took hold of the card on the top of the pile, flipped it over, and revealed to the table that it was an ace. Marisol shouted in amusement, while Carla breathed the air of relief. Hernandez put both hands on the flat pile and pulled in the twenty-some cards that were his as a result of being held accountable. His fiancée was laughing at him as he struggled to put them all into order, keeping their various identities hidden from his two opponents.

"Now you suffer," Marisol told her love.

"I will make a comeback," he promised, then turned to Carla. "How did you know?"

"I did not know," Carla corrected. "To be honest, I do not have a king, so I was going to get all these cards if I had been wrong anyway."

"You are smart, Carla," said Marisol. "So, your turn."

"I just admitted that I do not have a king. Por lo tanto, it is your turn."

"Three aces," said Marisol, putting down three cards.

"One moment," said Hernandez, still sifting through his large gathering of numbers and suits. "Okay then. Two twos."

Their game was interrupted by the soaring sound emanating from the outside. It was not from the desolate nature around the airstrip, nor was it the moaning engine of a land vehicle. The control tower was in another building on the property, with a pair of personnel guiding the pilot down to the tarmac. The three were able to see the descending ship from a window in the rec room, a shadow on the night sky punctuated with a few lights. It rumbled all the louder as it sped to the strip, its wheels revealing themselves. Carla and her peers did not watch the landing but got ready for the journey.

"Now, as a reminder, the plane will take you to the D.C. area first," Hernandez explained as the three got up, with Marisol cleaning up the cards and putting them away. "There, you will be debriefed by Mavis. After that, you will take a commercial flight back home. I am assuming that Josiah and Laila will be thrilled to see you again."

"If she still remembers me," said the mother of the toddler.

"You were only here for five weeks," said Marisol. "Kids aren't that stupid, are they?"

"Hopefully not."

"Ojala," Marisol said, nodding.

Carla had a rolling suitcase for which her various things had been packed. She left behind several other items, clothes and the like, which were part of her cover and thus viewed as expendable. She had been permitted a laptop, which she used to try and communicate with family. This was a challenge, as the signal strength for the wireless was of low quality. There were schedule issues, as she worked evenings at the restaurant while her husband worked during the day. The laptop remained in possession of the Agency, which erased any and all personal information.

"Your beloved chariot awaits," Hernandez stated as the three stood on the tarmac before the private airplane.

The vessel was smaller than the typical commercial plane, having only eight seats for passengers. No stewardesses or other travelers would be on the flight. The propeller was still rotating as a crew checked the quality of the frame and refueled the engine. It was an unsuspecting plane, with a generic white paint job and an alphanumeric identification marked along both wings and the midsection. A metal stair truck with railing was pushed to the open side of the ship. Given the slant of the body of the plane when on the ground, the top stair was not perfectly parallel to the entry. However, no one believed this to be a point of concern, as Carla lacked any mobility issues.

"Vaya con Dios, Carla," said Hernandez.

"Y tu, tambien," she replied.

"Adios, Carla," said Marisol as she and the agent hugged. "See you at the wedding?"

"Por supuesto," Carla answered with a smile.

Carla waved at the two with her free hand as she walked across the landing strip to the stairs. The crew had done their inspection and filled the tank. The pilot, who had taken the brief respite to walk up and down the aisle of the plane, was back at the cockpit. Carla dragged the luggage up the metal stairs, lifting the heavy suitcase over each step. She had to crouch down to get into the plane, again lugging her suitcase behind her. As the lone passenger, she had her choice of seats. As Carla sat down and buckled up, one of the crew closed the door to the plane. Within a couple of minutes, the plane slowly turned around, then sped up, and propelled upward into the heavens, sending her back to the United States.

II.

Governor Josiah Sharp was in a meeting at his office. The 30-something executive leader was in his usual business attire of a tie and slacks, plus a button-up shirt with collar. The dress code for the others in the room was of a similar level of formality. Women in the meeting wore either a dress or a pant-suit. The only man with a dinner jacket on was Attorney General Kyle Brown, who was the oldest figure present. This point was driven home by his all-gray hair and deeply wrinkled skin. Communications Director James Colbert, who also assisted with leading the staff, was one of the younger people present. He was growing out his curls again, at the behest of his girlfriend.

Sharp was sitting at his desk. It was a polished, thick piece of wooden furniture that had several drawers. Governor Sharp had placed a few personal effects on the top, including a wedding photo of him and Carla, a photo of his immediate family, and also two framed Bible quotes, which he'd had since his days as an assistant district attorney. The one on his right was Leviticus 24:22, "You are to have the same law for the foreigner and the native-born. I am the LORD your God." The one on his left came from James 2:10, "For whoever keeps the whole law and yet stumbles at just one point is guilty of breaking all of it." He also kept a Bible on a small table near his desk.

Other people present sat on office chairs with either three or four wheels, ranging in color from black to gray. To the right of Sharp were two windows made of bulletproof glass, which were covered by dark-blue curtains. The ceiling above was white, while a chandelier hung down from the center. To the left of Sharp were four framed posters, each one showing a former governor. Other portraits of past executives were found elsewhere in the building. All of them were in black-and-white. The wall behind Sharp had a sideboard and two filing cabinets, as well as an American flag and a state flag on opposite corners. When he had first arrived at the office a couple of years ago, he was taken by the chamber. As he held his regular staff meeting that morning, it was just another day in the same room.

"And what are the numbers?" Sharp asked Colbert.

"Very good, sir, very good," said the staffer with glee. "According to the metrics, the state economy grew for the sixth straight month. We created a total of 3,500 jobs, according to the data. That brings the official unemployment rate down to 3.2%."

"That really is very good," the governor remarked.

"I can remember my time in the previous administration," Brown commented. "Back then, we used to say that we would never see unemployment below six percent in our lifetime. I guess you proved them wrong, Josiah."

"Glory," he said under his breath. "You will be sure to have the press release out by lunchtime, right, James?"

"Just shoot me an email with a nice quote after the meeting, and I will have it out by brunch," Colbert confidently replied, getting a few smiles from the other staffers.

"Any litigation updates, Kyle?" Sharp asked Brown.

"Well," he began, one of the other staffers sitting by him and handing him some notes on the latest updates, "thanks to successful legal efforts elsewhere, the lawsuits filed against our abortion restrictions have effectively stopped. One got rejected outright by a court of appeals, while the plaintiffs in the second one have dropped it."

"That second one was the capital-based clinic, right?"

"Correct," said Brown, whose aide also nodded. "It was basically a technicality. You see, the clinic only had one official abortion provider on staff. He just retired, which means right now the clinic is only providing birth control and counseling. In other words, nothing particularly objectionable."

"Unless you're an ultra-strict Catholic," interjected one of the female staffers, getting a nod from the attorney general.

"As for the lawsuit about the freedom of information act, that one is nearing a settlement," Brown continued. "Basically, it looks like it was one big misunderstanding about some paperwork. We are working with the plaintiffs, and hopefully, their request will be successfully processed."

"Remind me, what were they looking into, anyway?" Sharp inquired.

"State files on elected officials who were part of the Cicero Organization. You know, things like personal memos and items like that. If I recall the details of the case correctly, the plaintiffs are two reporters trying to write a book about the Cicero group and its many political connections."

"Seems innocent enough," said Sharp. "Any other legal updates?"

"One more," Brown recalled. "A gun rights group just filed a complaint over our state's assault weapons ban. They claim it is an unconstitutional overreach and puts them in danger of being arrested for owning assault rifles that they bought before the law took effect."

"Correct me if I am wrong, but I seem to remember that law explicitly stating that it would not apply to assault weapons purchased before it took effect," said Sharp.

"Yes, it does. But, of course, objective facts have never gotten in the way of someone filing a lawsuit," noted Brown.

"That echoes my experiences in the Justice Department," Sharp said, getting a laugh and a nod from Colbert. "Well, if that is everything, I guess we can call this meeting adjourned."

"No motion or second?" asked Colbert, feigning seriousness.

"Shut up and get out of here, James," replied the governor.

The various staffers rose from their respective office chairs, either rolling them away from the room to return to their desks, or putting them to the side, as they belonged to the specific chamber where the meeting was held. They broke into assorted banal conversations, joking and chatting as they went away from the room. There were some light exchanges between Sharp and his peers lacking any business substance. Things were in a leisurely mood, as the state was improving on all fronts, with Sharp's approval rating remaining high. It was a good time to be in charge.

As the doors to the room were opened and staff members trickled out, a woman stood waiting to cross the threshold into the space. She had black hair that went down to her neck, having recently trimmed it. Her pale complexion and American upbringing made many assume that she was Caucasian, though in the geographic sense, she was Middle Eastern. She was fluent in English and Spanish, being semi-fluent in what was technically her native tongue. She was slightly taller than two of the three women who passed by her, though a couple of inches shorter than Colbert as he walked by. As the people made way and she stood alone, Josiah recognized her at once, and rushed to hug her.

"You're back!" he declared, the two embracing and kissing. "When did you come in?"

"Only an hour ago," Carla al-Hassan Sharp responded.

"How are you?"

"Tolerable," she remarked as Josiah closed the doors to the office. "I already saw Laila before coming here."

"She must have been thrilled to see you."

"Actually," said Carla as she sat at one of the chairs left over from the meeting, "she was still asleep when I got back."

"Yeah, she has been a good sleeper," said Josiah.

"Good to hear."

"Oh!" said Josiah, taking out his smart phone from his pants pocket. "I nearly forgot to show you the big development."

"What big development?" asked a confused Carla.

"Hold on..." said Josiah, looking down at his phone, hastily tapping away to get to a saved video. "Found it."

"Found what?"

"Check this out," he said, holding the screen in front of his wife. "This happened about a week after you left."

Carla looked down at the rectangular screen, her husband right behind her. Her confusion melted away as she saw the amateur video of her daughter. The cute little child, with the same pale skin and black hair that her mother had, was holding onto the seat of a living room chair. Her tiny back was against the phone, but she turned and smiled at the adult filming her. Carla was proud of the little child, who, with one hand on the seat, turned to the camera and took a few steps. With encouragement voiced off camera by her father, she took a few more steps before slowly falling to all fours. Carla felt like crying, perplexing Josiah as he looked at her, assuming that she would be happy.

"Amazing, isn't it?"

"Yeah."

"She will be happy to see you again."

"I hope she recognizes me," said Carla, looking down. "I never liked being away before. However, with Laila, I really hate being away. Every time I come back, I feel like I am missing years of her life."

"You already know how I would respond to what you said, so I will not say it."

"Thank you," said Carla, weary of the conversation that her husband always seemed to bring up whenever her profession interfered with having a normal life.

"You know, apart from crafting some quote for yet another press release, I do not really have anything scheduled for today," said Josiah, with Carla looking up. "I am sure I can leave the office early, so we can be together."

"Sounds good," she said, smiling.

* * *

"I think my favorite granddaughter should say grace," said George al-Hassan.

Carla gave a wry smile but agreed to the request. She and her grandfather crossed themselves in the Eastern manner, going up-down-right-left, while George's wife, Elnora, crossed herself in the Western manner of up-down-left-right. Josiah, the lone Protestant, simply bowed his head and closed his eyes. Laila, still small enough to require a highchair, slowly looked around at the adults at the table, holding her arms in a random posture. As Carla briefly gave words of thanks to God for the meal, the little one said "baa, baa, baa" for no apparent reason other than to get attention. The infantile comment was ignored by the adults, with three of the four crossing themselves shortly after.

The dinner was held at the governor's mansion. The Sharps and the al-Hassans had originally planned to alternate locations when having dinner together, bouncing between the landlord's apartment where the latter lived or the governor's mansion of the former. After a while, they agreed that, given the high profile of the Sharps, it was more practical to have their family dinners at the mansion. Furthermore, the security detail for the governor and his wife considered the mansion more ideal for safety, noting their greater familiarity with the space as well as the various measures already taken.

Three of the four adults at the table ate slices of pizza. This meal had not been delivered, but rather was prepared by the culinary staff. Carla had not yet partaken of the food on her plate, instead using a fork and knife to chop up a piece of pizza for Laila to eat. Her daughter had gotten to the point where she could feed herself, provided she focused on the effort. With the slice chopped into mostly square pieces, Laila was encouraged to eat. She smiled at her mother, took hold of one of the pieces while lightly kicking her legs in the air, and put the food in her mouth, slowly chewing it.

"I think Laila's table manners are improving," said Elnora.

"I have been training her well," Josiah said. "A month ago, she would have thrown the food on the floor and then laughed."

"Carla was the same way as a toddler," said George. "There were many days when whole meals were on the floor below her chair."

"Hey, Giddo," Carla said to George. "Please don't give Laila any ideas."

"What, you think she can understand me?"

"They say toddlers develop comprehension abilities faster than speaking abilities," said Josiah. "Just because Laila cannot form full sentences does not mean she cannot understand what we are saying."

"Full sentences?" asked Carla, staring at Josiah at the revelation. "You mean, she has already said her first word?"

"Words, actually," Josiah corrected her. "I have heard the occasional 'mama' and 'pa,' as well as the occasional 'no.' Though she does not use them regularly yet."

"And when did this happen?"

"Two weeks ago," said Josiah. "Sorry, but I keep failing to catch it on camera."

"Carla learned 'no' very quickly," said George. "As soon as she realized the power of the word, she used it all the time." George looked up in recollection. "Carla, eat your dinner. 'No.' Carla, time to take your bath. 'No!'"

"Oh, Giddo," stated the granddaughter.

"My eldest son's first word was 'hi,'" Elnora chimed in. "Every time I took him to the grocery store with me, he would say 'hi' to everyone he saw."

"I thought your son's first word was 'kitty,'" asked a confused George.

"That was my younger son's first word. You remember Oakley, right?"

"Oh, yes, now I do. The lawyer."

"Yes," Elnora said, nodding. "Well, before he became a lawyer, he was a baby who was enamored with my newly bought tabby cat. So, he always loved to say 'kitty' every time he showed up." Elnora started laughing. "When he got to be a kid, Oakley used to always chase the poor cat. He would shout, 'Chase the kitty! Chase the kitty!' as he did so. When he became an attorney, I told him that he went from chasing cats to chasing ambulances. He was somewhat amused."

"I bet he was," said Josiah.

"Ma-ma-ma," said Laila, getting the attention of the adults.

"Laila, eat more of your dinner," Carla kindly ordered, then turned to the others. "I am pretty sure that was just random syllables and not the actual word."

"I fear you are correct," said her husband. "She will get it down soon enough."

"Can you say 'grandpa,' Laila?" George asked the little one. "Grand-pa?"

Laila simply smiled, opening her mouth to reveal a mostly toothless interior.

"She is getting closer," George claimed. "Soon enough, she will know."

"Soon enough," Carla agreed. "It is good to be back. I really mean it."

"Same," said Josiah. "There were times in the middle of the night when I could tell Laila wanted you to calm her down and not me."

"And yes, Josiah, I will deal with her if she wakes up tonight."

"I love you, Carla," said Josiah, with him and his wife laughing at his remark.

"When are you planning to leave the country again?" asked Elnora, who, like her husband, George, was not fully aware of all the things Carla did for the Agency.

"For now, I am on-call," said Carla. "I have to go back into the office tomorrow. At that point, I will find out more."

"Don't they know that you have a young daughter?" Elnora asked. "Back in my day, employers gave more consideration for that."

"Yeah, I agree, Carla," said Josiah. "You should have a talk with Hernandez and Chalmers about staying here more. Maybe even retire."

"Sounds like a good idea to me," George interjected before Carla could respond. "I have been retired for years now, and it is a lot of fun."

"Maybe Josiah just doesn't like being the one who always has to wake up in the middle of the night to put Laila back to sleep," Elnora suggested.

"Being the only diaper changer is not fun, either," admitted Josiah.

"I will talk with Hernandez, and he will talk with Chalmers," said Carla, again looking to check on Laila's high chair table, which had only a couple of pizza pieces remaining. "Maybe something can be worked out."

"I pray for it, daily," Josiah whispered to Carla, who nodded in response.

"Pa-pa-pa!" said Laila, throwing one arm in the arm and looking at George.

"A very wise point, Laila," Josiah smartly remarked.

"She almost had it," said George. "Maybe next dinner."

"Maybe," said Carla.

* * *

Carla always got to her current occupation on time. This was not the product of being an especially punctual person. To the contrary, growing up, Carla often struggled to get to her shifts in the customer service industry when she was supposed to clock in. Rather, the way from the governor's mansion to the government building that housed the Central Intelligence Agency branch office was made clear by the short motorcade of black SUVs who got priority on the road. The onlookers of the city were never aware of who specifically was being ferried from the mansion in such a way, as Carla began her commute in the parking garage below the mansion, away from curious eyes.

She was rarely seen in her journey from the garage parking lot of the government building to the upper floor where her often abandoned cubicle was situated. It was a simple elevator trip between the two points. Carla did not socialize much with her coworkers either. There was no hostility, just only basic contact. There was not a lot of need for her to fraternize with them, as nearly all of her work involved her speaking with either her handler, Alfredo Hernandez, or the director, Mavis Chalmers. Fleeting statements of "good morning" and "hello" were exchanged as she got to her seat.

Carla was drowsy. She yawned much between the mansion and the building. Laila had decided to welcome her mother back by crying in the middle of the night on at least three occasions. Carla failed to get more than an hour of deep sleep at a time before the little one screamed. After the second time, Carla resolved to get out of bed only if the crying persisted. Unfortunately for her, that subjective measurement was easily broken. Each time she arrived to gently hold and comfort her daughter, Laila calmed down pretty quickly. When she finally got a long period of silence, Carla remained unable to fully rest. By that point, she kept wondering if the quiet was evidence of wrong.

Carla sipped coffee as she clicked on the icon on her desktop that allowed her to go online. She signed into her work email, quickly sifting through the mostly unimportant electronic missives. With that tab still up, she went to a couple of Spanish-language news sites, searching for updates on the death of the arms dealer. There were a few reports, often citing and linking back to the same original sources. The official story still held that the death was natural, most likely a previously undocumented heart condition. A few comments posted expressed skepticism, claiming that more nefarious forces were at work. However, no one had solid evidence of such imaginings.

Hernandez was drawing near. Carla saw him past her cubicle wall. She heard him banter with a couple of others in the office. She did not feel dread at his coming near, but she was focused on the development. She was going to put forth an old argument with new points. In a way, she had been desensitized by the effort, as the request had been made multiple times before sans harmful consequences. She got up from her office chair as he arrived, smiling and with a bottle of orange juice in his right hand.

"Buenos dias, Señora Sharp," he said.

"Buenos dias, Al," she replied. "Any new updates?"

"The wedding is still in the planning phase."

"Apart from that," said Carla, who drank some more coffee.

"Well, Marisol has learned that the deal is off," said Hernandez. "After the death of Delacruz, the inheritors of her company no longer want to have anything to do with the Torquemada cartel."

"And since her clients include other prominent cartels and factions, they will not have to worry about any repercussions," Carla noted.

"Exactamente, mi amiga," said Hernandez, sporting a big smile. "And what of the news?"

"Impunity, como siempre."

"As always, indeed," said Hernandez, who began to lean on the cubicle wall. "You know, sometimes this job gets a little too easy."

"Al, I need to ask you something."

"You want out, don't you?" asked Hernandez.

Carla nodded.

"You have wanted out pretty much from the moment I recruited you a few years ago. Sometimes, I admit, that you have had very good reasons to leave. What makes now any different?"

"Laila," she stated, causing Hernandez to shift his posture. "She is growing up and I am not there. She took her first walk and said her first words all while I was a thousand miles away plotting to kill someone that I had never met before."

"I see."

"I am really serious this time, Al. I need to be here, for her. I would think with the other reasons—the ones that never went away, I might add— that I have proven that I cannot work for the Agency anymore. At least, not in my current capacity."

Hernandez nodded in contemplation.

"Whatever debt I owe you, I must have paid it to the fullest by now, and more."

"Yes, yes, you have been very useful to the Agency," Hernandez conceded. "More to the point, you have served your country with your actions." He began to pace about. "What's more, we have not always been kind to you. There was that awful French incident, the temporary burning and all that. You were very forgiving about it all. Maybe because you had no choice, or maybe you are just a good person stuck in an evil situation." He stopped pacing. "Tell you what…Let me talk with Mavis about the matter. While an immediate dismissal is out of the question, something else could be arranged."

"I want to believe you," said Carla. "Can I believe you?"

"Like I said, I think I can get Mavis to agree to let you go. However, as with any major change, there has to be something that triggers it. Something major has to occur on the ground to justify it. I believe we are getting close to that moment. Like I said, I will talk with Mavis at once and see to it."

"I hope and pray."

"That is a very good idea," said Hernandez, smiling and pointing at Carla. "Anyhow, off to see the wizard I go."

* * *

More than a thousand miles south of where Carla and Hernandez discussed her future, a different meeting with very different people was occurring. The location was a well-guarded hacienda, which covered many acres of property in the hinterlands. There was a wall that stretched around the entire property, with an entrance at each cardinal direction. Inside the wall were multiple buildings, all of which were modeled off of the colonial estates of the old Spanish Empire. The barrier and the edifices had white-painted adobe walls, with shingled roofs comprised of dark orange tiles.

In the manor house were many bedrooms, bathrooms, and halls. The hacienda had many statues, paintings, and a host of employees whose professions tended to be legitimate, such as hired security, gardeners, delivery men, janitors, accountants, and maids. There were also servants' quarters and a couple of structures used as offices or for storage. A petite chapel stood within the walls of the property, although it was seldom used. From time to time over the years, cartel leadership had considered converting the holy space into some other purpose, though enough lieutenants were either too religious or too superstitious to give approval for such a secularizing project.

A gathering of these leaders within the largescale enterprise took place in a wide chamber normally used for formal meals. Its décor was akin to the rest of the ornate hacienda, with its ivory walls and detailed paintings, with chiseled marble bodies standing at each corner of the room. Raul Torquemada was seated at the head of a long mahogany table placed in the center. There were several others gathered at the table. Most were lieutenants who answered to Torquemada. Many of them were older than he, and took some exception to his leadership. Other lower-ranked figures were there as well, including Pedro Aguilares, who was one of the youngest at the meeting.

On the grand table between them, there were three pitchers of water and two opened bottles of wine, taken from the property cellar. Each figure had at least one glass before them, with most having had some of the fermented drinks. Closer to the center of the table were four ash trays, each containing a few simmering, twisted butts. The chamber windows were wide open to keep blowing the smoke away. There were several pads, tablets, and smart phones laid out, with a few being used to showcase the statistical reports on business for the cartel. The conversations were all in Spanish.

"Our sales in the United States continue to plummet," lamented Carlos Benedico, an older lieutenant with dyed red hair and a gray mustache. "Over the past three years, our profits have dropped at least 40% on an annual basis. Local markets are nowhere near enough to compensate the decline. Unless we find another source of income, we are going to be bankrupt by next fiscal year." Benedico looked directly at the head of the table, where Torquemada was seated. This prompted most of the others to do likewise. "So, Señor Torquemada, our fearless leader, what do we do?"

"I have been reaching out to various businesses," explained Torquemada, keeping his temper in check. "There are people who can either give us a loan, or can be used to help export our products to the United States and elsewhere through other channels."

"And how has that been going?" Benedico critically asked, nearly cutting off his superior with his query. "So far, all of them have either declined our offers or have turned up dead."

"It is clear we are being targeted by a resourceful entity," said Aguilares, coming to the defense of his boss. "Torquemada has been at the forefront of getting us more resources and finding ways to revive our industries. He cannot help that unknown forces are cutting off those avenues of relief."

"I am suspicious," said another lieutenant, seated beside Benedico. "Every time nuestro jefe tries something, it is thwarted. Is this incompetence or is it collaboration?"

"How dare you!" Torquemada declared, rising to his feet. "I have never betrayed the cartel. I have only wanted us to thrive." His tone stunned a few of his peers at the table, though many remained unimpressed. "I work hour after hour to make the cartel stronger, to pursue new revenues, to defeat our enemies, and to make sure every level of our business is working at the best capacity. You have no right to question my loyalty!"

"Muy verdad!" declared Aguilares in support, a fist raised. "We need to spend less time blaming each other and more time finding a solution."

"There is one solution to this problem," said Benedico. "We need a new leader."

All in the chamber looked at the lieutenant. Some were shocked that someone would utter such a suggestion in front of the very man who would be replaced in that scenario. Others were insulted by the idea, with Aguilares being one of them. A few felt uncomfortable, fearing that the audacious declaration would lead to violence. Yet many subscribed to the sentiment of Benedico, with a few heads nodding in agreement. Torquemada took a deep breath, his exhale loud enough to bring people's attention to himself. They waited for his response, yet the cartel leader took a few steps from his chair, pushed it in, and then slowly walked about the long, well-cut wooden table, each head turning to see him as he went.

"Un lider nuevo," said Torquemada in a contemplative, calm tone. "You want a new leader. Someone who can take on the responsibilities and obligations of this whole entire empire. A man who will bring us out of this dark age and into a bright future. That is what you want, correct? Lo quieres, sí? Here is the problem..." Torquemada stopped, confidently standing behind a pair of lieutenants who quietly agreed with Benedico. "You have no better alternative than me." Torquemada stood still for a moment, silence the only response. He then slowly yet confidently went back to his seat. "None of you have the energy, the ability, or the willpower to do what I do. None of you are able to travel as far as I can travel, put together a plan as I put together a plan. None of you has the balls to challenge me. You would rather stay along the side of the table, complaining about my rule, rather than have the stomach to take responsibility for all of this."

Torquemada was able to see the faces of his critics sink. He grinned as they shrank from their opposition, albeit grudgingly. Even Benedico, the most vociferous of the dissenting lot, chose to bow his head rather than select himself as a replacement. Aguilares was one of the smiling figures at the table, happy to see his boss putting the lieutenants in their place. Torquemada returned to his chair, his hands resting on its top. "We will get through this. We will find a way out. It will happen on my watch. None of you is willing to challenge me, because none of you can name a single man in the entire cartel who would be able to do what I can do. And that, mis amigos, is that."

Then, just as Torquemada was about to sit down, there was a loud pounding on one of the closed wooden doors leading to the chamber. The two armed guards nearest to the door cautiously approached it. They were unaware of who it might be, yet they were certain the party could not have been too hostile, as such an arrival would have been detected at the compound walls well in advance of reaching the main building. One pointed his assault rifle at the door, while the other slowly opened it. From the vantage point of Torquemada, the figure was unseen, as the door swung toward the cartel head. Yet the guard stood there, stunned by what he saw. A few others also cautiously approached, likewise unable to properly respond to the presence who had just been seen.

"Who is it?" asked Torquemada, staying near his chair. Two other guards briefly jogged to be at either side of their superior, just in case. A few others at the table were able to see the figure behind the opened door, with each struggling to explain.

Finally, the mysterious creature walked into the chamber, making his visage clear to all at the table. He was the grandson of German immigrants, which explained why he had natural blond hair and skin that was more pinkish than most of his peers. He had been fairly assimilated into Latin American culture, and thus knew little of his heritage. Fluent in both Spanish and English, he had risen through the ranks of the cartel as Torquemada had, although with a greater quotient of violence. Many stood to see him, most froze in their place as they saw the man, Fulgencio Brennenberg by name, slowly make his way to the mahogany table where he once sat on a regular basis.

He rested both hands on the edge, standing on the opposite narrow side of the table as Torquemada. The journey appeared to be a little demanding on him, as he massaged his upper chest, right around where the wound was given. As they all watched him, some in confusion and some in horror, he took out from his jacket a small breathing apparatus, which included a mask that fit over his nose and mouth. He took a few quick breaths into the device and then moved the small device back into his jacket. Upon finishing the act, he stood straight up, with a commanding posture. Before all of those shocked and horrified to see him among the living, he stared at Torquemada and gave a simple utterance:

"I challenge you."

III.

It had been a few months shy of two years, and yet he remembered the evening well. It was hard to get away from that night, and its lasting impact upon his existence. He remembered the failed kidnapping attempt, with the first lady successfully fending him off. Then he recalled fleeing the scene in a white van, his cohorts disappointed by the failure, yet fearful of questioning his right to lead. He was nervous when he realized that they needed to get gas, yet relieved when nothing happened as they stopped. He had been so confident after the station, thinking that they had escaped.

The darkness of night was made all the deeper by the canopy of leafless trees and the robust layer of clouds covering up the sky. Artificial lights from the pier checkpoint illumined the otherwise black eventide. The men inside of the van were able to hear the constant crunching of the gravelly roadway. Some of the route had little bumps and potholes, bouncing them a bit as they got closer to the entryway. He ordered the van to stop near the checkpoint, with its humble tollhouse and lone barrier gate.

There was only one guard, a heavyset man wearing denim jeans and a plaid jacket. As they came out of the white van and approached the checkpoint, the guard left his tollhouse station and met them on the minor roadway. The guard was a cautious man, having a pistol tucked into his pants and holding a shotgun. Although the barrel was pointed at the ground, it could easily be brought up to be aimed at the men. Yet Fulgencio Brennenberg was not concerned. He smiled at the guard.

"Good evening," he said to the plump armed man, his breath visible.

"Evening," the guard replied, also with visible breath.

"We need to rent a boat."

"Pier's closed, sir."

"Not anymore," said Brennenberg, who was quicker on the draw than the shotgun-wielding man, taking out a pistol and shooting him dead. The lone shot scared nearby wildlife, with several birds flying away in fear. However, the surrounding area remained quiet.

"Y ahora, que?" one thug asked Brennenberg.

"Necesitamos una bota," he answered. "Adelante."

The four men walked past the dead guard and his barrier gate, not even bothering to lift the pole when going by. So focused on getting away that they were unaware that a woman was following them. Instead, they scattered about the pier as it began to snow. A wooden walkway stretched along the edge of the land, with wooden poles with several boats tied to them. Vessels powered by motors, sails, and rows alike, with more docked along the pier. Various items were gathered on the open space. Many bright-colored canoe boats were stacked on top of each other in one area, while multiple piles of lumber were gathered several feet away from the canoes. Tackle and other fishing materials were in a pile near the water. There were a couple of small outbuildings, including a row of outhouses and a shed.

"Bien?" one henchman asked another, the latter being on deck of one of the motorboats.

"No," he replied. "Tenemos que tener las llaves."

"Como sobre esta bota?" asked another man to Brennenberg, the duo being about forty feet away from the other two, who left the motor boat due to a lack of keys.

"Tiene solamente remos?"

"Si, señor."

"Entounces, no."

He got off the boat and back onto the wooden surface. They looked around more, unaware that someone was watching from behind a shed. As Brennenberg surveyed the many boats before him, one of the henchmen shouted from the pier. He had found a boat with a pull-string motor. He smiled at his discovery, only to be shot in the chest a moment after sensing triumph. The blast was like a jet speeding by. The victim fell into the water, his corpse slowly turning to face down into the river. Brennenberg and his two surviving comrades threw themselves to the ground, crawling to cover. None of them had seen where the shot originated. Brennenberg was behind some barrels and netting. About fifteen feet from the barrels, the other two men were crouching behind a thick pile of lumber. Each rapidly exhaled breaths that looked like smoke in the winter air.

"Tu," stated Brennenberg, looking squarely at one of the men behind the lumber. "Vas a la bota." He timidly shook his head in the negative. "Vas a la bota!"

The henchman finally nodded in the affirmative, inspired in part by Brennenberg pointing a gun at him. The snow started to come down in thicker sheets. The man ordered to run to the motorboat jumped into a sprint, dashing upon the wooden planks while trying to stay low. Slowing down to reach the boat, he was shot in the lower back from an unknown party, and then fell on his belly and face, screaming in pain. In response, Brennenberg and the unwounded henchman lifted themselves above their respective obstructions and fired several shots each into the canoes. For less than a minute, they blew away pieces out of a stack and punched holes into a shed before crouching down again to reload their respective weapons. Then, they repeated their actions for another minute, before again ducking down.

"Ahora, que?" the unwounded thug asked.

Brennenberg was silent.

"Señor?"

"Vas a la bota," he ordered. "Providere fuego cubierta."

The third henchman agreed with the idea. As he faced the pier, he saw his wounded associate moving around, yet going nowhere while loudly moaning. Brennenberg gave him a hand signal telling him to go. As the henchman ran for the boat, Brennenberg rose up from his protection and opened fire, spreading his shots out. The thug hastily made his way to the motorboat, passing a wounded comrade who vainly stretched out an arm in an attempt to reach him, all the while losing more blood.

The henchman had gotten farther than the last fellow, reaching the boat and beginning to untie it before a shotgun blast struck the side of his head. The impact spun him around before he landed on the wooden surface.

Brennenberg saw the direction of the shot and fired three bullets, striking two outhouses. All became quiet, save the moaning of the wounded man. All was stagnant, save for the falling snowflakes. Then another shot rang out, finishing off the wounded man. The projectile blew away that part of his face.

In a decision he remembered long after, Brennenberg concluded that it was best time for him to make a run for the motorboat. He ran towards the vessel, sporadically firing his handgun to his right. He jumped over the two corpses in his way, nearly slipping on the wooden beams when he landed. Brennenberg finished untying the boat and started the engine. Then a shot ripped through the snowy air and struck him in the chest, causing him to fall into the river with a splash, amid trauma and pain. As he drifted, Brennenberg saw nothing but darkness. His body became numb due to the cold water, the droning motorboat noise the loudest sound. He thought he heard footsteps on the wood of the pier, but nothing conclusive as the numbness led him to sink into unconsciousness.

* * *

Sound was the first sense to return. It was a low beeping noise, which came and went at a regular pace. Then the sounds of the vents above him, overseeing the climate control of the facility. He could hear his own breathing, as his mouth and nose were covered by a clear mask. Feeling gradually returned. He was still numb, though not from the cold, but rather through the painkillers being fed into his system intravenously. There was the sheet covering his body, save his arms and head. The bandaging along his chest, the breathing apparatus that had been inserted into his mouth and down into his throat. The tape along his cheeks to help keep the tube and mask in place.

The room was a blur. His eyelids were slow to open, slow to process the objects around him. Nothing was moving, no one was there. He saw the light blue blanket covering him, his pinkish arms, the IV that was pricked into his right arm, and the beige handles along either side of his bed. He saw the bland walls, with the closed door in front of him. It was wooden, brown, and extra wide. He started to move his eyes, slowly tilting his head to the right to see the machine with its beeping, a bright line on a black background curving up and down, with little numbers indicating his condition. Lacking any reason to stay awake, he returned to his sleep, his memories blurring again.

"When did he wake up?" he heard someone saying, his eyes again shifting from a clouded view of the room to a sharper focus.

"I don't know, about an hour ago, if not earlier," replied the other, a woman.

The beeping, the climate control noises, and the general dull sounds of the machines went to the background as he listened to the two talking by his bedside. The woman may have been a nurse, wearing turquoise scrubs and a lanyard that appeared to include official identification. She had dark skin, possibly Somalian on the basis of the accent, and was much shorter than the man. He was wearing a white lab coat, a tie, and slacks. He was white, wore thick-rimmed glasses, and had a stethoscope around his neck. He laid still, his eyes looking at them, as they continued to talk, periodically looking back at him.

"No ID?"

"None," she replied. "I think he was robbed."

"Most likely."

"The fishermen said he was in the river when they found him."

The doctor walked over to the patient, his features becoming visible. He had a lot of age lines along his neck and face. His hair, which looked authentically brown when from a distance, now looked to be dyed. He had hazel eyes and thin lips. The doctor studied the patient. Then he took the stethoscope and used it, putting the buds to his ears and the end to the chest of the patient. After a few moments, he studied the man some more. Then he took out a small light and flashed it in each pupil, getting a flickering of the eyelids in response. From there, he took out a smart phone and jotted some notes on the screen. He walked toward the nurse, who had remained at the foot of the bed.

"No lasting effects from the hypothermia. Heartbeat is weak but within normal parameters," he explained. "It is the lung I am worried about. There was a lot of damage. He will need another surgery. A specialized operation."

"Doctor?"

"He can be moved, correct?"

"His condition is stable."

"Good," said the doctor. "We need to move him to Main Memorial. There is a pulmonary specialist who should be able to save his respiratory system."

"Doctor, are you sure that's a good idea? If he was robbed, the police will want to speak with him."

"Then we will give them an address to reach him, once he is well enough to speak," he said. "We have an obligation to save his life. They can investigate the robbery later."

"Yes, sir."

"Tell the EMTs to prep him for transportation."

"Yes, sir."

After they left, all was quiet once more. He fell asleep again. After an unknown amount of time being unconscious, he awoke to see people all around him wearing scrubs and facemasks. The broad brown door before him was wide open. He felt he was floating as the bed began to move forward. They were careful to keep the machinery in order, to maintain the stability used to keep him alive. He started seeing ceiling lights, with their long tubular frames covered by rectangular glass. He heard the noises of the hallway, conversations, and even laughter. As they turned a corner, he shifted his head to look to his right, where he saw someone who looked like a police detective go by. Unbeknownst to him, the figure was actually Alfredo Hernandez of the Central Intelligence Agency, who had narrowly missed discovering the cartel lieutenant at his weakest.

* * *

Again, it was noise that first greeted the wounded Fulgencio as he returned from the state of unconsciousness. More gentle beeping, but also the sound of outdoor wind. His room was a shelter from whatever was going on outside, yet the breeze was still audible. The sheets were comfortable, the bandages less so. There was no ventilator inserted into his throat, though a breathing mask still covered his face. As his vision returned, he was able to see sunlight through the closed drapes. There seemed to be less action behind the wide oak door that he faced, similar yet different from the one in the other room.

He felt something strange as he took deep breaths, an odd sensation in his right lung. It was as though it were smaller, that it somehow shrunk a size or two from what it was before. That side of his body was sore. He was unrestrained, so he moved his hands to gently glide along his chest. An odd texture; Fulgencio quickly realized that it was stitching. At some point from his fleeting memories of leaving the hospital to the present moment recuperating in bed, someone had worked on him. That someone entered the room a few minutes after he had regained awareness of his surroundings.

"I am Dr. Kontra," explained the forty-something-year-old woman in a white coat. Next to her was a younger woman, who appeared to be an assistant. "I performed the surgery on your lung. Are you able to speak?"

"Yes," said a raspy Fulgencio. He took a breath and continued, his voice clearing a bit. "Yes, I am able. What happened?"

"You were shot in the lung, apparently with a shotgun," she explained. "You were struck from behind. There was a lot of damage to your right lung. I had to remove one of your lobes and patch up another. As a result, you are going to have to be careful about overexerting yourself. I can provide you with a list of exercises aimed at helping you keep your remaining lobes strong enough."

"Sure," he said. "That sounds good."

"Before I do so, I need to get some basic information from you," she began, her secretary beginning to take notes. "First of all, what is your name?"

"John Smith," said Fulgencio. "Spelled normally."

"Place of residence?"

"Detroit, Michigan."

"Age?"

"41," he replied, his first truthful answer.

"Sex?"

"But we just met," he quipped, causing the secretary to chortle. The doctor remained professional, tacitly prompting Fulgencio to become serious again. "Male."

"What is your insurance?"

"Blue Anthem, or Cross Shield, or something like that," said Fulgencio. "I never really kept track. All that information was in my wallet."

"Yes, I understand," said Dr. Kontra. "The police will be coming here soon."

"The police?" asked Fulgencio, sitting up.

"Yes," she replied, a little surprised at his response. "You were the victim of a robbery. They will need to speak with you."

"Yes," he said, nodding. "Yes, that's right. I was robbed."

"Now that you are out of surgery, a detective will be on his way."

"Okay, okay," said Fulgencio. "I can talk to the police."

"Do you have any other questions?"

"Can I walk around?"

"Yes, but be cautious," said the doctor. "Remember that you do not have the breathing capacity you once did."

"All right," he said. "Thank you. I would like to be alone now."

"Okay," said Kontra. "Let me print out a few pages of exercises that you can do in order to help adapt to the reduced lung capacity. I will be back in a few minutes."

"Good, thank you."

Fulgencio felt what she meant as he got out of bed. His steps were slower, and his hand held to the foot of the bed as he walked about the room. He eyed a closet space to the left of the wide door. His instinct about what was there was correct, as his clothes from the night that he was shot were hanging there. He considered trying to escape. The facility did not appear busy, let alone well-guarded. Yet breathing remained harder than before. Fulgencio opted to change into his old clothes, but he remained around to speak with the police officer. The minutes of wait gave him ample time to fabricate a robbery.

* * *

Weeks passed, and Fulgencio was in hiding once again. A man claiming to be his nephew arrived after Fulgencio called him using a phone at the facility. The man provided insurance information for a "John Smith" that covered the immediate costs of the operation. Although the staff at the facility were confused about the patient's insurance saying he was Madison, Wisconsin, instead of Detroit, Fulgencio assured that this was simply an older address he used to live in before moving to the Motor City. They accepted these things at face value, and Fulgencio was allowed to leave.

As Hernandez and other members of the Agency combed the capital city looking for the cartel lieutenant—or his lifeless body—Fulgencio was about a hundred miles away. The man who posed as family was an American contact for the Torquemada cartel. He was surprised to learn that Fulgencio had survived the violence at the pier. Nevertheless, he was willing and able to assist the superior as needed. When authorities returned to the facility to speak with Fulgencio, they learned that he had disappeared without providing accurate contact information. Other efforts to discover who was responsible for the mass shooting at the pier also fell short, for want of witnesses or good forensic evidence.

"You are a good cook, Marlan," Fulgencio told his host as he ate the scrambled eggs and toast provided to him on that morning.

"Thank you, Mr. Brennenberg."

"Oh, come on, Marlan, you can call me Fulgencio," assured the cartel figure. "After spending this much time around each other, I would think the formalities would be gone."

"I like to be careful," Marlan replied.

"Very well," said the guest.

"Maybe I should call you 'El Artista.' I heard from others that that was your nickname back in the day."

"It was," said Fulgencio, looking forward into space. "It has been too long since I have created a masterpiece. Torquemada would make a good portrait."

Marlan wisely stayed mum as Brennenberg used a knife and fork to cut through the white and yellow scramble, placing it on top of the toast. Once lathered in the egg, Brennenberg would take a bite out of the bread, enjoying both aspects of his breakfast simultaneously. He was a slower eater than before, as blocking his mouth with chewing food made it a bit harder to breathe than before. Still, he enjoyed the meal and consumed it while watching the morning news. The banal local stories and information on traffic and weather did not concern him. Updates on the fatal incident at the dock were, however, of great interest. Authorities had gradually stopped providing updates for want of leads.

"Damn," remarked Fulgencio, getting the attention of Marlan.

"What is it?"

"Nothing new on the shooting."

"Yes, um, Fulgencio."

"I would love to know who did it," he commented, having just cleaned his plate. "If nothing else, I might offer that shooter a job."

"A job?"

"Someone that powerful and that deadly...I would much rather they be on my side than someone else's."

"I see. Yeah, that makes sense," said Marlan, walking up to the seated Fulgencio. "I can take your plate, if you're done."

"Thank you, Marlan. Although, maybe having the public lose interest in the shooting will be to my benefit. Fewer people will care about the killer and myself. It will make it easier for me to remain obscure if no one is looking for me."

"That's what I don't get," Marlan commented as he turned on the faucet to rinse the plate and the glass he took from his guest. "One phone call, and one of the lieutenants could help get you out of here. You know, send you back home. Don't you want that?"

"No," Fulgencio firmly stated. "I do not want Torquemada or any of my friends to know I survive. I do not want them to know that I am still alive. Let them conclude that I am dead. Let them accept it, embrace it, and move on. Then, when I show up, they will be in awe. They will do what I want."

"I just don't understand," said Marlan, walking back to where Fulgencio was seated. "Why don't you want them to know?"

"Because, Marlan," he patiently replied, "they are failing us. The cartel is failing. We need new leadership. You realize that, right?"

"Yeah, of course."

"Good."

"So, when do you plan to take over?"

"Not yet," said Fulgencio. "I want things to get worse. I want them to be desperate. I want as few people to stick up for Torquemada as possible."

"When will be bad enough for you to take over, but not so bad that things will be destroyed?" asked Marlan. "I mean, there's got to be a balance, you know?"

"I know, Marlan," said Fulgencio, calmly explaining the situation. "I will know when the—as you call it—'balance' is struck. And when it is struck, I will strike. That way, my conquest will be a simple one."

"Yes, Fulgencio."

"I challenge you," declared Brennenberg, standing on the opposite end of the long mahogany table in the formal dining room of the hacienda, a wide-eyed Raul Torquemada looking on.

All of the other lieutenants and leaders of the cartel were aghast at the arrival of the man presumed dead. They looked on at the man, many a mouth gaping, then gradually turned to face the head of their criminal empire. They wanted a response; they sought some sort of rebuttal to the declaration.

"This meeting is over," stated Torquemada, pounding his fist on the table and storming out of the room, barely making eye contact with anyone else. Pedro Aguilares got up from his seat and followed Torquemada.

No one knew for sure what to do. It was not as though the cartel held formal elections for their central leadership. There was more of an informal system of promotion and demotion, with both usually entailing a level of violence. Brennenberg breathed easier, seeing that his fellow lieutenants gazed upon him in reverence and fear rather than anger or opposition. They started to get up. A few left the room, mostly to simply process the unforeseen situation. Others went up to Brennenberg, offering handshakes and welcomes, idle chatter, and expressions of sympathy. He took it all in quite well.

IV.

For centuries they came, using the plaza square for commerce. They had been there before the first Europeans had arrived, bringing crops and goods for barter, with the nearest temple offering human sacrifices to keep the sacred order alive. Their business practices continued even as the temples were shut down and churches took their stead. As the Spanish built new buildings around the plaza, they came to buy and sell. As the old empire collapsed and chaotic independence was achieved, farmers and merchants still gathered. Even as the twentieth century brought offices, cars, and a global market, those of the working class remained committed to the plaza market.

Marisol Contreras was there among the many vendors, placing their assorted grown goods along the tables set up in lengthy rows. Many brought canopies, some of which were simply sticks propping up homemade blankets. Others had the more sophisticated tents, with their metal stands, bolts, and mass-produced covers. Each vender had their pattern of agricultural variety, large baskets, or barrels full of locally grown fruits and vegetables. Some cooks brought ample loaves and pita breads for sale, along with sauces that they themselves created and personally bottled. A minority of them had fish or chicken for sale, kept fresh via several coolers filled with ice. These vendors tended to be the first to go, as the humid warm climate was not friendly to the preservation. Still, with a good enough early crowd, they could make a fair amount of peso for their labors.

Contreras carried a basket, its woven handle sometimes being held by her hand, and sometimes being held by her bent arm. She analyzed every tomato, potato, or apple that she encountered, judging as best she could by touch, sight, and smell. Paying for the items was not a simple transaction, as haggling was commonplace. Being a pretty young woman, the male farmers seemed to charge her less than most. Some of the women out there at the tables knew her family, and thus gave her a nepotistic discount. She knew some of them as well, having run such errands since she was a tweener.

Marisol was putting a few apples in her basket, having just agreed on a price with the elderly farmer, when she caught a glimpse of a stranger. He was standing two tables to her right. She did not directly look at the figure, though he appeared to be paying her a great deal of attention. He looked a little young, with a smooth face and thick black hair. Initially, she brushed it off. The figure would not be the first man to check her out while she shopped. Since he gave no whistles or catcalls, she considered it more minor than most. Yet, as she went to another table, mostly just to view the produce, she briefly glanced him walking in her direction, looking at her more than the tables.

She did not know the man and felt him menacing enough to not want to know him. Yet, he seemed to persist. She kept going down the line of tables, feigning interest in the harvested and picked products. He persisted in following, failing to provide subtlety for his effort. He was young; this might have been his first assignment. His presence made her all the more uncomfortable. The young man appeared to be trying to close the gap, spending less time searching the produce and more time walking closer to her. Marisol decided to make a more overt effort to get away, halting her perusal of the tables and making a fast walk down the row, squeezing by the crowds inhabiting the plaza.

"Marisol!" said a man in front of her, causing Contreras to nearly jump backward. This man was different. He was taller, more muscular, and had a short black beard. He was familiar, which gave her some ease amid the apparent stalking. "Estas bien?"

"Pedro," she said in relief. "Sí, yo pienso que estoy bien."

"You look scared," he said, the two continuing their discussion in Spanish.

"There was a man," she began, turning to face the crowd of oblivious patrons. "He was..." She squinted but did not see him. Turning back to Pedro, she smiled. "I guess you scared him away."

"I am glad that I am useful," he said, apparently meaning something else in his comment. "I was looking for you. We need to talk in private."

"Por que?"

"Por favor, venga conmigo."

"Por que?" she asked, mildly impatient.

"It is too important and too sensitive to explain here," he said, taking her arm. "Just come with me, please."

"And if I say no?" she asked, becoming more serious.

"Marisol, por favor."

Contreras was unsure of what to do next. Theoretically, she was safe out there. There were plenty of well-meaning people going about the tables. If Pedro did anything wrong, some people would come to her rescue thanks to a high-pitched scream. Yet he wanted to leave the safety of the plaza market. She thought about resisting right there, having thought that maybe Pedro had figured things out about her and why she was really interested in him. There was something more serious about him than in their past get-togethers. Yet she dismissed the idea, as she always questioned his intelligence.

"All right, I will come with you."

He smiled but kept his hold on her arm. It was not a tight grip, yet it did serve as a reminder that he felt a need to compel her to come. As they weaved through the other people, she again saw the young man with the smooth face. Pedro saw him as well and nodded at him. The nod prompted a smile from the young stalker, who then disappeared into the crowd. Marisol looked at Pedro, who grinned at her as though he had successfully pulled some prank on the young woman. She felt odd, as the revelation of collusion made her feel both relieved and worried about what was coming.

They got past the tables and their vendors, the patrons, and the tourists, and then went among the surrounding buildings. There was an alleyway, shaded even amid the afternoon sun, which Pedro guided Marisol toward. She became more apprehensive, her walk slowed. Yet Pedro tightened his grip on her arm, tacitly insisting that she continue into the space between the two buildings. There were still folk milling about the sidewalk, and Marisol was confident in her screaming abilities. Regardless, her guts were feeling awful, and she began to sweat, her breathing more rapid. There were moving shadows in the dark, figures of men who were affiliated with Pedro.

Her heart skipped a beat when they entered the alley, going several feet from the relative succor of the sidewalks. Her eyes widened when she realized that the central shadow of the alley was none other than Raul Torquemada. He had on dark red slacks and a jacket, with a black shirt covering his chest. His hair was in a ponytail, and his eyes seemed darker than the night. Marisol looked around and saw that the young man from before was standing at the mouth of the alleyway, as though to block any effort to run. One of the other shadows moved along behind her, presumably to help surround her. Torquemada took a few steps closer to Marisol, while Pedro let go of her arm and walked a few steps backward. She looked around her and saw no escape. Then, she saw only Torquemada.

"Is this your girlfriend, Pedro?"

"Sí, Señor Torquemada," Pedro stated, formally.

"Why am I here?" she asked.

"You are the reason we failed."

"What are you talking about?"

He took a deep breath, then continued. As he spoke, he paced around the timid young woman. "My meeting with Alba Delacruz was kept secret. Only a few members of the cartel knew the details. Pedro was one of the few. When Delacruz was killed, I started asking questions. Pedro is not only my employee; he is my friend also. And as any good friend would do, he confessed that he told one person, una mujer, about the meeting. Because he is a friend, I forgave him. However, because of this mistake, I demanded answers. He told me that the woman he talked to was you. You knew about the meeting."

"Señor Torquemada, por favor," Marisol pleaded, putting down her basket and clasping her hands together. "He told me about the meeting, but nothing more. He did not say where or when. I know nothing else about it. Nada!"

"I agree," said Torquemada, who stopped his pacing so that he was standing behind her. This prompted Marisol to cautiously turn and face him. "I know he did not tell you those details. However, he told you enough. You then told someone else, someone with enough resources to find out the rest. They learned the rest, and they killed Delacruz."

"Señor Torquemada—"

"Shut up!" he declared, causing Marisol to bow her head. "You know some powerful people. I suspected one of our rivals, yet they were just as surprised at the death of Delacruz as I was. Many of them have profited from doing business with her and would never dare harm her. So, it must be someone else. Someone who has international power, someone who wants to destroy me. Americans, perhaps?"

Marisol kept her head down, holding her arms.

Torquemada stepped closer. "It is the Americans, true?"

Marisol kept silent, shaking in her place.

"It better be the Americans, or else I will kill you."

Marisol looked up in confusion.

"Contestame, ahora!"

"Sí, sí, sí, sí!" she answered. "My friends are American. I admit it."

"Good," Torquemada calmly stated. "Then you are going to be very useful to me."

* * *

That night marked the third evening in a row that the Sharps were given a full shift of sleep. Carla regained consciousness as sunlight pressed against the closed drapes. She saw the rays outline the edges of the fabric used to obscure the view of the capital. Josiah was stirring, yet his eyes remained closed. She pulled away the sheets from her body, the excess flopping on top of the covers already blanketing Josiah. She sat for several moments on the side of the bed, her bare feet touching on the floor. A deep breath and she stood, still a bit drowsy, yet satisfied with the amount of sleep she had gotten.

Carla shut her eyes after closing the bathroom door. A flip of one of the switches illuminated the lights just above the mirror. She then opened her eyes, learning from experience that such a practice helped her pupils adjust to the new brightness. She heard more movement in the bedroom, rightly presuming that it was her husband getting up from the bed. Her hair was still not as long as it had been before the latest assignment. To properly wear the wig, her mane had to be half the length it usually was. The ends of the strands stopped just above her shoulders. While the shorter cut had its advantages, Carla was more comfortable with it being longer.

Then she noticed something, something that gave her a bit of pause. Maybe it had been there before, maybe it had just emerged. Regardless, it was more visible in the present moment than it had been before, if had been there before. It was not a frightening realization; however, it was not welcomed, either. There was a gentle knock on the bathroom door.

Carla turned to face the closed portal. "It's occupied!"

"All right," he said. "Down the hall I go."

Carla smiled at the deference he gave her and continued to get ready for the day. She showered and changed clothes, and brushed the hair, including the follicles that caught her attention earlier this morning. Soon enough, she was downstairs, eating breakfast that was warmed via microwave. Josiah came down minutes later, also cleaned up and fully clothed. Without speaking, he went to the pantry and found something to have for his first meal of the day. He then went to the refrigerator and took out the orange juice, pouring some in a cylindrical glass that was four inches tall. With a plate of food in one hand and the glass in another, he sat down at the table, facing opposite his wife.

"Laila is sleeping very well," Carla noted.

"Yeah, I guess we will wake her in about a half hour."

"Yeah," said Carla, who paused to finish her breakfast. "Josiah, do you notice anything particularly different about me?"

"You mean the shorter hair?"

"No, aside from that."

"Maybe," he said, getting up from his seat. "Let me get a better look at you." Josiah approached his wife, comically bending forward and staring at her.

"Oh, stop," she said, laughing. "I am serious."

"Well, your hair seems a little lighter on one side."

"It is not light, Josiah. It's gray."

"Gray?" Josiah again got closer to look, this time in a less humorous style. "Yeah, I think I see them. A few of them by your ear."

49

"Yeah, that's where I found them this morning," said Carla, sighing. "I was kind of hoping I could at least get to 40 before I had to worry about grays."

"Honestly," said Josiah as he sat back down before his breakfast, "given how stressful your life has been, I am a little surprised you did not get them sooner."

"There is that," she acknowledged, as her husband said a brief silent prayer over his meal. "I wonder if I should color it."

"I don't know," Josiah replied, as he began to eat his meal. "I think it gives you character. Something alluring and mysterious."

"Alluring and mysterious," Carla repeated. "I kind of like that."

"And it makes you look distinguished."

"Okay, now you have gone too far."

"Sorry, sorry," said Josiah, hands raised. "I guess that is only a compliment for men."

"Exactly."

"Well, if it makes you feel better, I have some hair problems of my own."

"Yeah, I noticed it was thinning out a couple of weeks ago."

"You did?" asked Josiah, shocked.

"Of course I did," said Carla, almost surprised that he was surprised. "It is really obvious whenever you bow your head."

"And you did not say anything?"

"I had a feeling that you already knew."

"Well, in fact, I did," said the governor. "Although, I had hoped it was not too obvious to the casual observer."

"I mean, I have looked at your head more than most people, so it would be obvious to me," said Carla. "If you do not bow your head in public, few people will notice."

"Thank you," said Josiah with a wry smile. "If it gets any worse, I will definitely look into a treatment of some kind."

"Okay, but I will warn you about my cousin Albert..."

"The bald one, right?"

"Right," she said. "Albert has done a bunch of treatments over the years. Some of them worked, but the problem was, according to him, he had to keep taking things. After a while, he just did not want to bother anymore."

"Well, here's hoping technology has advanced since he last tried."

"Yeah," said Carla, whose phone went off. The device had been silently resting on the kitchen table, several inches away from the baby monitor. She picked up the phone and recognize the caller. A push of the button the screen and she began to speak to the interrupter.

"Yeah?...I was already planning to...How important?...Okay...Okay...I will leave at once. Bye!"

"Work?"

"That is right," said Carla. "Alfredo just told me that he had an important assignment for me, one whose details could not wait another hour."

"You know, every time you get a call from him or the office, a little bit of me wonders if it isn't a trap of some kind."

"Same here."

* * *

"You're late, you're late, you're late," said Alfredo Hernandez.

"You know me," said Carla as she walked toward her handler. "Arab standard time."

Hernandez smiled at the remark. He was not so much concerned over her belated arrival as he was excited. Carla was able to read him well, with his enduring grin and bidding that she follow him to the office of their superior. Hernandez had not given the details as to why he was so enthusiastic, let alone why Carla needed to arrive as quickly as possible. Confirming that no traps were set was nice, though also expected. Then again, she still had to meet with Mavis Chalmers, so the idea remained on the fringes of her thoughts. Carla regularly wondered if she had forgiven too quickly for having initially burned her over the death in Paris over a year earlier.

Carla did not bother to press Hernandez over what the morning meeting was about, as she knew he would be evasive and that the answer would be arriving soon. Like a gentleman, Hernandez held the office door open for Carla, who saw their superior seated at a desk, sternly looking at a computer screen. Chalmers was a gray-haired African American woman and

51

grandmother who rarely ever loosened her professional demeanor when on the clock. As Carla entered the room, her arrival did not alter the executive director's expression in the faintest. She had speculated that the strict commitment to this stoic propensity came from being a minority female in an Agency historically dominated by white men, and thus a greater demand for employee quality was implicit. This was, of course, mere speculation on the part of Carla, though not easy to dismiss.

"Morning, Director Chalmers," said Carla as she sat down.

"Mrs. Sharp," stated Chalmers, nodding. "Take a seat."

Carla did so at once, as an armless office chair was placed between the desk and the door. Hernandez opted to remain standing, walking to the side of their superior and leaning against the wall. Chalmers returned her focus to the screen, whose pixelated surface was invisible from where Carla was seated. Chalmers was like a doctor reviewing a patient's files, while Hernandez was not unlike a nurse, smiling and consoling the patient in question. Carla felt like she was in a doctor's office, so the comparison stood firm. The pause in speech made her wonder, then made her a little nervous. Yet, she refused to believe that bad news was coming, as her handler was much too jovial. Finally, Chalmers clicked her mouse a few times and then directed her attention back to Carla.

"Hernandez tells me that you want to leave the Agency," said Chalmers, sans emotion.

"Yes, I have wanted that for a long time."

"That is understandable," Chalmers replied. "We have rarely treated you well. The many times we have sent you into danger, the times we have distanced ourselves when you needed us, and then there was the burning not long ago. Your request is understandable."

"There is also the time away from my family," Carla audaciously added, head down as she spoke. "That is becoming harder for me, now that I have a daughter."

"Yes, I can understand that," said Chalmers, who paused before continuing. "I think I have a solution that will give you most of what you want."

Carla went from nervous to excited, yet she kept herself composed as her superior spoke. Hernandez folded his arms yet remained his happy self in the background. Chalmers bent to one side, looking down at one of her desk drawers. Carla heard the noise of a drawer opening, with a short-lived metal rumble. Chalmers sifted through some folders, then picked out one. She then grabbed a folder, straightened up, and placed the item on her desktop. The folder was a very light orange, with only a couple of pages inside. Chalmers nodded at Carla, who gently took hold of the folder and opened it.

"It is an official contract, transferring you from the Agency to the FBI," said Chalmers, as her agent looked over the dense written details. "You will still work for the government, and there is still the occasional danger, however you can now remain stateside. That way, everyone gets something."

"Yeah," said Carla, flipping through the contents with restrained hope.

"If you will note on the last page, there are two signatures missing from the agreement. The first, of course, is yours. And the second is mine."

Carla looked up. "You want me to do something to earn this, right?"

Chalmers nodded in the affirmative.

"What do I have to do?"

Chalmers looked over her shoulder at Hernandez and nodded. He unfolded his arms and took a few steps forward, leaning on the desk of their superior. "Marisol is the reason why this is possible. She called me this morning, early hours, informing me of a fairly interesting in-person meeting that she had with none other than Raul Torquemada."

"She met with Torquemada?" asked a surprised Carla.

"Well, it was more Torquemada had some goons of his bring her to him to talk," said Hernandez. "Regardless, Torquemada informed her that he wants out. Out of the cartel, that is. According to him, a lieutenant we assumed had been killed is actually still among the living and is winning over the rest of the leadership. Torquemada does not expect to survive the challenge to his rule, so he is coming to us for help."

"What does he want?"

"Witness protection, relocation to the United States, and, as you would expect, total immunity for all the crimes he had committed."

"What does he offer?" asked Carla. "I assume he will give us something in return."

"Indeed, he will," said Hernandez, smiling once more. "Torquemada knows everything about the inner workings of his cartel. He knows the locations of weapons stockpiles, which plantations are being run by his organization, bank accounts, you name it. He has full access to everything. Y quiero decir todas las cosas."

Carla nodded. "You told me that in order to get out of the Agency, there would have to be a major change, like the Torquemada Cartel being destroyed."

"Exactly!" declared Hernandez, especially upbeat. "We are very close to ending that cartel once and for all. And when it is gone, a whole lot of people will be free from its grip. So, if you can help make this become reality, then we will finally be able to start removing resources from the area. Resources such as yourself."

"Sounds good," said Carla, who was sedate outside yet increasingly feeling joyful on the inside. "What do I have to do?"

"You and I will be going down South to help oversee his extraction. Once we get Torquemada safely within U.S. borders, your job is done."

"A simple extraction?"

"A simple extraction," Hernandez assured her. "However, we do need to make haste on this little effort of ours, so we will need to leave early tomorrow morning. The sooner you get home and get to packing, the better."

"Hold on," said Carla, keeping her wits about her. "This extraction will involve me meeting Torquemada, correct?"

"Yes, most likely."

"What if he recognizes me?"

"Recognizes?" inquired Hernandez, who paused and then remembered what she was getting at. "Oh, yes, his efforts to kidnap you in order to get your husband to do his will. I remember that."

"What will happen if he remembers me, or starts to figure out that I might have been the reason why he has been put in this situation?"

"I don't think it will be an issue," Hernandez assured her. "At this point, what choice does he have but to get help from you?"

"There is that, I guess," said Carla.

"You are my best agent, Carla," Hernandez began. "You know how to thrive in a horrible environment. You know your way around that part of the world. And you have often prevailed against the cartel. If there is anyone more suited to go with me to extract Torquemada, I have not encountered them. So, can you get ready to leave?"

"Okay," she said, getting up from her chair. "I will do so."

"Remember," Chalmers stated, "Torquemada needs to go into custody. He needs to be here for the mission to be a success. If the cartel kills him or he changes his mind, then this deal does not happen."

"I understand, Director Chalmers."

"I don't know about you, but I am super excited about all of this," said a giddy Hernandez. "This means that Marisol and I can finally stop delaying our wedding."

"I was wondering when it was going to happen," Carla commented as she and Hernandez left the office side-by-side.

"Muy, muy pronto, thanks to this operation."

"Have you sent any invitations out?" Carla asked.

"Ah, no, not really," said Hernandez. "It will probably be a small ceremony. She doesn't have a lot of family, and I can barely stand my relatives." He again held the door for Carla, getting a fleeting thanks in return. "In a way, this extraction operation will be like having a honeymoon in advance of the ceremony."

"She is going to be involved?" asked Carla, previously unaware of this information.

"She has to be," Hernandez answered. "Torquemada requested it. For the time being, he only trusts her as a proper go-between."

"I see."

"She has worked with us on dangerous assignments before. Compared to past efforts, this one should be quite safe."

* * *

Josiah never forgot where he came from. He remembered his family, his faith, and his professional experience. Over the past few years, even with the hectic schedule as governor, he often met with family, both on his side and on Carla's side. Thanksgiving still meant going to his parents' house. He attended the same Methodist church that he had before being elected, with his pastor father occasionally preaching a sermon from that very pulpit. People who had helped his campaign ended up in his administration, and people he had feuded with were still among those he dialogued and civilly debated. This combined with his legislative progress and economic record made him a popular elected official.

Carla knew that her husband remembered his roots, and relied on them as she informed him of the development at the office. She handed him the contract for his review, knowing that he had a respectable legal background. Josiah was between meetings, and thus was able to make time to see what was being promised. He scanned each line, each clause, and each paragraph. She waited in silence, patiently sitting across the desk from him. She looked at his face, seeing his focus and trying to locate any sign of concern upon his countenance. A few shifts of the eyebrows, a long blink here and there, and yet nothing that seemed too worrisome. Finally, he perused the last page, which had the least amount of content included, and then looked up at his curious wife.

"It looks good," he said, almost surprised.

"Really?" she asked, tinged with optimism.

"I mean, this is the CIA we are dealing with," cautioned Josiah. "They have the ability to forge documents and contrive whole companies to pull off operations."

"And you think this is an example of them lying to me?" Carla insisted. "There have been times when Chalmers has been misleading, and Hernandez has failed to uphold his promises. Yet, to have them both lie to me on something like this?"

"I know, I know," said Josiah. "It is hard for me to see them go that far, either. And they are not entirely done with you, if this contract is honored."

"You mean the FBI part, right?"

"Right," said Josiah. "The talk of 'mutual cooperation' means that you might still have to work alongside Hernandez."

"I am okay with that," Carla said. "He can be a bit much, but by himself he is not the problem. And besides, ultimately, we both owe him a great deal."

"I guess we do," Josiah conceded, putting the contract back into the envelope on his desk. "So, when does it become official?"

"When I get back."

"One more time, huh?"

"Yeah."

"You just got home," said Josiah, as a lament. "Laila will not be happy."

"She is not the only one," said Carla, getting up from her chair, prompting her husband to do likewise. "However, this final job should not take as long as the last."

"What is the last job, anyway?"

"I cannot talk too much about it, but I have to help get someone here, someone who will finally destroy the Torquemada cartel."

"Hernandez must be expecting trouble if he wants you there."

"It should not be anything that I have not seen before."

"You *have* seen a lot," Josiah noted. "And done a lot, thanks to them."

"I know and I know," she replied.

Carla walked toward the windows. She moved one of the curtains to get a better view of the outside world. Before her was the green flat lawn of the governor's mansion. There was the occasional security guard patrolling the grounds. From there, she saw the imposing iron fencing that protected all sides of the property. The occasional camera topped the barrier, pointed downward at the city and its people. From there, sidewalks and streets with cars and pedestrians going about for numerous reasons, business and casual. Beyond that, the buildings that made the urban forest of the capital. Only the sky could be seen past all of that, its view of the future invisible from her position in the office.

"I agree with your optimism," said Josiah. "This is the best chance we have at getting you out of that world. When do you leave?"

"Early morning," said Carla. "Before the sunrise."

"I am sure Laila will help you wake up," said Josiah, causing his wife to snicker.

"Yes, she probably will," said Carla, turning to face her husband. "I hope she wakes me up a lot in the near future."

V.

Pedro Aguilares was pacing about the bedroom. For the time being, he was alone. Before him was a king-sized bed, which had a tall wooden headboard that had detailed carving of vines and flowers. The sheets were slightly disheveled but were mostly in good order. The top layer had an open suitcase on it, which had an ever-growing supply of folded clothing inside. Near it was a black laptop case, which included the device in question, as well as a battery, a set of headphones, multiple thumb drives, some pens, and some paper. He caressed his beard as his soon-to-be former superior walked in.

Raul Torquemada barely looked at the man he knew was there. The cartel leader was busy adding more things to the suitcase, including a few more shirts and a transparent zipped plastic bag containing toiletries. He pushed the plump bag into a corner of the case, the stacked clothing ceding much ground to the new arrival. He knew that he could not take everything with him. His choices were strictly utilitarian, as he had few personal items of a cherished nature at hand. Torquemada was unmarried, had no children, and was distant from his extended family, some of whom had been old rivals.

Torquemada walked away from the bed once again, going across the interior of the large chamber to an opened dresser drawer, where still more clothes were to be found. He grabbed a bunch more items, this time a dozen pairs of socks, and carried them over to the bed. Each pair was rolled into itself, making them like potatoes or pears. One arm kept the bulbs close, while he placed them one at a time inside the case. The luggage was nearly full by this point, which was more a relief than a concern. Torquemada finally turned to face Pedro, who had been silent for some time.

"Are you packed yet?"

"Why are you leaving?" asked Pedro. "You can fight Señor Brennenberg. He is a weak man. You saw how he needed that thing to breathe."

"He has power," Torquemada responded. "Power with the others. They see weakness as strength. To go from being dead to being wounded is a miracle."

Torquemada returned to looking at the insides of the case. He faced downward, his index finger pointing at various items stacked and packed in the case. The cartel leader checked off each item, his mental list being explored. So many things remained outside of the luggage, from paintings to jewelry to other clothes to DVD copies of his favorite films, and the dishes and glasses from the kitchen. There were no religious objects put in either case he had on the bed. As he saw it, anything spiritual he might need could wait for his final destination. There was no prized family Bible with milestones written in the opening pages, nor a rosary handed down through the generations for prayer.

"I could talk with the others," Pedro insisted. "There are lieutenants who are neutral. If I could reason with them—"

"No," stated Torquemada firmly. "It would be a waste of time. Brennenberg has come at my weakest hour. He knew when to come."

"Sí, Señor Torquemada," said Pedro, head bowed.

"Have you packed, yet?"

"No," replied the subordinate. "I am not leaving."

"Pedro," he said, turning away from his luggage to face Aguilares. "When Brennenberg takes power, he will purge any allies of mine. And he will do it the way that El Artista is famous for doing it. If you want to be spared that, you need to come with me."

"I am staying," said Pedro, folding his arms. "I do not run. I will not run."

"You need to come with me," Torquemada insisted.

"I will be a good soldier. I will keep out of trouble. Brennenberg will not worry about me. He will see me as loyal and leave me alone."

"You do not understand," said Torquemada. "There will no cartel when I am done with the authorities. I will tell them all of our weaknesses. I have everything I need to end it in my head and on my laptop and drives. When they get these things, the cartel will be destroyed. You will be destroyed with it. I do not want that to happen. Come with me, take advantage of the immunity I will be getting. Tell them what you know, and I will make sure you can also start a new life in the United States."

"Lo siento, Señor Torquemada," Pedro said. "But I cannot go. I do not want to move to the United States. I will take my chances here."

Torquemada did not immediately respond. He was disappointed, but otherwise untroubled. He turned to face the open suitcase. Again, he double-checked that everything he needed was there. No weapons were there; however, he felt no need to carry one for this journey. Again satisfied that all he needed was inside of the case, he took hold of the top of the case and flipped it down, closing the luggage. He had to push a little to get the lid closed enough to begin zipping the case shut. Nevertheless, with a few jerks to one side, he was able to seal shut the case, the zipper pushed to the other side.

"Very well," Torquemada conceded. "I will be sure to tell the authorities to go easy on you. Ojala, they will give you a light sentence, at the worst."

"Gracias, mi jefe."

"De nada."

"When will you meet with the Americans?"

"Tomorrow morning," said Torquemada. "However, I need to get out of here now. Just in case Brennenberg suddenly moves fast."

"Good point."

"Do you need anything else, before I leave?"

"No, Señor Torquemada. You have been a good leader. No matter what the others may say, I think you did an excellent job as our jefe. I think things will get worse under Señor Brennenberg. If I were more connected, if I had more influence, I would stop him. But I guess it was not meant to be."

"No, it was not," said Torquemada, who then took hold of his luggage. He put the strap of the laptop case along his right shoulder, while pulling out the handle for the suitcase, and putting its wheels to the marble floor.

"Ten cuidado, Señor Torquemada," said Pedro.

"Cuidate, Pedro."

* * *

Carla al-Hassan Sharp woke up before the sunrise. As Josiah slept, she showered and changed. Her suitcases were already packed. As the skies shifted from black to dark blue, she quietly entered the bedroom of Laila. Blowing a kiss to her child, she then went down the stairs and, from there, down another level to the garage. As the first beams of light began to color the horizon, Carla set out. She was in one of three black jeeps, which went at top speed directly to the airport. When the sunrise was at its glorious beginning, she was checking in to a private jet parked on the tarmac. She was ten thousand feet above the ground by the time most of the capital was at work on that weekday.

The plane encountered some turbulence about halfway through the aerial journey to Central America. For a brief while, Carla almost found humor in the idea that her final assignment with the Agency was going to abruptly end via a plane crash. She was able to joke about such things, as the remainder of the trip was smooth. As they neared the airstrip, the familiar sights were there. Outside of her window, she saw an endless layer of jungle, periodic enclaves with skyscrapers. Like veins in a body, there were roads wide enough to be seen from her vertical position. It was quite the chore for the public sector to keep the vines and branches from taking over the various routes.

Finally, came the airstrip. It was not unlike the location she had been to several days earlier, though it was located a couple hundred miles south of that previous destination. There were few people there, as only a few were needed to keep it in operation. The facility was surrounded on all sides by thick jungle, with an electrified fence along its borders to keep out the more menacing wildlife. However, plenty of bugs flew about unabated. There were a few buildings on sight, bland in their décor, and none of them being higher than three stories tall. One road led to and from the property.

"Estamos aqui," Alfredo Hernandez commented as the plane touched down at the hidden airstrip. "We are now one step closer."

Carla simply nodded. She was taking in the gravity of the situation as the plane finally came to a full stop. She and Hernandez were the only passengers in the main compartment of the plane. The cockpit had a pilot and co-pilot. All four unbuckled their belts and headed for the exit along the side of the vessel. Ground crew placed a metal stairway at the edge of the opening, allowing them to disembark. Carla and Hernandez hauled their own respective luggage down the stairs. Once they set foot on the tarmac, the two used the wheels on their cases to roll the items to a nearby building.

Marisol Contreras was there, waiting for them. She and Hernandez hugged each other, then kissed. Carla smiled at their affection. Once Marisol let go of her fiancé, she hugged Carla next. She took one of Carla's suitcases as the three continued to walk, with Marisol leading them to the corner of the building, which had been sectioned off through a network of curtains suspended from poles. There were six poles altogether, forming two rows of three. A total of seven curtains were hung between the poles, creating two small temporary bedrooms, which had cots for beds. The two cut off spaces were next to the only full bathroom located on that floor of the two-story building.

"Pick your poison," Hernandez quipped when Contreras showed them the cots.

"I am picking the one closest to the bathroom," she said, using one hand to push away a curtain and another to roll her suitcase. She and Marisol placed her two cases next to the cot, which had one pillow and a lone blanket for comfort. Carla turned to face Hernandez. "What do we do now?"

"We wait until tomorrow morning," said Hernandez. "For the time being, we should go over the plan once again."

"All right," said Carla, who sat on the edge of the cot, while Marisol stood.

"Stage one," began Hernandez. "We meet at a factory owned by the Primera Vez Milk Company. The business is technically legitimate; however, they also have strong ties to the Torquemada Cartel. Torquemada himself will meet us there. He will park in the back and enter into the main factory building. We should basically be alone, as he already allowed the workers to take the day off."

"How nice of him," Carla commented.

"Stage two," continued Hernandez. "A group of National Guard units will arrive. They will be posing as factory workers, ready to ship products out of the country. This is not an uncommon practice for the factory, which often deals with exporting products to the USA and elsewhere. To the outside world, it will like just another convoy of goods heading out. In reality, it will be fourteen vehicles, including nine trucks and five SUVs. Carla, myself, and Torquemada will be in one of the trucks."

"And where will I be?" asked Contreras, who, unlike Carla, had not yet heard the full details of the extraction operation.

"Aqui."

"Aqui?" she asked in lament. "Por que aqui?"

"Because I said so," stated Hernandez, who sounded more like a school-master than her fiancé. "Besides, you will not have to wait long."

"Okay," she conceded, at least outwardly.

"Stage three," Hernandez said. "As we get on the highway, all but three of the vehicles will peel off and head toward here. This will include the truck that we are in, plus two SUVs with armed personnel. This is, of course, where we will be at our weakest, due to smaller numbers. However, the overall convoy of trucks should serve as a fairly good distraction for any other commuters. From there, we make our way to this very spot, we depart from the truck, we board the plane, which should be all gassed and ready to go, and we fly out of this place, landing in the United States within a couple of hours."

"It sounds so easy," said Carla.

"Maybe because it is," said Hernandez with a smile. "Few people know the full plan. Even among the National Guard units that the government has loaned us, none of them will know which truck Torquemada will be in, and none will know which vehicles in the convoy will be breaking away at the opportune time. In other words, Orwell might have had something when he claimed that 'ignorance is strength.'"

"In this case, ignorance does help," Carla said.

"Ellas tienen algunas preguntas?"

"No, not at present," responded Carla.

"How long from the factory to here?" Marisol asked.

"No more than an hour, at the most."

"Good," said Marisol.

"Any other questions?"

Carla shook her head no, while Marisol remained silent.

"Excellent!" Hernandez declared, sporting a great smile. "Well, now if you will excuse me, that cancer stick will not smoke itself."

Hernandez walked away from the temporary rooms, going toward the nearest exit. Carla leaned back so that she was resting on the cot. Above her was a beige ceiling with various brownish spots, some abandoned spider webs, and some faint cracks. The climate control was working, the faint moans of the cooling units dominating the background. Everything felt still, everything felt solitary. Even though Marisol was there, Carla felt a strange sense of ease that comes from being alone. The cot made her feel like she was floating, as though drifting away from the violent obligations of her profession.

"If you need to rest, I can leave," said Marisol.

"Do what you want, I feel fine," said Carla, still looking upward. "I have not felt this well in a very long time."

Marisol smiled, patted Carla on the shoulder, and then walked away.

* * *

Carlos Benedico, one of the oldest lieutenants in the cartel, had gotten to the formal dining room of the hacienda before most of the others. As other lieutenants trickled into the long space with the great mahogany table, they easily spotted the man with artificial red hair and a sincerely gray mustache. Some nodded in greetings and then meandered elsewhere; a few stopped to make conversation before the impromptu gathering. One cartel figure, a man about half the age of Benedico, was standing at one of the corners of the long table that was near to the main entrance of the chamber.

"Like I said, Miquel, there is no real established process," Benedico explained to the younger leader. "It is not as though we have elections or formal rules of debate."

"Then, how have we chosen our leaders?" he asked.

"We just do, based on what feels right at the moment," said Benedico. "Sometimes—most of the time, really—whomever has the fire to demand it gets it. Señor Torquemada became our leader that way. After his predecessor was killed, he all but stormed into a meeting demanding that everyone follow him. There were many who thought they could do a better job, yet no one had the courage or the confidence to stop him."

"Until now."

"Quiza, Miquel. Quiza."

"So, what if both Torquemada and Brennenberg come here and stake claim to the cartel? What will we do then?"

"I would like to think that a simple vote would resolve the debate," said Benedico. "I can think of two occasions where it came down to that. One of them we raised our hands. The other one, we used paper and pen. Regardless, they were bloodless affairs."

"Ojala," said Miquel, who quickly crossed himself.

"Then again, I do not recall the situation being as desperate then as it is now," Benedico noted, raising his fist as he continued. "We need someone with power, someone with drive. We need a figure who can stop us from imploding."

"Does this mean you support Señor Brennenberg?" Miquel whispered.

"Honestly, I have not yet decided. I just want one of them to be made the clear victor. One of them needs to take the helm. I fear any alternatives."

"Alternatives, Señor Benedico?"

"Have you not heard the others?" Benedico asked his peer, who shook his head. "I have heard some of my more arrogant fellow lieutenants claim that they can lead us. They claim that they should be in charge. And they will spill blood to do so. The only thing keeping them from these foolish egotistic crusades are Brennenberg and Torquemada. If one of them fails to unite us all, then we fall apart. So, I am going with whomever everyone else supports. It is the best way to keep us all together."

"Yes, Señor Benedico."

"I believe you must do the same."

"Then I will, Señor Benedico."

The doors to the dining room chamber pulled open once more, revealing an entourage of lower ranked cartel leaders and less notable lieutenants. At the center of this group of people was the man of the day, the figure of the hour. Fulgencio Brennenberg was at the center of the collection of people, walking to the table. He stopped shortly before getting there, taking out a breathing mask from his jacket, quickly inhaling and exhaling four times before going any farther. The mask went back into his jacket, and he went back to the task of getting to the chair at the head of the long table, both hands resting on the top of the seat. All the idle chatter vanished at his presence.

"How can a man so weakened by a wound be so terrifying?" Benedico whispered to Miquel.

"In Revelation, the beast that came from the sea looked to be fatally wounded, and yet he ended up ruling the whole world," Miquel replied.

Brennenberg remained standing, sometimes leaning against the chair, sometimes towering on his own power. When he arrived, there was a tacit realization that the meeting should soon begin. In silence, figures representing the various businesses and plantations and soldiers and administration of the cartel took their seats. Sometimes they dared to look at the returning figure, other times they looked at each other to try and read what the general sentiment was of his call to power. Brennenberg surveyed the seated, looking over them as a king looks over his kingdom.

"Bienvenidos, cabelleros y lideres de la cartel," began Brennenberg, continuing his remarks in his native tongue. "I come to you as a voice from the dead. I am here to lead you into new life. A new life for our organization, a new life for our enterprises. When I was dead, I had much to think about. I thought about how our beloved cartel had become weak and timid. We have so much fear. We have fear of the Americans, we have fear of other organizations, and we have fear of exploration. Look at us. Look at what has happened under the rule of Torquemada. Just as he gave up on trying to regain our business in the EEUU, so he gives up on other efforts. He goes cap-in-hand to businesses, pleading for their support. He has fear; he is full of fear. And he has made us all fearful."

Pedro Aguilares was among those seated along the table. He was one of the last to come to the table before the entourage of Brennenberg had arrived. He sat far from the speaker, both out of habit and out of personal objection. As the once seriously wounded figure continued to list his grievances against the current leadership, Pedro turned with sadness to face the empty chair that was at the other end of the table. It was the very place where Torquemada normally sat when he dealt with leading the cartel. And yet, it was vacant. Pedro knew where his former boss was yet said nothing. He knew that speaking up would threaten the life of a man for whom he maintained much respect.

"However, mis cabelleros y mis lideres," declared Brennenberg, who grinned. "I no longer have any fear. The dead do not fear. I am here to lead you. I am here to destroy your fear. I have come back to this cartel to drive out its fear and make it strong again. We will become the dead. We will become what people fear, what people respect, and what people are not able to avoid. That is my promise to you, to all of you. Yo soy el muerte, ellos son los muertes. Somos los muertes. When I take control of this cartel, there will be no mercy, for death never shows mercy. There will be no more coming to others in weakness; we will come to them as death comes to an old man lying on his final bed. We can be the dead. We can be powerful again. Pero, this can only happen under my rule."

Many of those seated at the long table listened with intent, many who may have doubted the resolve of the man before them doubted no longer. Without Torquemada present to object to his allegations, and with the situation so horrid, few felt that there was a better alternative than the speaker who claimed to have died and come back. Pedro kept mum, recognizing as the others did that no one could truly stand against Brennenberg. No one asked for a raising of hands, no one asked to hand out pieces of paper and pens. This was because, by the end of the meeting, no one disputed who was in control of the cartel.

* * *

"Estas seguro que quieres a inviter su hermana?" asked Marisol. "Mariana?"

"Sí."

"Hey, yo amo mi hermana," Alfredo insisted, the two continuing their conversation en Español. "I mean, she can get a little annoying with her complaints about my job, yet she is still family. What is a man without his family?"

"Okay," Marisol conceded. "She was nice when she visited."

"There! My point is made!"

Marisol and her fiancé were at the airstrip, inside the building that included the two sectioned-off cots for Hernandez and Carla. They were at a round card table, with Marisol taking notes on her smart phone. It was evening, and the three had gone over the plan for the following morning at length. For the time, they were simply relaxing, aware of the heavy obligations of the morrow. The two had talked about these matters before, yet as they were finally looking to fix a date, they became a topic once again. Both of them seemed to get a sense of comfort from talking about the issue.

"Como sobre su tio?" Hernandez asked Marisol.

"Cual tio?"

"El tio que no le gusta el EEUU?"

"Ah, you mean Uncle Norman?"

"Yes. Him."

"He will behave. Yo te prometo."

"I do not agree. I think he will be a problem."

"Oh, come on, Alfredo. Do you think your sister will misbehave?"

"No."

"Then give me the benefit of a doubt. If necessary, I will talk with Uncle Norman before the ceremony. You know, set him straight."

"Okay. Whatever you want."

"Muy bien," she said, beaming.

"Estoy curioso," Hernandez inquired. "How did a guy who hates Americans get a gringo name like Norman?"

Marisol laughed. "In honesty, I have no idea."

"Really?"

"Verdad."

"You never asked?"

"I never cared."

"Ah," noted Hernandez. "Well, that should take care of the guest list."

"We are having it at my church."

"I never disputed that idea."

"You did, at first."

"Well, I just thought that since my side of the family is bigger, maybe it would be better if we held the ceremony in the United States."

"I grew up in that church. I was baptized there. I had my quinceañera there. There are no alternatives," Marisol stated.

"Yo se, yo se," he conceded, hands raised. "You win and you win."

"You know? I think I am going to like being married," she said, smiling.

"Tambien."

As the two chatted over wedding plans, Carla was at her cot. The suspended sheets were closed, giving her a privacy from the other two. She was seated on one end of the cot, with a small laptop placed on the opposite end. The device was on loan from those overseeing the airstrip. She was able to reach out to her family via a secure channel. She had first talked with her grandfather, with his wife by his side. It was a light conversation, with George al-Hassan acting with his usual dry humor and wrinkled smile. Carla initially tried to call her husband through the laptop, however he did not pick up. She waited twenty minutes, having figured who was responsible for the delay, and then tried again. This time he was patched in, with the two viewing each other through screens.

"Laila was a bit stubborn tonight," Josiah explained. "I finally got her down. She misses you, but you already know that."

"Yes, I do," said Carla. "Everything going well for you, Laila notwithstanding?"

"Yes, all is well."

"I am glad to hear it," she said. "I will be even happier when this assignment is over, and I will be back for the duration."

"How long is this supposed to take?"

"God-willing, I should be back by tomorrow, possibly the day after tomorrow at the latest." Carla paused. "On paper, it should be easy. Just a simple extraction and then back home. It almost feels like a victory lap."

"And yet, you wonder," said Josiah.

"I do."

"I had a grandfather who served in the army. He passed before we met. But he used to joke that military plans never go according to plan."

"Honestly, I am not sure that I find that funny right about now."

"Well, years later, I have wondered if he was joking," said Josiah. "You will be in my prayers, as always, Carla."

"They are appreciated," she said.

Through the screen, Carla could hear a minor disruption. Josiah heard it as well and groaned. Carla saw him looking down, her husband wincing once again. He returned his focus back to his wife. "Laila isn't happy."

"You better get to her, then."

"Yeah, I better," said Josiah, who was about to get up but stopped. "Carla...As the hymn puts it, God be with you till we meet again."

"And you also, Josiah," said Carla, who kissed three of her fingers and then lightly touched the screen with them while her husband was still on the screen. As she signed off, she took a deep breath, removed the laptop from the end of the cot, and then leaned back, again dreaming while still conscious.

* * *

It was not a grand feast. The kitchen served steaks, with salad and red wine. There were many who were absent from the occasion. Lieutenants and other ranked figures in the cartel had gone home, content that a new leader had been selected. Only some of them remained, partly out of genuine loyalty to Fulgencio Brennenberg, and partly to get on his best side. Many of the seats at the long table were empty, which was acceptable for the new head. Suspended lights gave vision to the chamber as the night sky reigned. The tone was surprisingly informal for the venue and the occasion.

Brennenberg still wore his best suit to the dinner, sitting at the same end of the table that he had been standing at days earlier when he made his triumphant return. He felt no need to occupy the seat of Raul Torquemada, as he saw the seat and the man to be of little consequence. Next to him was Carlos Benedico and his wife. The dinner had more women around than the business meetings. Girlfriends and wives occupied some of the seats. As many conversations went about the table, Benedico leaned into the new leader, occasionally speaking business and occasionally reminiscing about old times.

"I was glad to hear that the uniforms came in as quickly as they did," said Benedico. "I think it is good to set us apart like that."

"I said we would become death to our enemies and to any who cross us. I did not lie when I promised that. The new gear will showcase this quite well, I believe."

"Sí, Señor Brennenberg," said Benedico, who drank the rest of his wine so that only the dregs remained. "And what will you do with Torquemada?"

"You mean, to Torquemada, mi amigo," said one of the lieutenants seated near Brennenberg and Benedico, swinging his wine glass around.

"Estoy pensando," said the new leader. "I am not entirely sure that I want to kill him. While clearly not up to the task of running our cartel, Señor Torquemada had some strong points. He could be useful in getting the peasants to work harder."

"You are correct, Señor Brennenberg," Benedico nodded. "Plantations under his direct control always produced more crops."

"So, you demote him to local manager?" asked another lieutenant between bites of his steak. "That might be a worse fate than death!" The comment prompted him and his lay friend to laugh hysterically.

"All options are still being considered," said Brennenberg. "Although, leaving him alive is a bit awkward."

"Yes, it is, Señor Brennenberg," said one person at the table.

"Yes, of course, Señor Brennenberg," chimed in another.

Their banter continued for some time, as the people at the table finished their meals and opened another bottle of wine. Some left, as the hour was getting late. Benedico felt a need to remain as long as possible, even though his wife was clearly uncomfortable with the situation. They exchanged looks as the night wore on. Nevertheless, the topics of discussion became increasingly trivial. There was a rousing debate over who played the best football, or "soccer" as Brennenberg had come to call it due to his time in the United States. A few more left under good terms and in good spirits.

As the door was about to shut from the latest person to exit, it was stopped from latching. The portal then opened wider to reveal Pedro Aguilares. The new cartel leader was unafraid of the younger man. If nothing else, the new arrival was unarmed, while Brennenberg had multiple guards at multiple sides of the table. Pedro was sober and a bit tired, as he had been walking a lot around the hacienda. There was a chair, vacant and pulled out of the table, which Brennenberg motioned for Pedro to sit in. He was still very much filled with festive sentiment over his quick conquest of the cartel. Meanwhile, Pedro simply moved a few steps forward, but tacitly declined to be seated.

"I need to talk to you," Pedro told Brennenberg. He then looked at Benedico and his wife. "This is a private affair."

"Pedro, show some respect," Benedico dissented. "We are all friends here."

"I want to talk with Brennenberg alone," Pedro said, doubling down.

"But Pedro—"

"Everyone, leave," said Brennenberg, who felt compelled to repeat his order. "I said, everyone, leave! Now!"

"Adios, jefe!" said one of the lieutenants as he followed the command.

"We will talk later," said Benedico as he stood up, his wife openly relieved that they were exiting the chamber. "Good night, Señor Brennenberg."

Pedro stood there, patient as the rest of the people left. They straggled about, some having consumed a fair amount of fermented liquid. More well-wishes were bestowed upon Brennenberg by those departing for the evening. They ranged from the vocal to a simple nod of the head to an enthusiastic verbal salute. Only a couple even acknowledged Pedro, with one giving a light pat on the back as he walked by. He remained still and quiet, wanting the last of them to leave before he uttered another word. Pedro looked at the armed guards standing about the table. A part of him wanted them to leave as well, however Brennenberg would not permit the request. Pedro knew this and did not ask of it.

"The door is shut, the guests are gone, and we are effectively alone," Brennenberg observed. "Did you see the new uniforms the men will be wearing? I feel they symbolize our new commitment to power."

"I saw them," said Pedro. "They seem practical."

"You win wars by scaring the enemy. You scare the enemy through the fear of death."

"Sí, señor."

"Que quieres, Pedro?"

"What do I want?" he repeated, more in contemplation than as a query. "This is not about what I want. I will never get what I want. I know that. This is about what I need. I need the cartel. I need this. I need all of this. I have always needed it. I want it, sometimes, but I need it. That is for sure."

"Get to the point please," said Brennenberg, who took out the breathing device from his jacket pocket and quickly inhaled and exhaled into the mask a few times.

"Torquemada has left the hacienda."

"That does not surprise me," said the new leader, brushing off the news. "No one has seen him since this afternoon."

"I know where he is going."

"Again, I do not understand why this is important," said Brennenberg, who picked at the steak bone on his plate. "I have debated what I plan to do to my predecessor. Sometimes, I want him to live. Sometimes, I want him to die. If he wants to disappear, start a new life elsewhere, I am okay with that."

"He is going to the Americans," said Pedro, who leaned forward, fists on the tabletop. "He is going to turn himself in. He is going to tell them everything about us. He wants to destroy the cartel. He wants to destroy us."

Brennenberg presented no evidence of emotion. He lacked any surprise. He just kept picking at the steak bone. He then gave a faint grin. "You are his friend, correct?"

"I was."

"Why would you betray him?"

"He is betraying us," Pedro insisted. "As you know, I am opposed to you taking control. I wanted Torquemada to stay in power. However, he cannot be allowed to destroy us. He chose to betray. We must stop him."

"Bien. Muy, muy bien," said the new leader. "I like this. I like your reasoning. I had my doubts about you, but they are vanishing away."

"Gracias."

"Now, tell me all that you know about his plan to leave."

"Sí... mi jefe."

VI.

Carla al-Hassan Sharp felt oddly at home as they neared the milk factory. The imposing industrial edifice reminded her of the many abandoned facilities outside of her hometown back in the United States. It was a fitting comparison, as the milk factory was likely tied to the history of her homeland. As the factories in the Great Lakes area of the United States closed down, they were moved to southern states, where wages could be lower, and the union presence was weak. Some of those jobs continued to travel downward, with globalization making their owners conclude that Latin America was a better place to reap profits. It was possible that some of the older manufacturing machines at the milk factory had gone from the Rust Belt all the way down to that city in Central America.

Marisol Contreras was driving Carla and Alfredo Hernandez. There was little conversation among them that morning as they ventured to the rendezvous location. The shower at the airstrip only had cold water, which made for a less than pleasant preparation. However, there was no small child to have to get ready, either. Hernandez had a cigarette before they drove out, the smoke smell still leaving a faint aroma inside the vehicle. Carla and Hernandez were armed, while Marisol was not. Hernandez was wearing slacks and a tie, both brown, with a white shirt. Carla was wearing a factory uniform, which consisted of a light blue pants and jacket. It was part of the deception.

As Marisol stopped the car, the trio found themselves shaded by the dark walls of the factory, a crowded loading dock before them. Several trucks were lined up. They were of bland colors and lacked any logos or flashy imagery.

Plain and simple exteriors, with empty semi-trailers attached to each one. Others moved about the dock, both on the elevated platform that directly led to the interior of the factory and the lower level where the trucks were parked. Some were in factory worker uniforms, while others were in military uniforms. None of them actually worked at the facility. The truck drivers were the only ones there not employed by the local National Guard or the Agency. Carla and Hernandez exited the vehicle, while Marisol remained in the driver's seat, her window rolled down.

"Vaya con Dios," Marisol said to her fiancé and to Carla.

"Y tu, tambien," Carla replied.

Hernandez responded by bending forward and kissing Marisol on the lips. She stretched out her arm and touched his tan cheek with her fingers, the digits slowly gliding down his face. Hernandez grudgingly took a few steps back, while Marisol put the car in reverse, turned around, and then drove away. Hernandez remained focused on the departing vehicle for a few extra seconds, until a tap on the shoulder brought him back to the assignment. The men on the ground were loading up the trucks, while the person of interest was inside the factory, hidden from their immediate view.

"Are you excited yet?" Hernandez asked Carla, a smile upon his face.

"Not sure I would use the word excited."

"Be of good cheer, as the Good Book puts it," Hernandez assured her, as the two walked up a rampway along the side of the loading dock. "He comes to us for help. Even if he finds out who you are, it will hardly be a dealbreaker. He has no other options."

"Inshallah."

Large silver vats abounded within the factory, each one twice as tall as an average-sized man. A complex network of pipes and tubes wrapped around the units, which in turn connected to other machines. Most of the main room was occupied by the thin, twisting conveyor belts, which had railings along both sides to prevent the newly sealed bottles from spilling. The machines, which often produced great noise as well as many products, were silent at that hour. Carla and Hernandez walked by the quiet, empty conveyors to meet the man who was standing on the opposite end of the large room.

He had a suitcase on the ground beside him, his fingers contorted as though about to form fists. He was wearing dark blue slacks and a dinner jacket, with a black T-shirt. His hair was almost as long as Carla's, but unlike hers, it was fashioned into a ponytail. He had a mustache and goatee, which was black, like his hair. Serious was his demeanor, and he initially showed no pathos as the two Americans drew nigh. Carla suppressed her emotions, as she remembered that the last time she saw the man was the year before, when she nearly put a bullet into his brain. Only her dark thoughts had prevented the operation from succeeding. She and her handler stopped within six feet of the figure.

"Señor Raul Torquemada, I presume," said Hernandez.

"Yes," he said, speaking English.

"We are the Agency representatives assigned to take you out of here," said Hernandez. "When the trucks are ready, we will pick one and get moving."

"Will the drivers know which one?"

"They will only know which of them will be peeling off from the convoy when we roll out. The less they know, the better."

"I agree," said Torquemada, who started to focus more on Carla. "Once I get to the United States, I will tell you everything."

"I am very happy to hear that," Hernandez said as he smiled even more.

"You look familiar," Torquemada said to Carla. "I know I have seen you before." Then it clicked for him. "You are that governor's wife. I remember you now."

Carla remained silent.

"We tried to kidnap you. We wondered if you had fought off our soldiers. Then, I wondered if you were a double instead of the real wife. You are the real one, right?"

"Yes, she is," said Hernandez. Carla and Torquemada looked at him. Hernandez eyed Carla. "We might as well be honest, at this point. Are you really worried about Torquemada knowing this now?"

"I do not care," Torquemada assured her. "This explains why we failed. We did not know that you were an agent. You are someone trained to kill."

"Your ignorance was my advantage," Carla finally spoke up. "I confess, I have done a lot to harm your cartel."

"Did you kill Delacruz?"

"Yes."

"How?"

"I was the waitress. I dropped a pill in her wine."

"Interesting," said Torquemada, who paced about in contemplation. "Verdad, I am more impressed than angry."

"Thank you."

"Are we ready yet?" Torquemada asked Hernandez.

"Let me check with the guard officer," said Hernandez. "You two keep having fun."

"Who else have you killed?" Torquemada asked Carla as Hernandez walked toward one of the men wearing dark body armor.

"Many," she said, coldly.

"How many?"

"I do not keep track," said Carla. "I may be good at what I do, but I do not like it. I do it because I have to."

"I knew people like you in the cartel," Torquemada observed. "They do it to make a living, nothing more."

"And you? Did you like what you did?"

Before Torquemada could answer, Hernandez returned, smiling once again. "We are ready to go now, so let us do this."

"God," she prayed in a whisper. "Please let this work."

* * *

"Number one, number one, do you copy?" Hernandez inquired over a walkie-talkie.

"Number one here. I copy," responded the static-laden voice.

"How long until next step, over?"

"Next step coming up in three miles, over."

"Copy, number one. Over and out," concluded Hernandez.

"Over and out."

Their environment had become a windowless gray shell. The floor moved, though the figures inside remained balanced, thanks to the shock absorption. There were several crates along the walls, as well as a few chairs for sitting. Torquemada stayed by his suitcase, the luggage leaning against his seat. Hernandez was near the front of the semitrailer, while Carla walked about one of the sides. Two National Guardsmen in gray body armor and helmets were there as well, carrying assault rifles. The outside world provided only noises—mostly, the roaring engines of the motorcade.

By and large, the trip had been a smooth one. After the guardsmen and other personnel entered the trucks or the two-axel vehicles present, Carla, Hernandez, and Torquemada picked one of the lorries and secured the back. There was an initial jolt from the vehicle beginning its forward motion, and the occasional jerking due to periodic sudden breaks. This was the kind of upheaval expected when riding out to the airstrip. The passengers had felt the truck revving up as the convoy got onto the highway. Hernandez smiled at that step being accomplished without incident. He remained positive.

"How much longer?" Torquemada asked.

"A few more miles, so maybe five or six minutes until we split off from the main body," said Hernandez. "From there, it will probably be another half an hour to get to the airstrip. And then from there, no more than ten or fifteen minutes until we take off."

"Muy bien," the former cartel leader stated.

"I hope we can say the same when you turn over all of what you know about the cartel."

"You will," assured Torquemada. "I have details on everything. Personnel, plantations, business ties. As you say, 'the works.'"

"Out of curiosity, is it all memorized, or do you have it on some hardware?"

"You will know when I get to safety."

Hernandez thought about pressing but decided against it. At that moment, he did not feel a need to know more. A part of him felt that even if Torquemada had exaggerated his level of knowledge about the cartel, anything he could provide must be of value. There was a moral victory about having someone as prominent as Torquemada in custody, especially given how actively involved he had been in the operations of his criminal organization. Seeing him sitting there, demoralized and hunched over, looking down for much of the trip, gave Hernandez a sense of inherent triumph.

"How do you do it?" Torquemada suddenly asked Carla.

"What?"

"How do you do it?"

"Do what?"

"Be the wife of a governor and kill people for the CIA?"

"It is not easy," she said. "I guess—"

BOOM! A loud explosion, heard over the dominant droning of the engines, made the truck come to an abrupt stop. The semitrailer swung to one side, throwing everyone to the floor, causing chairs and even crates to fall over. One crate smashed upon a guard, crushing his leg. Another chair flew upward and slammed into Hernandez, knocking him unconscious. Torquemada and Carla nearly collided as they landed onto the floor. Two other guards impacted one of the walls. The suitcase hit a couple of the crates that had been at the ground level, the impact being such that the luggage was cracked along one side. The latch remained secure, so no clothing was tossed about.

Half a moment after the initial blast, another crashing noise was heard, as the front of the truck slammed into the semitrailer ahead of them. The crunching of metal was a crooked painful note that was all but blinding to those already unable to see the outside. Passengers continued to be thrown about, the unconscious body of Hernandez flying into the wall, while another crate crashed into another guardsman, knocking him senseless. Carla and Torquemada likewise were flung around. Loud thuds of objects and bodies flung around sounded like a pounding of protest upon the frame of the semitrailer.

As everyone was on the floor of the container, another great explosion was heard, the echoes coming from behind them this time. Carla expected another impact at this second, a vehicle plowing into the frame of the once moving chamber, however none came. After a few moments that felt like forever, the semitrailer was stopped. All fell still within the unit, as neither body nor object was being hurled about. Carla had a couple of bruises from the impacts, and her uniform had a couple of small tears. Otherwise, she was okay. Torquemada's jacket had a rip in the back that was about five inches long, and his body was sore from being thrown into things. Yet, he was otherwise unharmed.

Carla and Torquemada were the only ones on their feet at that point. On the floor were the other passengers. Hernandez was still out, with a shattered crate covering most of his body. One guard was writhing in pain, his leg broken in two places. The other two guards were gathering their wits, as their armor prevented any serious physical harm. A couple of assault rifles were laid upon the floor, as were splintered pieces of crate. More blasts were heard, sounding like artillery shells. They seemed to be getting ever closer to their semitrailer, as they picked off the others. Carla and Torquemada knew what to do, as they each took an assault rifle from the floor and then headed for the rear doors.

"Can you open it?" Carla asked Torquemada.

He simply nodded in response, rushing to the end of the unit as yet another explosion was heard outside. That one sounded as though it were the vehicle right in front of them. Torquemada slung the assault rifle on his shoulder and used both hands to work on the latch. After some moments, he was able to push the latch free, causing one of the doors to shift in its freedom. Carla and Torquemada both gripped their respective assault rifles, pointing their firearms at the two doors. Torquemada looked at Carla, nodded, and then kicked open the loose door. They darted out of the unit, one at a time, jumping down and scanning with their guns, pointing wherever an enemy might be found.

Before them was a highway filled with carnage. The bright morning was darkened by the black clouds from the explosions. A thunderous background noise of the fires served as ambience, with a canon of honking horns and emergency noises from distant vehicles trying to get through the lanes of thick halted traffic. Shattered cars were around them as well, with the SUV that was behind them having been thrown off to the side and landing upside down. Smashed glass and twisted metal covered the ground. Wreckage abounded, with a few bodies scattered on the wide road in the distance.

The two kept looking around, moving away from the ruined transport. They expected to use their weapons, yet no bullets were fired. The enemy was invisible. No one was greeting them with resistance. What few people they saw moving nearby were either on the ground wounded or were the able-bodied helping treat those in need. Torquemada and Carla stayed close, going to one side of the crashed truck to check on the situation. They struggled to see anyone else from the stopped convoy. There were some people moving outside of the vehicles about a couple hundred feet away. Although, the figures might have been the unknown assailants trying to finish off the passengers.

As they went across the highway, they finally got a better look at the damage in front of them. Each of the vehicles in the motorcade was stopped. All of them appeared to have been severely damaged or outright totaled. Semitrailers were blown to bits, with giant holes where there were once solid metal walls. Each was like a funeral pyre, dedicated to the guardsmen and others who once inhabited the units. The drivers did not appear to have been much better off, as trucks and SUVs crashed into each other at full speed, some to the point of fusing together with the vehicle ahead of them.

Carla and Torquemada struggled to see the destructive panorama, as the winds changed their flow and began throwing the smoke in their direction. Both breathed hard, trying to grasp what had happened. Carla wanted to go back to the unit to get Hernandez. The last she saw of him, he was knocked out by the blast. Once the safety of Torquemada and herself seemed sure, she wanted desperately to go back to the semitrailer. She believed that he was most likely alive, as no one else in the container had appeared to suffer fatal injuries. Carla saw a guard jump out of the back.

However, before she could act upon her desire, loud motorized noises were heard to her left. She and Torquemada turned to see a new convoy. There was a wave of dark jeeps and pick-up trucks modified to include machine guns in the back. While it was unclear who was in the vehicles, the lack of flashing emergency lights told Carla and Torquemada plenty. Torquemada led the way as they fled from the roadway, leaving the concrete and venturing into the adjacent jungle growth. As they got among the trees, Carla took one last look at the line of broken vehicles, knowing that she was leaving behind a friend and colleague, then dashed into the growth as the nefarious ones drew nigh.

* * *

Fulgencio Brennenberg walked amongst the wreckage. He was within several feet of the line of ruined trucks and cars. His shoes crumpled shards of weakened glass, his skin was warmed by the dying fires, and his eyes were slightly irritated when he saw the bright red flares placed along the effected lanes. Above him was a thick layer of smoke, making much shade for those milling about the destroyed convoy. As he went along the side of one totaled vehicle, he noticed a rearview mirror on the ground. He picked it up, seeing that it only had a faint crack. With the mirror held in one hand, Brennenberg used his fingers to adjust his blond hair, making sure the strands were in place. Once satisfied with his makeover, he tossed the rearview mirror, giving it no further thought.

Traffic cops were nearby, guiding the gridlocked lanes into the one free avenue of travel. Two lanes of commuters had to awkwardly slide to the left, hoping to find a kind soul behind another wheel who will allow them to merge. Once they went beyond the narrowed way, cars sped fast. Few wanted to be anywhere near the dark presence that persisted at the crashes. A gust of breeze came as courtesy to each vehicle that went by, the drivers flooring the gas lest they garner suspicion. A mixture of fear and corruption prompted the police to keep their distance from those at the totaled vehicles.

Around Brennenberg were the newly uniformed figures of his newly acquired cartel. Each soldier of the criminal enterprise was wearing black pants and hooded jackets. Their countenances were covered with sunglasses and surgical facemasks that resembled the bottom half of a skull. Most of those walking on the road carried assault rifles, as well as handguns. Some remained in the back of pick-ups, standing by machine guns mounted to the bed of the vehicle. They scanned the environment, looking for any potential threat. Laid on either side of them on the dirty hard surface of the bed were RPGs and bazookas. These were the means they had used to take down the convoy.

While others patrolled the carnage, a small number of the cartel figures went into the fiery wrecks, both to finish off any survivors and to try and confirm the demise of the target. It was a complicated effort, as many of the corpses were charred well beyond recognition. Some were not, and thus were eliminated from the guessing game. Many of the blackened bodies were laid alongside each other, without dignifying them via a sheet to cover their bodies, much less a priest to give last rites. They were of interest when it might have been the man they were after, and dismissed when confirmed that they were not. Several became nauseous as the aroma of burning flesh filled the air.

Brennenberg was standing above a row of a dozen bodies. A few of them still had on the body armor meant to protect from bullets. Such shielding did little to protect from the flames and the intense explosive power of the cartel artillery. Others—the bodies more torn up by his destructive power—were dressed in factory uniforms. Brennenberg surveyed the dead, figuring out that they were not Torquemada. They were too short, or too fat, or too scrawny, or too tall. Brennenberg and a few other cartel figures were inspecting the corpses, able to make good judgments on whether they were the target or not, because they knew the target and had known him for years.

"We still have not found him," explained one of the masked figures to Brennenberg.

"What of the ones too burned to be identified?" asked the new leader, who took out his breathing device and used it yet again. The thick, rising smoke had required him to use the device more than usual.

"There are only a few that bad. We will get them to the lab back at the hacienda."

"Muy bien," said Brennenberg, looking down at the row of dead.

The masked soldier nodded and went back to work. People were going back and forth, with some cautiously entering the smoldering units. Some of the bodies were unable to be reached, having been crushed into the wrecks. A quick look inside was sufficient. One of the few cartel figures who lacked a hood and facemask who was prowling about the scene was Pedro

Aguilares. Although lacking the skeletal mask, he still wore a black shirt and pants to reflect the garb of his peers. He stood taller than most of his peers, which helped Brennenberg see him coming from several feet away.

"Report to me, Pedro."

"According to the soldiers I spoke to, at least two people went into the jungle before we secured the area."

"Was one of them Torquemada?" asked Brennenberg with some angst.

"They were not sure."

"Damn," he said under his breath, before returning to face Aguilares. "Have men search the jungles. If they were on foot, they cannot have gotten that far from here."

"Sí, Señor Brennenberg."

"Also, have another group of soldiers return to the ammo warehouse and get more long-range weapons. We nearly used them all up on this little operation."

"Sí, señor."

"And find me a map."

"A map?"

"Yes, an old-fashioned map," said Brennenberg, who paused to take out his breath mask, quickly inhaled and exhaled four times, and then continued speaking. "I want to get a good look at where Torquemada might be heading."

"Right away," said Pedro, who then ran off to fulfill the orders bestowed upon him.

Brennenberg saw more vehicles speeding by in the left lane. Most were solitary commuters in office attire. Some were women with children in the back. Many faces turned to see the devastation, only to immediately turn back when they realized the source. Brennenberg took in the fearful looks. He was honored by the gesture, viewing it as comparable to subjects bowing before a king. As he stood near the left lane, he put his hands into fists and rested them on his hips, staring forward with his blue eyes. Cars trickling out of the gridlock veered more to the left to avoid him.

"Señor Brennenberg! Señor Brennenberg!"

The cartel head turned to see a young man coming his way. While his face was still obscured by sunglasses and the skeletal mask, his hood had drifted backwards, revealing a shaved head. He was a few inches shorter than Brennenberg, even though he was wearing boots. He looked up to the leader both literally and figuratively and seemed disappointed as he halted before him to bring his news. As though a teacher before a student, Brennenberg nodded to give him permission to speak.

"We have recovered all the bodies we can. None of them are Señor Torquemada. Well, maybe the five that are really damaged, but we do not know."

"Have the five tested at the lab."

"Sí, señor," said the young soldier, who ran past Pedro as he came back, a paper map under his arm.

"You have a map?"

"I do, Señor Brennenberg."

Pedro kept hold of the map, unrolling the document and spreading it out so that his superior was able to view it. It was the usual cartographic design, with a legend in the upper left-hand corner, names of cities, towns, and villages, lines representing streets, and assorted appellations for natural topographic features. Brennenberg knew his present location, having charted the plan of attack the night before, thanks to Pedro telling him of the planned extraction of Torquemada. In silence, he studied the map. After several moments, he stretched out a finger, pointing at their spot on the highway, and then gliding just above the map. He was initially unsure of his movement, but then smiled, and had the fingertip press against the illustrated features, going a specific way.

"I think I know where he is going."

"Donde, Señor Brennenberg?"

"A few villages that are not far from here," said Brennenberg, who raised his head and stared forward. "He thinks he will be safe."

"Should I get the men ready, señor?"

"Yes, do," said the cartel leader.

"It will be good to stop him, Señor Brennenberg. He was going to ruin us all. He wanted to destroy the cartel. We need to stop him for that reason."

"Yes, that reason," said Brennenberg, still staring forward. "However, there is another, maybe greater, reason."

"Señor Brennenberg?"

"It has been a long time since I have made a masterpiece. El Artista is starving for a new canvas, a new work of brilliance. I long to create a fitting work of art to celebrate my rise to the top of this operation. There must be a great sculpture, a masterfully crafted portrait, a symbolic monument to this new vision of death. It will inspire devotion in my men and fear in our enemies, and submission to the rest. Yes, there is something very important that Torquemada must do for us. A part of me now almost wants him alive, so that I can make him a great paragon of triumph."

"So, do you want us to take him alive after all?"

"If possible, yes. Otherwise, feel free to kill him. I could always use others for my cultural endeavors," said Brennenberg. "The men said that they saw someone who might have been Torquemada into the jungle with someone else, right?"

"Yes."

"Then, maybe kill our former leader and keep alive the other man. Maybe the honor of a monument can be reserved for him."

"Her."

"Que?" Brennenberg asked.

"The person who fled into the jungle with the man who might have been Torquemada was a woman."

Brennenberg smiled. "So much the better."

VII.

Carla al-Hassan Sharp was batting away countless little flying beasts as she and Raul Torquemada went deeper into the jungle. The ground was an uneven patchwork of grassland and thick tree roots, mud, and puddles. Carla or Torquemada often splashed as they walked, darkening their respective pant legs. There was no way to go too fast, as the ground was neither flat nor fully stable. Vines got in the way, with the two either ducking or slapping them away. Contorted branches full of leaves and birds were arched above, blocking out most of the beams from hitting them.

They kept looking back as they were moving away from the carnage of the destroyed convoy. There were no humans in sight. Trees crowded the view of the background and the way ahead, as though human civilization itself had vanished amid their plights. There were no sounds of automobile or factory, of lawnmower or vacuum. Only the hoots and hollers and buzzes and screeches of the wilderness. Only the occasional bug, mistaking an ear for a flower, diving into the two people walking. They both slapped a lot, both concerned about itching and disease, despite their vaccinations.

Carla felt miserable. She kept thinking of Alfredo Hernandez and the others, those left for dead amid the great attack. She felt sorrow for Marisol Contreras, as she would likely be the one to inform Marisol that her fiancé was murdered. Carla did not know where they were going, or where the airstrip was from their current position. Her feet were wet inside her damp shoes and socks, and her clothing had a growing number of tears and blemishes, while her legs and upper body had a thin layer of sweat. The fully loaded assault rifle she bore felt twice as heavy as it did when she first took it from the semitrailer. Torquemada was looking little better, with his clothes being soaked by sweat, and the physical demands of their retreat was getting to him more than to her.

After a couple of hours of fervent travel, the two stopped at a clearing. The space was lit by a few descending beams of light that broke through the thick jungle canopy. Hard roots formed several little arches inches above the ground, rising up from the dirt and then burrowing back into the terrain. Brown dirt and sporadic clumps of green grass formed the flooring for the space, with scores of bugs flying above them in circles. Dozens of vines hung from the branches, a couple of them ripped by the two human beings who went into the clearing, where they stopped and tried to gather themselves.

Carla did not want to sit down. In addition to the perpetual concern of the enemy catching up, there was the sense that sitting down on a thick root or leaning against a tree trunk would be an open invitation for the swarms to crawl all over her and inside of her clothing. Carla laid her firearm against the trunk and took off her jacket, putting it under her arm. Torquemada seemed less worried about infestation, as he pressed his back against a tree on the opposite end of the clearing and caught his breath. He held his assault rifle with one hand with the muzzle pointing to the ground. Torquemada looked down for a time, seeming to struggle to face the woman who had fled into the wilds with him.

"We cannot stay here long," said Carla, trying to be professional. "They will realize that you are not among the dead. They will fan out and try and find you."

"I know."

"We will have to find another way to the airstrip. There might be another way. I have to get a map of the area, but I think I can—"

"No."

The rejection surprised Carla. She waited for a response.

"If they knew what we are doing, then they know where we are going."

"How? How could they know?"

Torquemada looked down. Carla became incensed.

"You told someone."

"Yes," he confessed. "One of the other leaders. I thought he wanted to come along. He has always been loyal to me."

"Well, he wasn't loyal this time," she stated, putting her tarnished light blue jacket back on, and taking hold of her assault rifle. She brushed it a bit, just in case some ant or spider had opted to make her weapon a new home. "We need to go to the airstrip."

"I said we cannot go there."

"Then where?" she asked, fist clenching.

"There's a town, a few miles from here. They know me."

"Are they as loyal as your friend?"

Torquemada refused to respond to the question. "They will shelter us. We need to go."

"Are you sure you can trust them?"

"Where would you go?" asked Torquemada, who became visibly angry. "Back to the highway, where they're waiting for us? How about the airstrip, where they are waiting? We can't go anywhere else! We go to the village, or we rot here!"

Carla wanted to shout back; she wanted to pour out her frustration against the man whose enemies led them to the jungle. She just knew that the extraction would not be as simple, yet she hardly fathomed the level of destruction reaped. She realized that an outburst against the former cartel leader would be pointless. Torquemada may have lacked a foolproof plan, yet she lacked an alternative. Instead, she gripped her assault rifle and deferred to Torquemada to lead the way. He gave a weak smile, and the two continued to make distance between themselves and the bloodthirsty adversary.

* * *

Around him were buildings; below him was pavement. His location was an old parking lot for a condemned office. A recent earthquake had made the structure unusable, with the foundation being severely compromised. It was scheduled for demolition some time ago, but the actual performance of the deed kept being delayed. Various supplies from the building had been taken either by the former owners or by thieves. It was dark inside, with only piles of debris occupying the ruined interior. Other buildings that were in the immediate background were still in use, for business and for pleasure.

Fulgencio Brennenberg was waiting around. There were three SUVs parked at the lot. Two of them were back-to-back, while the third was stationed off in the corner. He was among them, knowing that others were going to join him. Walking about the lot were a few men wearing black clothes, Day of the Dead themed facemasks, and sunglasses. Each bore an assault rifle, with a couple of them having pistols holstered. They faced outwards for purposes of keeping their leader safe. Brennenberg was thinking about things, ranging from the recent ambush to plans for a new work of art.

Attention was given to two new vehicles. They slowed down as the lot entrance drew nigh, turning into the space without competition. There were few people around that part of the city, anyway. What few did frequent that stretch of streets kept away once they saw the dark-clad men waiting around the lot. Brennenberg caught a glimpse of one of the passengers. He had dyed red hair as well as a gray mustache. He knew it to be Carlos Benedico. The new arrivals parked side by side, several feet from those standing around. A small group of cartel lieutenants and guards exited the vehicles, being led by Benedico and flanked by Pedro Aguilares. Their security also adopted the morbid attire of Brennenberg's men.

"What the hell happened?" Benedico shouted, still walking toward Brennenberg.

"I ran out of missiles," Brennenberg deadpanned.

"You said you could kill him just like that! You said that you would eliminate him in one great swoop and then we would not have to worry about him anymore."

"I was close," Brennenberg said defensively, as the new group stood in front of him. "I think it was a pretty good showing, all things considered."

"A good showing?" asked an exasperated Benedico.

"Yes!" declared the cartel leader. "You did not see the fear of those around us because of what we did. The police stayed away until we left, and the people fled in terror. We showed that we are the dominant force in this country. Not the United States, not the government, not the National Guard. Us. And us alone!"

"Torquemada still lives," Benedico countered, softly. "As long as he lives, we are vulnerable. He cannot leave this country alive. He cannot talk to the Americans."

"Yo sé, yo sé," declared an annoyed Brennenberg. "I know, I know."

"Do you even know where he is?"

"We have a couple of ideas. We are going to visit some of the villages near here. We know he has some contacts. Even some friends."

"The other lieutenants are not as patient as I am," Benedico warned. "A couple of them have told me that they are having second thoughts about letting you take control."

"Name them and I will be sure to change their minds," said Brennenberg, a sadistic grin upon his face. "Or I could make them a gallery to my new authority."

"Señor Torquemada," said the older lieutenant. "If you are going to lead us, you need to respect dissenting views. When Torquemada was in control, you were given a wide latitude to criticize his actions."

"That was because there was something to criticize," countered Brennenberg. "Death does not make mistakes. It may be unknowing, but it is also unstoppable."

Benedico had no response.

"Torquemada will be found," Brennenberg assured the lieutenant. "And he will be made an example of. As will anyone who is found to be supporting him."

Brennenberg said goodbye by simply giving a smile at Benedico. He turned away from the cartel officer and went to one of the SUVs. He signaled for the other soldiers who had come with him to join his motorcade. They went to the passenger seats or behind the wheels, engines revving up, and rolling out. Pedro walked up to Benedico, patting the shorter cartel officer on the shoulder. As the last of the SUVs departed the old lot, Benedico looked back at the younger Pedro and shook his head.

"This was a bad idea," Benedico told Pedro, the rest of their entourage milling about the parking lot. "I knew it was, but I let it happen."

"Señor Benedico," said Pedro. "If you want to blame anyone, blame me. I could have stopped Torquemada when he was still at the hacienda. I did not."

"Yours is a mistake of loyalty," said the older cartel figure. "You were hesitant to kill a friend and a mentor. That is understandable."

"Pero, I was not hesitant enough to let him go."

"That was smart of you," said Benedico. "You show nuance, discernment. Not bad for a young brute."

"Gracias, señor."

"It is our new leader that troubles me. His bloodlust knows no nuance, no discernment. He has become infatuated with inflicting suffering."

"You supported him."

"I did," said Benedico, "but only because I saw no better option. We need to rally behind someone. We need one central man in charge of everything, or else it all falls apart. I do not have that power. You definitely do not have it, either. That power can only be found with Señor Brennenberg. Whether we like it or not."

"And it sounds like neither of us likes it."

"Maybe he is right," said Benedico, as the two walked back to the vehicles remaining. "Maybe he will succeed. I could never imagine Torquemada doing what Brennenberg did today, let alone doing so with relative impunity."

"Death usually has impunity," said Pedro, getting a stare from the older cartel officer. "What? Even I can see the appeal."

"You, plus many others."

* * *

There was still sunlight abounding as Carla and Torquemada neared the village. They crept softly as they got closer to the unpaved main street. They crouched down as vehicles went to and from the settlement. Each one could have been tied to the cartel and thus linked to the mission of targeting the former leader. Thus far, the two had been fortunate. The men who had so swiftly destroyed their convoy had not caught up with them. They speculated that either the cartel had presumed Torquemada to be dead, or they had failed to predict his whereabouts after the highway ambush.

The village was quiet. Few people went about the dirt roads, and even fewer cars were present. Most of the homes were barely a story tall, with a couple of domiciles having two stories. They were brick dwellings with metal roofs, with nearly all of them having electricity, refrigerators, freezers, microwaves, and ovens. One building was a laundromat; another was a barbershop; and another, a tiny library whose major appeal was that it had a pair of old computers that were donated several years ago. Running water was an occasional convenience, as it was often shut off or was contaminated. A well was located in the middle of the town and was still often used by locals.

"Where is everyone?" Carla asked Torquemada.

"They are working at the plantation," he explained. "There is a farm about ten miles from here. It grows coffee beans and narcotics."

"I take it one serves as cover for the other."

"Yes," he replied. "That plantation alone provides about ten percent of our cartel's annual income. Several small villages like this one serve as the workforce."

"I see."

"That one was for free," Torquemada stated, briefly facing Carla as he spoke. "Other important information will come when you get me to the United States."

"I hope so."

"We need to go," said Torquemada, rising from the jungle cover. "Sigueme."

"Okay."

Carla followed Torquemada out of the jungle and onto the clear street. The dirt path was wide and dry, making for an easy trek. This was welcomed, as the two had been walking for hours through the thick growth of vine and branch, their limbs very sore from the journey. Both of them had darkened their attire with blobs of sweat, as well as added little tears here and there on sleeves and pant legs. Both casually carried their assault rifles, having yet to fire them either in anger or in practice. No alarms appeared to be sounded as the two walked into the center of the village.

"Over here," said Torquemada, veering right of the well. "That house."

"Friends?"

"They should be."

"Should," Carla stated, doubt drenching the succinct comment.

Torquemada persisted, walking up to the house that had two stories. Windows were open to allow for a decent cross breeze. Centralized climate control was rare in those parts. There was a screen door and a metal door behind it. Torquemada slung his rifle upon his back, opened the screen door, and then knocked on the metal barrier. There was no response, initially. A few seconds later, he knocked again. Carla massaged her legs with her free hand, waiting for the claim of friendship to be proven true. After the second round of knocking, the two heard some conversations in Español behind the door. Then, the sound of lumbering steps before the metal door was opened.

Before their view was an elderly man, wearing a white T-shirt that barely covered his hefty waist. He was wearing blue jeans and sandals as well. He had wrinkles on his face, neck, and arms, with a mostly gray beard on his cheeks. His dark eyes were stoic at the initial moment of introduction, then passionate when he saw the figure standing before him, but then confused when he beheld the circumstances. It was a lot to take in, seeing Torquemada armed, weary, and accompanied by a strange woman.

"Raul? What is happening?" he asked.

"Long story, Felipe," Torquemada replied. "Can we come in?"

"Sure, Raul, sure," he replied, waving them both into his dwelling place.

Carla entered a modest living room. There was an old couch, comfy yet discolored and with several rips in the fabric. It was originally a solid green but had worn over the years. There were two additional chairs on either side of the couch, one that had permanent stains over various parts of the faded blue cushioning, while the other was simply all wooden. An old cubic television set with a cable box was situated prominently on one side, the furniture all facing it. In the corner was a white fan blowing slightly cooler air in the room. The blades were each fifteen inches long, and the upper half of the device slowly moved back and forth in a quarter of a circle. It was on its highest rotation level.

"Come, sit down," Felipe insisted.

Carla and Torquemada obliged, with the former cartel leader picking the couch while Carla selected the chair with the faded fabric hue. Both of them put their assault rifles on the ground, with Carla also removing her shoes. Felipe checked the windows, peering outside to see a village square mostly devoid of movement. He made sure the curtains remained closed, pushing the two open ends closer together in an effort to make it that much harder to detect his guests. Torquemada leaned back into the couch, as the seat was comfortable in spite of its rugged appearance. Felipe lumbered away from the windows so that he was standing in front of the television set.

"Que pasó?" asked the homeowner.

"There has been a coup in the cartel," said Torquemada. "Do you remember Señor Brennenberg?"

"The hombre with the blond hair?"

"Sí, eso hombre."

"What about him?"

"He is trying to take over the cartel," said Torquemada. "He has gathered up a lot of troops. He even ambushed me, which is why I am here now."

"Muy terrible, Raul," Felipe commented. "I saw the men with the skeleton masks and black clothes. Those are his men, correcto?"

"Sí, correcto."

"Well then, what is the next move?"

"I do not know," admitted the former cartel leader. "For now, I need you to tell the others about what happened. Tell them I am still alive and that we need to meet up."

"Sí, Raul."

"And be careful."

"Como siempre, Raul," said Felipe, smiling. "By the way, who is this nice lady you brought with you?"

"Mi nombre es Carla Sharp," she said.

"Ah...Ha," Felipe replied. "She looks like a good one."

"Oh, no, no, no," said Torquemada, waving his hands. "It is not like that. She is serving as security. That is all."

"And I am married," Carla stressed.

"Ah…I see," said Felipe, who smiled at Carla. "A pity…Ella es muy bonita."

"Go and tell the others," Torquemada reiterated. "Is the stockpile still in your basement?"

"Yes."

"Good."

* * *

"Lo siento," said the doctor.

Those two simple words elicited great sadness for the two women who stood in front of him, for they knew what they meant in that dark moment. A mother and a sister to one of the many dead National Guardsmen, who had been assigned to the convoy. They had kept hoping and kept praying, yet the dreadful news was the same. Both recalled the many times they expressed concern for the man who was a son and a brother. They remembered the many times he brushed off their worries. His commitment, his valor, and his service. The medical professional could not stay long, as others needed his care. He simply guided them to the chapel that was attached to the hospital, where others mourned in prayer.

Marisol had seen the same performance played and replayed in that waiting room. Many mourning wives, mothers, brothers, and fathers. She saw the fullest spectrum of melancholy. There were those who had a stiff upper lip, keeping everything bottled inside. Stoic and solemn, accepting with quiet sadness the news. A few others were so intense, so public in their pain that their screams were heard throughout the facility, with sympathetic people holding them and taking them elsewhere until the peak suffering had passed and that grudging acceptance of life's cruelty took its stead. Some left in anger, and others remained to take in the new reality of their lives. One had to see a doctor due to the shock.

As Marisol paced about the chamber in waiting, her stomach in knots and her arms folded, the frenzy of the building continued in earnest. National Guards and police were going in and out of the automatic doors, as were gurneys and stretchers with more wounded and ill. By this point, those being rushed into the hospital suffered their injuries from other incidents. Once in a while, another figure would come limping in, or carrying another. This brought some hope to those in wait, to those wondering if their loved ones had survived the barrage of the newly minted Brennenberg Cartel.

Law enforcement had set up a quasi-field headquarters at the hospital, interviewing survivors and witnesses, gathering what information they could on the new menace. Highway commuters spoke of death coming in the form of a wave of armed militants, with shadowed eyes and skeletal faces. Their smiting of the convoy seemed almost supernatural, as the explosions came from long distance weapons. Their cold leader had ice water for eyes, giving death stares to each person who went by him on the blocked road. They thought nothing of the corpses, the harvest of destruction left behind. And then, as phantasms on the end of the Day of the Dead, they sped away amid clouds of smoke.

As she looked around, she saw many armed personnel milling about the facility. There was also a pair of armored police vehicles outside of the entrance nearest to the waiting room. There was a fear among many that the cartel would next attack the hospital, having been so emboldened by their victory on the highway. Going back and forth like a pendulum, she noticed that a doctor was coming her way. He was fairly young, probably only a couple of years older than her. He was clean-shaven and had black hair. Dressed in blue scrubs, he had an identification card hanging from a lanyard that bounced around as he walked into the space for waiting. She soon realized that he was looking for her, specifically. Her pacing slowed; her stomach began to feel worse.

"Senorita Contreras?" a doctor inquired, prompting her to stay in place. "Si?"

"Sigueme," he ordered.

She followed him as requested, having to have an extra pep in her stride as he was walking a brisk pace. They both automatically veered to the left as another team of emergency personnel rushed someone on a stretcher. It looked to be a child wearing a T-shirt and shorts, with large blood stains on his chest and legs. Marisol did not know if this latest critically injured person was another victim of the cartel. She had her doubts, as the convoy would not have included minors, and what civilians were harmed in the explosions would have already been taken to the hospital hours earlier.

She kept following the doctor, leaving the waiting room just as another woman could be heard crying. They went past several rooms, where people of various ages and backgrounds convalesced from wounds accidental and intentional. There was a pair of armed and armored guards on either side of the wide entrance to the hospital room that the doctor guided her to. He pointed her in, and Marisol gave a nod of gratitude. The medical professional did not stay, however, as other patients needed his help.

The very first person she saw was Alfredo. Her beloved fiancé was laying on the bed nearest to the entrance. His pants and shoes remained on, however was naked from the waist up. A bandage was wrapped around his head, the center of the white cloth a faint red. His left arm was bandaged up as well. His tan skin did not obscure the presence of multiple bruises on his chest and arms, as well as one on his left cheek. His demeanor, which had been mildly sullen, perked up when Marisol entered. She felt like crying, even though he ultimately was okay. For the time, she kept it in and simply rushed to him, careful in her embrace lest the tight grip of the hug accidentally reinjure him.

"You are alive, you are alive!" she declared. "Gracias a Dios."

"Muy verdad."

"What about Carla? Torquemada?"

"I do not know," he said solemnly. "I lost consciousness when the attack began. When I came to, I saw some cartel thugs walking about. I guess…I guess they did not see me. They kept moving on. When I heard a bunch of cars drive away, I rightly assumed that they had moved on."

"Then they must be alive," said Marisol, her voice fueled by hope. "If they were dead, they would have stopped searching."

"Mi amor, they did stop searching," said Hernandez, getting to a seated position on the bed. "I told you, they left."

"But they left quickly. Why leave quickly if they had found them?" she maintained.

"I do not know," said Hernandez, who took a breath before continuing. "I would argue more, but my head hurts a lot."

"She is right," stated a newly entered officer in the National Guard, grabbing the attention of both Marisol and her wounded lover. "Our local contacts say that the cartel soldiers are patrolling villages on the outskirts of town."

"And you are?" Hernandez inquired.

"Captain Enrique Dager," said the figure, briefly bowing his head in greetings. "High Command assigned me to oversee the response team."

"I see," said Hernandez. "Well, I recommend getting as many National Guard units as you can. And get some tanks and helicopters while you are at it. You need big guns for this one."

"I understand your desire to strike back," began Dager. "I have the same urge. I had friends on that convoy. Still, we need to be cautious."

"Cautious?"

"You are right, we need to gather our forces," said the commander. "However, we need time to do that. And to plot our next steps."

"Captain...?"

"Dager," he clarified. "Captain Dager."

"All right, Captain Dager," Hernandez said, getting to a standing position beside the bed. "You may have the time to take it slow, but my friend and my person of interest do not. We need to find them and get them out of this lovely little country of yours. Immediate action is not requested, it is mandatory."

"Again, I respect your opinion, Señor Hernandez," said Dager, trying to be patient. "However, this is not the United States. You have no authority here. Your government was given a lot of deference in this affair. As a result, a lot of my men are dead. In other words, you had your chance. You failed. I am now in command. And my first objective is to secure those who remain. From there, we will get the materials needed to strike back. Then, we will plan out our strategy. And then and only then, we will attack. We are not 'cowboys,' Señor Hernandez, and the cartel are not 'Indians' with bows and arrows. They are far more powerful, and they need to be taken with greatest caution."

Hernandez was not strong enough to resist the sternly standing commander. He was still feeling sore in much of his body, and his balance had not fully returned to normal. With much apprehension, he ceded to the new authority. "All right. I agree. I will follow your instructions. Keep me posted."

"I will," said Dager, who looked down at his wristwatch. "There will be a meeting with government officials in about ten minutes. I suggest you join me."

"Could I have a few minutes alone with Marisol first, before I...before I join you?"

"Very well," said Dager. "I will wait outside."

Hernandez sat back down on the bed as the commander exited the room. Marisol looked at the door, waiting for the figure to be out of sight. As the door shut behind the National Guard officer, the two returned their focus to one another. Hernandez was in pain, yet it felt muted by the presence of his fiancée. She was touching his shoulders, and her eyes looked into his. He tried to smile, to give his usual grin of assurance. Yet it was harder at the moment. She started to brush the bruised cheek, as though the massaging motion would heal the injury in moments. Hernandez leaned in closer, not for intimacy but for secrecy.

"Carla and Torquemada will need help," he said at a whisper. "I hate to do this, but I need you to get out there and try to help them."

"How?"

"I do not know. Whatever comes to mind."

"That works," Marisol said, giving a brief smile. "What do I do if I find them?"

"Find them first, then we will figure it out from there."

"Okay."

"Marisol?"

"Sí, mi amor?"

"Please, be careful."

She smiled, kissed him on the lips, and exited the room.

VIII.

Felipe's wife, Maria, was the one who got things moving in the mornings. She was the one who prepared breakfast, the one who turned on lights as needed, the one who woke up her husband, and the one who said grace over the meal. When they were younger, she was the one who helped get him prepared for work and who made sure he took a lunch with him. She did much the same for their five children, four of whom were now adults and one had tragically died in a car accident years ago. She was an early riser by nature and was always the first to fall asleep in the evening.

For the first time in some time, Maria prepared breakfast for more than just her husband. One of the two guests was a fairly young woman, who nevertheless had a couple strands of gray hair amid her otherwise black crown. The other was a familiar face, though usually he came better polished and less beaten by the labors of the day. She mistook them for a couple, although this assumption was dashed when the woman volunteered to sleep on the couch while the familiar man slept upstairs in a guest room. As she did her usual early morning routine, she was troubled by the woman, who seemed to be struggling in her sleep. Maria accurately guessed it to be a nightmare.

Carla al-Hassan Sharp and Raul Torquemada joined the elder couple at their dinner table, which was an old round card table. Although the furniture piece itself was a bit worn and informal, it was nevertheless topped with a well-stitched tablecloth that Maria herself had knitted together. Maria prepared eggs and toast, with locally made orange juice to drink. Margarine was used for the spread instead of butter. The plates and utensils used were of sturdy content, having been used in the family for generations. Carla noticed that her plate, as well as the others, used to have detailed painted imagery on them. However, decades upon decades of bearing hot food and being washed had largely removed the imprints.

Maria said grace, with three of the four people at the table crossing themselves in the Roman manner, while Carla crossed herself in the Eastern manner. She expected a comment or two after doing so, but none came. Carla enjoyed the meal, especially the scrambled eggs. She quickly realized that the reason was the means of how it was cooked. For years, Carla made the dish without adding salt or butter to the eggs, due to health concerns for her grandfather. Even after he got better and she had moved out of their apartment, Carla continued to prepare her scrambled eggs in this healthier recipe, out of habit. Tasting the salted variation for the first time in several years was a surprise treat.

The dining room was a modestly decorated space, with only a bronze crucifix adorning the wall. The paint job was a light blue meant to resemble the skies. However, there were several cracks in the layers, allowing an attentive onlooker to see the original white paint job underneath. There were also several dark brown splotches along the walls, where bugs had been squashed by either Felipe or Maria. Similar spots were found in the other rooms, though not with the density as found there. Two doorless archways led to the living room and the kitchen, respectively. A fan plugged in at a corner made the room bearable in the summer, its blades providing a decent moving breeze.

"So," Raul began, "how is your son, Eddie, doing?"

"He is still at that IT company up north," Felipe explained. "He does not visit as much. However, he always sends nice presents for Christmas."

"I remember you said something about him moving recently."

"Planning to move," Felipe corrected, Raul nodding in concession. "Yes, he wants to move to the capital. I think his wife has family there. Wives can be bossy, after all."

Maria looked up at Felipe, who sheepishly grinned in response.

"And Elena?"

"Still living in the United States," said Felipe, the name-dropping of a familiar place causing Carla to perk up to attention. "Yes, Senora Sharp, my daughter married a gringo."

"She was studying abroad in Washington, D.C., when she met him," Raul explained, getting a nod from Felipe. He then looked at his elder host. "They have two kids, right?"

"Three," Felipe clarified. "My second grandson was born last year."

"Of course, now I remember," Raul said, pausing to drink some orange juice. "When she last visited, she was pregnant again."

"That is right."

"She named him after Felipe," Maria chimed in. "I think she could have done better."

Felipe looked at his wife, who smiled at her husband with the same smile that had melted his heart for decades. "They do not visit as much. I do not blame her. Between the little ones, the pregnancy, and...and, well, how things tend to be here... I do not blame her."

Raul simply nodded.

"Things are going to get worse, right?" Felipe asked the former cartel leader.

"Right," he replied. "That is why I am very thankful that the young men have already taken what they can from the stockpile and headed off to the rendezvous point."

"Rendezvous point?" asked Carla.

"It is clear that Brennenberg wants me dead. It is also clear he will not let me leave the country. I will have to face him. And when I do face him, I will need help."

"Where is this rendezvous point?" the lone American inquired.

"An old Lutheran mission," Raul answered. "It is about twenty miles from here. It is located near the mountains, so anyone attacking it has to go uphill. It is also enclosed around some heights, making it harder to hit with long range weapons."

"Years ago, Raul and I were checking on possible sites for a new plantation when we stumbled across it," Felipe told Carla, who finished her breakfast as he spoke. "They still have an active church there, if I remember right."

"Yes, they do," said Raul. "I have kept in contact with the missionaries there. They know me and I know them."

"Are they tied to the cartel?"

"No," he replied. "I made sure they were written off, so to speak."

Carla sipped her orange juice, then figured it out. "You knew there was a chance that someone would oust you from the cartel leadership. You made sure the cartel did not bother with that space, for your own sake."

"And for the sake of the others," Maria said. "People at the mission are safe. It is a place where the less fortunate and the victims of gang violence can go and be at peace. I have known people who have lost everything who speak well of the missionaries there. If we did not have as much as we did, I would suggest Felipe and I go with you."

"Also, to be honest, I doubt I am in shape for the trip," said Felipe to Raul. "The young men of the village told me that cartel soldiers are all over the streets. They are waiting for you and your woman friend to get on the road so they can track you down."

"In other words, we have to go through the jungle again," said Carla.

"We have clothes from our children that you can use," Maria suggested. "We keep them as hand-me-downs for the grandkids, when they get older."

"That would be helpful, thank you," said Carla.

"No problem, Senora Sharp," Maria explained. "Anyone who is a friend of Raul will be a friend of ours."

"We should leave soon," Carla said to Raul.

"Yes," said Raul. "Our next stop will be the shack." He turned to face Felipe. "It is still there, correct?"

"Right," said Felipe. "I checked yesterday after spreading the word about the mission. Everything looked to be there."

"What is this shack?" Carla inquired.

"It is what we call it. A shack," Raul replied in a matter-of-fact tone. "It is a large, abandoned building in the middle of the jungle. I think it used to be part of some old military installation that was uprooted last century. I stocked up the shack with some supplies, things needed for the trip to the mission. Once in a while, I check on it, put in new supplies, take out damaged ones. You know...maintenance."

"It will be necessary for the journey to the mission," Felipe added. "And it should be a safe journey. Few people ever drive to the shack. The road is always covered with vegetation."

"I take it you do not have a plane hidden there."

"No, not at all," said Raul, who appeared vaguely amused by the idea.

"I could only hope."

"There is still hope," Maria assured her. "As long as you can get to the mission, Señor Brennenberg will have a hard time winning the battle."

"Of course, we still have to get there," Carla replied.

Raul pushed back his chair and rose from his seat. "Well, in that case, we should change and go as soon as possible."

"Sounds good," said Carla, who likewise got up from her seat.

"Feel free to take some food from the fridge," Maria invited. "And no need to bring back any of the clothes you take."

"You have been very kind to us. Thank you," Carla said to Maria, as Felipe and Raul were speaking to each other.

Maria leaned in. "After all the times that Señor Torquemada was there for us when we were in need, it is the least we can do."

* * *

A meeting room at the hospital had been converted into a headquarters for the government and its armed forces. Officers in the National Guard were present, as were some police and special forces figures. Several laptops were opened and had state leaders present via virtual means. Mavis Chalmers was among those present, her visage visible on one of the screens. Sitting next to her was a Spanish translator with the Agency, so she could understand what was spoken. Alfredo Hernandez was there in person, a button-up collared shirt and tie hiding the bulk of his bandaged wounds. Both were respectfully silent as Captain Enrique Dager gave an update to all of those gathered, in the flesh or online.

"With the emergency order granted, we have now activated five thousand National Guardsmen within the past hour, to add to a force that already totaled six thousand," Dager explained. "We are moving to first secure various places of primary importance. As a result, we have put units of National Guard at the Capitol building, at Congress, and at local municipalities and courthouses. Additional units have been also placed outside the homes of various government officials and other figures of interest. Mobile units have secured all the major roads and are actively patrolling our largest cities. With the additional newly activated guardsmen, plus an expected additional three thousand personnel by the end of the day, I expect us to have full control over the situation by tomorrow evening."

Most of those in the room or listening online displayed approval to the update, with heads nodding and smiles given. Hernandez was more reserved, folding his arms in response to the confidence of the officer. Chalmers betrayed no emotions, yet inside she felt much the same as the wounded agent. Dager had a small laptop, which was connected to a device that allowed him to display images on a white board placed behind him. Although he had not been using it up to that point, he went to the laptop and, after a short bit of typing, was able to put a map of the Central American country on display behind him. There were bright red spots of varying sizes alongside various points.

"This map shows our current deployments," Dager told those gathered. "As you can see, the bulk of our forces are concentrated in the cities and points of political importance. As you go farther out, there are fewer personnel present. Also, many of the major roads outside of the metropolitan areas remain unprotected. As we activate more units, we will be directing them to these points of interest. Are there any questions?"

"Tengo una pregunta," said Hernandez.

"Sí, Señor Hernandez?"

"Have your men encountered any cartel soldiers since the initial convoy attack?"

"Desgraciadamente, no," Dager responded. "They were as fast at leaving the attack site as they were in getting there."

"When do you think you will be ready to start searching for Senora Sharp and Señor Torquemada?"

"As I said, by tomorrow evening the whole country should be safe again."

"Captain Dager," said Hernandez just as the National Guard officer was about to answer another question. "You are saying that they will be alone from now until tomorrow evening? It will be only them versus the entire cartel?"

"Señor Hernandez," stated Dager, suppressing his true feelings. "I know that you might be frustrated by this approach, but it is the best plan we have for the present time. We need to make sure that no cartel soldiers are going to surprise attack us…again. We need to secure our immediate environment, then we can start searching the jungles and the villages and the backroads for your agent and Señor Torquemada."

"You could have just said yes, by the way," Hernandez replied. "I mean, why waste all that oxygen just to tell me something you could have summed up in one word?"

"Señor Hernandez," Dager stated, clinching his teeth. "I believed that you needed to understand the situation. You Americans do not seem to understand how things work in this country. Neither, quite honestly, do you understand how much of a mess you made today. We are cleaning up your failure as best we can. Do you understand now, or was that also a waste of oxygen?"

"Gracias, Captain Dager."

The National Guardsman continued to take questions and give comments from others, with the exchanges being far less provocative than the conversation with Hernandez. The Agency representative thought about continuing the back and forth but decided against it instead. A part of him felt that Dager had made too good a point on his culpability in the destruction of the convoy. Hernandez wondered what he could have done differently to prevent the attack. However, nothing was entering his mind. Then again, he was still using some of his brain to pay attention to Dager.

Then, his phone went off. It was not a loud ring, but the vibrating noise was enough to turn a few heads near him. They gave him either curious or judgmental looks; Dager seemed to not notice at all, as he was occupied with speaking to someone else in the meeting room. Hernandez gave a smile to those who had looked in his direction, and then got up from his seat. Dager saw him get up, but Hernandez simply lifted up his phone to indicate that it was a personal matter. The National Guard officer accepted the tacit explanation and continued to address those gathered in the hospital room.

Meanwhile, Hernandez exited the room to be in one of the many hallways of the large medical facility. This was a less hectic wing of the building, as they were two floors above the emergency services. Most of those walking by the meeting room wore business casual with a white lab coat or were support staff like janitors. Non-medical officials were there as well. There was also a pair of armed guards who were milling about the entrance. As there were other detachments of guards between them and the outside world, they were laxer in their duties. Patients were rarely seen.

Hernandez leaned against the wall and put in his passcode to view his new message. It was from Marisol Contreras. She had simply texted, "Llamame ahora." Hernandez obliged, selecting her saved number and pushing the green button to begin the call. There were a few rings before she picked up.

"Sí?" she asked.

"It is Alfredo. What is new?"

"I have not found them yet, but I learned that they went into the jungle after the attack. Some people saw them heading to a village several miles away. If I remember correctly, it is one of the places that Torquemada used to personally oversee."

"In other words, the people there like him."

"Claro que sí."

"Did the people that you talked with tell you if either of them was wounded or injured?"

"No one knew for sure. They sounded like they were okay. Someone said they made a fast run to the jungle, so maybe they are unhurt."

"Quiza. Ojala," said a hopeful Hernandez. "Anything else?"

"Hold on..." she said, the pause lasting several seconds.

"Marisol, are you still there?"

"Sí, estoy aqui."

"Que pasó?"

"A bunch of cars just went by. Jeeps and SUVs. They were all painted black, and they had a bunch of men wearing hoods, sunglasses, and facemasks. One of the few that was not wearing a hood might have been Señor Brennenberg."

"Are you sure?"

"It was hard to tell. They went by very quickly. But one of them had blond hair and seemed to be in charge. He was in a back seat, and he looked like he was ordering the driver. Something like that."

"Where were they headed?"

"Toward the village. The one Carla and Torquemada probably went to."

"You think there is any chance we can warn them?"

"Tengo dudas," said Marisol. "We both have tried calling Carla before and we got nothing. Either her phone is dead, or it's off, or something."

"They really are alone," said Hernandez, more to himself than to Marisol.

"Alfredo," she said. "Maybe they will be gone. If either of them has any intelligence, they will know that they cannot stay there for very long."

"I know, Marisol, I know," said Hernandez, who sighed before continuing. "Can you tell me where specifically they are going, so I can at least tell our friends in the National Guard?"

"Sí. Claro."

* * *

Carla felt an itch behind her right knee. It was a small irritation, restricted to a diameter about the equivalent of a quarter, or maybe a silver dollar. She had started feeling it several minutes ago. It began as a faint bit of discomfort but was starting to become more noticeable as she and Torquemada continued to venture through the vines and branches of the jungle. She already had a dark pink rash on her right arm, which she received courtesy of a brush with some poisoned plant. That one remained mild in its discomfort, suggesting that the contact between skin and leaf was not close.

Felipe and Maria had provided the two with repellent. In a place like that, people were always well-stocked. Carla was sure that she had rubbed enough on her person that no miniature beast would dare to attack her. Still, from time to time, one of the stinging creatures with the long, bent

CARLA: THE VIA DOLOROSA

legs and high-pitching buzz would land on her arm or head, with her quick to swat them away. Perchance, one brave little bug desperate for her blood had found the small gap between her sock and her pant leg, flew into the dark cavernous path, and took a bite out of her before the repellent could take effect.

She was several steps behind Torquemada, as he alone knew the way to the shack. Or, at least, he claimed to know it. Carla was aware of how universal male behavior was and thought of the times as a child driving with her grandfather, who would greatly extend the time it took to get to a destination solely because he refused to ask for directions. A similar episode happened once with her husband when his GPS device died on him unexpectedly, midway through a trip to an unknown restaurant. It took him a good ten minutes before he finally asked a random pedestrian for help. Two men, wildly different in age and background, yet reacting the exact same way. Carla wondered if this was yet another man having yet another bout of that distinctive strain of pride.

Both of them were modestly dressed for the journey toward the secret place, and both of them had darkened their clothes with circles of sweat. Given the humidity and heat of the jungle, there was a sense that dressing in scant attire would have done little to ameliorate the situation. Furthermore, the more skin exposed, the greater the target for poisoned plants or infectious bug bites. Like professional travelers, they limited their consumption of water, lest they run out too quickly. Each bit of liquid that Carla drank every several minutes felt amazing. Every time she was tempted to chug.

Torquemada stopped beside an especially large tree. It looked to be so old that, perchance, it had seen the arrival of the Conquistadors, if not the mysterious disappearance of the Mayans. The shade was especially dark under its protection, providing a minimal amount of relief for the two exhausted people. The former cartel leader was keen to not rest his hand upon the broad trunk, as the arboreal giant pulsed with veins of ants going up and down it in long lines. Instead, he looked about it, searching for something. Carla watched him as his eyes darted about, and then saw him crack a smile.

"What is it?" she asked.

"We are almost there," he said.

"How much farther?"

"Half a mile, at the most."

"Muy bien," she said, tired.

"Esta manera," he replied, pointing northwest of their location.

With Torquemada still leading, the two left the cover of the large, infested tree, going down a bit of a hill. Continued care was made to avoid tripping over thick branches or puddles that were several inches deep. The bug attacks seemed to increase; Carla assumed it was because the repellant was wearing off. Weaving through the trees, cutting through more vines, batting away more little flying creatures. Carla could not yet see the promised destination, yet her guide walked an amplified confidence. She hoped and prayed that this was built on a solid reasoning, rather than hubris.

Then, it became visible. Through a network of twisted vines and contorted wooden arms, amid the darkness of the canopy and the blurriness of weary eyes, Carla was able to see a sizable manmade structure. She was beginning to echo the confidence of Torquemada, getting a minor jolt of strength given to her sore legs, one of which was getting itchier behind the kneecap. The guide turned a little to the right, leading the two to a clearing. It was a beaten path, paved only by periodic car usage. Skinny plants were once again trying to stretch across it, as the jungle sought to take back the vacant corridor.

"Estamos aqui," stated Torquemada.

"Gracias a Dios," she replied.

The facility looked military or industrial—dark gray walls, boarded up windows, and a single door on one side. Attached to the structure was a generator whose hue was likewise drab. Parked a few feet away from the edifice was a vehicle, which looked to be old yet useful. It was equipped with rugged tires that looked capable of scaling a mountain. There were no license plates, and the blue paint job was mostly worn off, as were the letters to the company that were once fused to the side. It was as though the car was camouflaged, stripped of anything that would make it known to a witness.

"Tell me it works," she said as they walked toward the building and the automobile.

"It worked two weeks ago, when I used it last," replied Torquemada. "Once every few weeks, either I or someone from the village comes here to check on things. You know, turn stuff on, drive the car, fix any issues, etc."

"So, when do we leave?"

"After nightfall," he said. "Assuming Brennenberg is as intelligent as I think he is, he will go to the village by the end of today. He will have people looking around the outskirts. They will stay on the roads, knowing that we cannot stay in the jungle for long."

"Do they know of this place?"

"Only the villagers and myself know of this place," said Torquemada, with the same certainty he had expressed earlier after looking at the old large tree. "Come inside. We could both use a rest."

Carla nodded as she went away from the vehicle and toward the entrance to the facility, where Torquemada was standing. He kept going, opening the door without a key. Carla thought of asking why he did not secure it but felt that the esoteric nature of the location was a lock unto itself. She entered the building as Torquemada put down his things and started turning on the electricity and, of great importance, the climate control. The walls growled as cold air began to be blown into the main room.

Four lights suspended from metal rafters illumined the simple accommodations. There were crates of supplies stacked in the corner, which included nonperishable canned foods, rolls of toilet paper, a few guns with ammunition, some grenades, bandages, blankets, and two First Aid kits, among other things. There was a cooler with several bottles of water located inside. Two smaller rooms were located to her right. One of them was originally an office used by administrators. The other was a lavatory.

"Home sweet home," Carla quipped.

"Here," Torquemada said, handing her a wonderfully cold water bottle. "Drink as much as you need. Bathroom is the door in the corner."

"Gracias," said Carla, who finally got to chug pleasantly cold liquid. A few seconds later, she returned for air. She took out her phone, which had no signal. Nevertheless, it informed her of the present time. "It should be another three hours before sunset."

"We will leave in six."

113

"I would like to oppose your idea, but right now I need to use the bathroom."

"Go ahead."

Carla smiled and walked to the lavatory, being able to feel the cold water coursing through her system. For his part, Torquemada closed the door. From there, with his female company behind another door, he removed the clothes covering his upper body, took another unopened water bottle, twisted off the cap, and then poured the cool liquid over his head and body. It was the closest that someone could get to having a shower in the facility. After that, he went to the door and peered through the very thin break between the door and the archway, seeing nothing of concern outside. Now more at ease, he slowly sat down on the concrete surface of the shack, pondering what had become of his empire. He even wondered about the village, realizing that they were left defenseless.

Carla had to put some extra effort into getting the water to work. The knob at the sink was a little rusted, and thus was harder to budge. Still, she was persistent and got the water to rush into the upturned dome. Pipes moaned at their usage, as though sorrowful for her presence. She splashed the liquid on her face, then splashed more of it on her arms. It took some effort to get the knob turned back to the original point as well, yet the water did eventually stop dripping. From there, she opened the lavatory door and beheld something she had not seen before. It was her guide, the once threatening Torquemada, seated on the floor, hunched forward, eyes looking dreary. He looked as he bore a great burden, a painful guilt that was finally beginning to break him. A moment passed, and he saw that Carla was looking at him. He straightened up, returned to his stoic composure, got up, and then went about foraging for supplies among the crates that could heal the physical wear of the jungle walk.

* * *

Felipe was watching the network television news while his wife began preparations for dinner. He could smell the pleasant aroma of the vegetables and the pita bread being cooked in the oven. The bulk of the coverage was about the devastation on the highway, with the destruction of the convoy and the many subsequent deaths. He leaned back into the old yet comfortable couch, sitting where he always sat. Not even having an unexpected guest sleep there had undone his indentations. His wife continued to work dutifully in the kitchen, a burden she gladly took upon herself.

His watching and her cooking were distracted by the loud motor noises outside. Felipe rose from his couch and Maria exited the kitchen to join each other at the front entrance. Through a window, they peered at the central space of the village. Black jeeps and SUVs circled around the well, kicking up mud and dirt as they sped into the quiet settlement. The old couple knew that it was the cartel. Yet they also dismissed the significance. Over the course of the day, one or two vehicles had patrolled the area. Felipe returned to his couch, while Maria walked back to the kitchen. Both were confident that the rumbling of the engines would pick up again, only to depart the village shortly.

And yet, as Maria took out the vegetables from the oven, carefully handling the hot edges of the sheet with her discolored oven mitts, both she and her husband realized that the noise was not stopping. They did not hear the vehicles leave. Some were silent, but their quietness was as a leopard in the bushes. While both tried to brush off the unusual activity, they began to hear voices outside. There were shouts of orders, steps running about the plaza. People were lamenting, more shouts were uttered. They heard a few more cars come and stop their engines, more house doors swinging open and car doors slamming shut. It was transforming into something beyond the typical.

Again, Maria and Felipe walked over to the window by the door, glimpsing the center of the village. This time, as assumed by what they were able to hear, more black vehicles had parked in the village. Additionally, armed men were milling about the quiet cars, wearing skeletal facemasks and sunglasses. Most of them were walking along the plaza, but a few were in pick-up trucks, standing watch as they gripped large machine guns attached to stands that had been bolted to the bed. Their friends and neighbors were lined up on the opposite end of the plaza, kept in order by shouting armed men.

"Should we hide?" Maria asked her husband.

"Too late," he replied, looking out the window and seeing a pair of masked cartel soldiers coming toward their door.

Felipe decided to be cooperative, opening his door before the armed men could get within knocking distance. They still shouted, with their guns pointed in their general direction. Felipe was calm, and his wife drew strength from his example. They both put on their sandals and walked without coercion to the plaza. The soldiers seemed to respect the example, as they neither pushed nor offered additional shouts. As they got to the plaza, their acquaintances looked at them with much trepidation, asking with their eyes what they needed to do to survive. A couple of them had already broken down and were crying.

Felipe and Maria were handling the situation as best they could, when Felipe saw a man leave one of the SUVs. He seemed to be putting something in his coat pocket as he got out, something that looked medical in nature. Yet, Felipe's attention quickly shifted to the countenance of the figure. He was blond-haired and had bright blue eyes, a rarity in those parts. The others showed him deference. Felipe soon realized that it was none other than Fulgencio Brennenberg, a cartel lieutenant he had only met once or twice over the years. He was clad in dark clothes, like the masked men around him.

"Who is it?" Maria asked in a whisper.

"Señor Brennenberg," he whispered back. "I thought he was dead."

"Raul told us he had returned."

"From where?" asked a nervous Felipe. "The grave?"

Brennenberg was walking toward the elderly couple, but then he stopped to look at the people lined up to his right. They were in four rows, consisting of fewer than one hundred individuals. Most of them were older, either in their forties or beyond that. A few struggled to stand and were kept steady by younger, healthier people; a few others balanced with canes. Even as the sun was setting, there was still ample light to view all of those, in the plaza. Felipe saw that the figure was openly disappointed by the population. He sighed, then continued his walk to meet Felipe and Maria.

"Buenos dias," Brennenberg said.

"Buenos dias, Señor Brennenberg," said Felipe, both he and his wife bowing their heads in respect. "I am called Felipe, and this is my wife, Maria."

"You know my name," said the cartel leader. "I like that."

"We have met before, Señor Brennenberg."

"I see," said Brennenberg, who did not recall the occasion. "You are a respected leader of this village, are you not?"

"Yes, Señor Brennenberg."

"You are responsible for these people. You guide them in their daily lives…like a priest, but without the collar. Am I correct?"

"I try to, Señor Brennenberg."

"Tell me then…Felipe, correct?"

"Sí, Señor Brennenberg. Felipe is my name."

"Felipe, tell me what is wrong with what you see," said Brennenberg, turning to face the rows of villagers, nervous and shaking.

"Well, um, Señor Brennenberg, I do not know."

"You do not know?" asked an incredulous Brennenberg, looking back at Felipe. "You mean, you cannot see what is amiss here?"

"Lo siento, Señor Brennenberg, but I am not able to."

He laughed with incredulity. "Where are the young people?"

"Well, um, I assume they are still working. I have heard that the plantation has increased the work hours, since the days are longer."

"That was a nice attempt, Felipe. I mean that," said Brennenberg. "The way you are covering for them. It was nice."

"Pero, Señor Brennenberg, I am not covering for anyone. I believe they are still at the plantation, working in the fields."

The cartel head laughed. He stretched out his left arm and patted Felipe on the shoulder. "I just came from the plantation. They are not there."

"Señor?" asked Felipe, trying to play stupid.

"I also know that your village is missing some weapons," said Brennenberg, who walked a few steps away from the elderly couple. "You see, before I came, I had my men check the stockpile that is supposed to be here. They told me nothing was left but a few rusty rifles." Brennenberg lowered his voice. "Are they at the plantation, too?"

Felipe remained silent. His wife gripped his arm.

"Felipe," said the cartel leader, inching closer to the man. "Where are my workers, and where are my guns?"

Felipe looked down.

Brennenberg laughed some more. "I guess you do not know, do you?"

Felipe shook his head.

"You did not check things before going home, did you? All these things happened here without you being the wiser. Estoy correcto?"

"You say so, Señor Brennenberg."

"Young people, right?" asked Brennenberg, smiling. "They do so many bad things. Their parents never find out. They are like your children, correct? They are delinquent children, right? You have no idea what mischief they are up to."

"Sí, usted esta correcto," replied Felipe, not knowing what else to say.

Brennenberg laughed a little more, bringing no comfort to Maria or Felipe. He again patted Felipe on the shoulder, giving a smile that showed most of his pearly teeth. It was a prompt on his part, and Felipe knew it. Nervously, he joined in with the jovial expression of amusement, knowing that, deep down, neither he nor his guest found it particularly funny. Brennenberg started to walk away. He then stopped, looked at the elderly couple, and turned to walk a few more steps. Felipe was confused as to the reasoning, with a faint hope that maybe Brennenberg was going to leave soon.

Instead, the cartel leader went to the nearest guard and ordered him to give him his assault rifle. The masked and spectacled figure obeyed, handing over the gun, along with a spare ammunition clip. Maria gripped the arm of her husband all the tighter as Brennenberg went several steps toward them, gripping the weapon, with a finger near the trigger. Felipe stood firm, oddly optimistic that nothing horrible would happen. The cartel leader lowered his weapon, giving a nice smile to the elderly couple. It was as though he was tacitly assuring them that he would not harm them.

Brennenberg turned to face the rows of nervous villagers. He tucked the spare clip into his pants, putting a firm hold on the assault weapon. He looked at the elderly couple, his body still facing the direction of the lined-up villagers. Then he raised the muzzle of the rapid-fire device so that it faced high up in the sky. Felipe and Maria watched in confusion as Brennenberg pulled the trigger, firing a line of bullets into the darkening sky, as though they were fireworks. The lined-up crowd was scared by the loud firing, but otherwise were as puzzled as Felipe. Then Brennenberg looked at the couple a second time, turned his attention back to the rows of people, and lowered the muzzle so that it was pointed a few feet above the heads of the villagers. Again, he let out a flurry of bullets. This time, the terror was palpable. Brennenberg looked at Felipe a third time, smiled, lowered the muzzle to be at gut level and then turned to face the crowd, of which a few were screaming.

"Alto! Alto!" shouted Felipe, preventing a third flurry of bullets from leaving the gun. "Please stop! All right! All right! He was here." He breathed in sadness. "He was here. Torquemada was here."

"When?" asked Brennenberg, rifle still pointed at the rows of villagers.

"Yesterday. They left this morning. The young men left ahead of them."

"Where is he going?"

"To the Lutheran Mission."

"The Lutheran Mission?"

"It's near the mountains."

"Oh, yes, I think I know the place." He lowered the weapon, to the relief of many. "Did he come here alone?"

"No, Señor Brennenberg," he replied, calming down. "There was a woman with him."

"What did she look like?"

"She was tall. Average weight. She had black hair and pale skin. She was definitely American. Maybe Arab."

Brennenberg shrank back, suddenly given to weakness. He took his right hand off of the weapon and caressed the spot on his chest where the slug had hit him. The gun was held casually as he paced about, lost in thought. A couple of his guards worried about their leader, approaching him to console if necessary. He brushed them off, assuring with his free hand that he was well. Still, he wondered about the description. *It sounded just like her*, he thought. *It must be her. Why is she here?* Brennenberg gathered himself, took a deep breath, and walked back to Felipe and Maria, who remained in their place.

"It is a long journey from here to the mission," said the cartel leader. "They must be gathering supplies. Where would they go for that?"

"I do not know, Señor Brennenberg," replied Felipe.

Brennenberg looked at him with disbelief, gripped the assault rifle, switched out the used clip for the fresh one, and then pointed it at the rows of villagers.

"All right! All right! He went to the shack."

"The shack?"

"We call it 'the shack.' It is some abandoned building northwest of here. It is in the jungle. Most cars cannot get there."

"Does it have a road? A road for cars?"

"Yes, one path. Not paved."

"Where does the path go to?"

"It goes into North Street, the village of Quetzal," Felipe admitted.

"North Street, Quetzal," repeated Brennenberg for assurance.

"Sí, usted esta correcto, Señor Brennenberg."

Brennenberg smiled.

"That is all I know, Señor Brennenberg, I swear."

"Estas seguro?" inquired the cartel leader.

"Yes, I am very sure. I know nothing more."

"Muy bien," replied the Brennenberg, who pointed the gun at the elderly couple and opened fire, mowing them down.

A great chorus of screams came from the villagers, with many of them cowering to the ground in terror. The cartel soldiers kept them from running, having boxed them in from all sides. Like ranchers with cattle prods, the masked thugs forced them to remain in their rows with outstretched firearms. As Brennenberg walked over to the group of villagers, he saw that nearly all of them were on their knees and some were even on all fours. The cried, they pleaded, they continued to scream. Many were keeping their frightened feelings to themselves, putting their heads down into the dirt and breathing in the dust.

Brennenberg took in the fearful adulation, fueled by their sentiments. He stood tall before almost all of them. The growth of his ecstasy was tempered when he found four of the villagers were still standing. None of them had the fullest of confidence; they were simply not scared enough to fall prostrate like the others. They were all men, ranging in age from forty to fifty-five. Three were married, while the fourth was widowed. One of the masked guards, eyes hidden behind shades, walked up to Brennenberg.

"What shall we do with the rest of them?" he asked, a youthful voice coming from the disguise. "Do we shoot them?"

"Hell no," stated the cartel leader. "We need them to tend the fields and tell the stories of what happens when people resist death." He smiled as he looked at the four standing men. "I would, however, like to create a few new works of art before we leave."

IX.

It was snowing, but it was also hot. Carla was sweating, even as she could see ice and snow all over the place. It was dark, yet everything was visible. Carla could see the bright paint jobs of the buildings and the boats. She saw all the fish swimming about the frozen river. Then they were still, captured in the ice. Sometimes they moved, sometimes they were frozen. Sometimes they were trapped in ice cubes, but the cubes themselves glided underneath the waters. At times, the river flowed, and other times it was frozen solid. It seemed incapable of choosing one or the other.

Carla perspired. She felt hot and disheveled. Her hair was longer, twice as long as it actually was. It went pretty far down her shoulder blades. She was wearing gloves and a jacket, and she could see her breath, but she was sweltering. Her legs were sore and itching. The worst of winter and the worst of summer were hitting her all at once. Around her, it was clearly winter. Snow everywhere, snow falling, ice on the water, ice on the pier. The wooden beams were all frozen together, as though glued by the frost. She breathed hard; she needed to. Then she didn't. It was like she was shifting from a fast run to suddenly being rested. Gusts of visible breath before her, a visible night around her.

She saw men on the pier. They were running away. No matter how fast they went, they were still about fifty or sixty feet away. They were shadows, without any distinguishing mark. No skin or clothes, just black. They turned to face her, shooting guns. Carla wanted to duck, she wanted to run. She was stuck, trapped in place. Yet the bullets missed. They went everywhere but at her. Then she realized that she had a gun in her hands. It kept changing form. Sometimes it was a rifle, other times a musket, other times a machine gun. The colors altered; the detail vacillated. Its general purpose and size, however, remained the same. It was a consistent tool for killing, consistent through the ages.

Carla fired back. One by one, the shadows disappeared. One screamed with a comically high-pitched squeal. It was almost funny; it was almost fun. Like a carnival game, picking off the little monochrome targets to win a prize. They popped like balloons, no blood or guts. They were gone, the snow kept falling, the heat endured, and the river was solid ice, yet still had fish moving under the surface. Then, they were not moving. They never could stay the same. They even disappeared and reappeared. Carla felt alone. Even the fish seemed distant. She wanted to get closer, yet she could not. She was stuck there, looking at the snowy pier, sweating as though it were noontime in the summer.

Then, another shadow emerged. It was bigger than the others. It was slower and more lax than the first ones. It did not frantically run about, nor did it shoot at her. It was just there, leaning against the sky. It was coming toward her. Carla fired the musket, the musket that became a machine gun. She fired it again, it being a Tommy gun at this point. Lots of bullets were streaming like a fire hose. Nothing happened. He kept coming. He was walking with a strut, a hand in the pocket. It was like he was some cool kid on the block. She kept firing, and she kept missing. Or were the bullets simply entering him without harming him? Her mind pivoted between the two ideas.

He was close. His hair was blond. She saw a smile; she saw wavy yellow hair. He stretched out his arms, as though he were about to embrace her. She kept firing, her gun now an eighteenth-century pistol. It fired many bullets at once; they all bounced against his deepest of dark bodies. Somehow, she never ran out of ammunition. Somehow, there were no shell casings littering the pier. The snow was covering everything. The whole city and river were blanketed by the erasing whiteness. Soon, it was just the blond shadow, blinding whiteness in the background, and Carla with her useless gun. Knowing not what else to do, she just kept firing, and he just kept getting closer and closer.

"Carla," declared Raul Torquemada, shaking her awake.

"What? What is it?" she asked, her head hurting.

"We need to go," he replied. "It is dark out."

"Okay," she said, taking a breath. "Okay."

Carla al-Hassan Sharp had been asleep for about three hours by that point. She had taken a few blankets and put them on the hard floor, using a backpack with a few supplies in it as a pillow. She remained fully clothed, save for her shoes, which she had removed upon lying down. Apart from being groggy, she was well. The itchiness of the walk through the jungle had disappeared through a mixture of rest and ointment. She stretched her arms and legs as she got to a sitting position. From there, she put her shoes back on and tied the laces. She rose up and stood beside Torquemada.

They talked little as they got their things together. Carla and Torquemada both had packs, and they filled them with bottled water and First Aid materials. Even with the vehicle at their disposal, they wanted to take precautions. Torquemada was considerate enough to turn off everything as they left. Carla entered an outside world that vaguely reminded her of that horrid dream. There was night, with the bits of brightness coming from the detailed constellations. Yet it was humid and warm. The bugs were at their loudest, an epic chorus of chirps and buzzes. Some mammalian howls and hollers were heard as well. Torquemada walked past her in order to unlock the car.

It was a compact vehicle, worn and rough on the exterior. And yet, the inside appeared to be in pretty good order. There was little trash or dirt, and the seats lacked any rips in their upholstery. The inside was stuffy, but that was expected. Each passenger fastened a seatbelt, as the driver turned the key to ignite the engine. It took a second or two longer than usual, briefly making Carla wonder if they would have to walk after all. Thankfully, the grumble of the motor was eventually heard, causing numerous little creatures to scurry away from the clearing. Torquemada slowly pulled the vehicle forward, the car bouncing a little as they went about the unpaved dirt pathway.

"No lights?" asked Carla, who observed the odd tendency of the driver.

"It is camouflage," he said. "Do not worry. I have driven at night with the lights off many times."

"Of course," Carla acknowledged. "Where to next?"

"The path eventually leads to Quetzal," Torquemada explained. "It is a village about four times the size of the one we just came from. It is more of a town, I guess."

"Or a small city?"

"Regardless," he stated after they took a slightly bigger bump than normal. "It is our next stop. After that, we will head to the mission to join the others."

"We should go to the airstrip," insisted Carla. "Your plane is there." Torquemada ignored her, so she changed the subject. "Is there a plane at this mission site?"

"Maybe, I am not sure," Torquemada answered. "For a time, they had a small strip to fly in supplies. However, when I was there last, it had been damaged by an earthquake. They talked of fixing it but admitted that they did not have the funding."

"I see," she said.

"Besides, it is not about escape," Torquemada said, making a slight veer to the right in order to remain on the path. "It is about defeating Brennenberg. Killing him, if possible."

Carla became frustrated. "You made a deal with us. You agreed to go in, to tell us everything about the cartel. You cannot do it if you are being held up at a broken-down mission station. You are supposed to be our informant."

"And you were supposed to get me out of the country yesterday," he countered. "So, I guess we are all failing each other, aren't we?"

"Wasn't it your friend who you told about our plan?" asked Carla.

"Pedro Aquilares," said Torquemada. "He was a loyal supporter. I urged him to come with me. He told me he could not. I thought he would at least let me go in peace, but I guess I was wrong."

"Then it isn't *our* fault, after all...It's yours!"

"Yes, yes! You are right," he declared, his anger rising. "You are right, okay? I made the mistake! It is my fault! Are you happy? Are you thrilled? Does it solve our current problem? No, no, it doesn't! We are going to the mission, not your little airstrip." He paused for a few moments as the road became very bumpy for a short stretch. He continued once it smoothed out. "Besides, it is not like you or I even know how to get there from here."

Carla nodded in concession. "True. Although, once we get to the town, this Quetzal, we should have reception for our phones. At least, I should be able to contact my handler."

"Hernandez, right?"

Carla was about to say "right" in response, but then she stopped. She realized that she was unsure if Alfredo Hernandez was still alive. The last she saw of him, he was unconscious inside one of the totaled trucks of the convoy, with the cartel soldiers coming en masse to their position. It was natural for her to assume that he was there. Carla felt deep melancholy at the epiphany that no one may answer.

"Actually, I guess I should call Marisol instead," she realized. "She was not with the convoy. It is more likely that she is alive."

"Whatever works, I guess," said Torquemada, veering left to stay out of the way of the trees. "Nevertheless, my position stands. We are going to the mission."

"Torque—"

"It is not just about me," he insisted. "There are already plantation workers gathering there. Scores of them, at least. If Brennenberg shows up before I do, if I never appear at all, I will have betrayed them. We both know what he will do to them because of their decision to stand with me. We both know what he has done to those we left behind at the village. I can't run. I have to be there, too."

Carla kept silent, processing what the driver was telling her. She studied his eyes. She looked about his face. He seemed sincere. Carla pondered the matter, curious as to how such a cold cartel leader could actually care about his underlings. He kept focusing on the dark road ahead. It was a winding journey, with Torquemada narrowly missing another cluster of trees. It felt faster than it actually was, as he kept below thirty miles an hour. And yet, without the artificial lights to illumine the route, objects appeared to emerge ex nihilio with great suddenness. Nevertheless, Torquemada did not lie when he noted having experience with such methods of travel, and the car continued to successfully traverse the wilds, giving them shelter from bugs and fairly decent air conditioning.

* * *

"We are almost there," Captain Enrique Dager told Alfredo Hernandez, their conversation being in Spanish only. "The village should be coming up."

"We should have gone there sooner," the American agent protested. "We have known about this location since last night."

"Look around the area, Señor Hernandez," said Dager.

Hernandez humored the national guard officer. As they were in a jeep with its top off, he was easily able to view the surrounding jungle growth on either side of the road they were taking. The darkness under vegetative canopy was present even with a morning sun that beat down upon the land. Thick trees and thick branches would have made for excellent cover, with the motorcade unable to properly protect their flanks. The roughness of the terrain also compromised their ability to go top speed. Slower and slimmer, barely able to make out creatures more than several feet off of the road.

"Okay, you may have a point in your waiting," Hernandez conceded. "We will see what the villagers have to tell us."

It was a well-armored convoy, even if it was vulnerable to sneak attack. There were only two jeeps, as the rest of the vehicles were camouflaged hummers. Each one had bulletproof siding and was topped with a machine gunner, whose turrets could turn a full 360 degrees. Hernandez was the only person in the group not wearing full body armor. Although, at the behest of his peers, he did have on a bulletproof vest and a ballistic helmet, the latter covering up the bandage around his head. Apart from Dager and Hernandez, the other personnel also wore black masks that covered most of their faces. This was done, as there were concerns that being recognized would lead to being personally targeted. Each man in the convoy was aware that they were entering enemy territory.

As the hummers entered the village, they slowed to swing around the well, the line of military vehicles curving around the old stone structure. Rather than see armed hostiles, the National Guardsmen beheld a more macabre sight. Motors turned off, camouflaged doors opened, and masked figures got out, with high-powered rifles and assault rifles at the ready. Few people were around as they secured the area. They searched the windows and the rooftops, only to see few, if any people, let alone cartel soldiers. Most were trying to ignore the gruesome display that was placed at the well.

Dager and Hernandez did not turn from the sight. They slowly walked toward it. At the well were four bodies, or what was left of them. Two strands of rope were used to tie them, the ends of each strand having a pair of bound hands. These strands formed an X-shape over the well opening. The corpses were shirtless and barefoot. Each man was placed sitting on the ground, their hands over their heads and backs to the brickwork of the well. Each figure had their chest opened wide, with their vital organs missing. Swarms of bugs were crowding the bodies, flies laying legions of maggots in the carnal caverns. On a hunch, Hernandez drew closer, using his left hand to cover his nose and mouth. Taking a flashlight from the hummer, he clicked it on and peered down the well.

"Just as I thought," he commented.

"What?" asked Dager, keeping distance.

"He threw the organs down the well," said Hernandez, turning off the flashlight and moving away from the sickening display. "He could have at least been a good boy and donated them to the local hospital."

Dager had no idea whether his company was being humorous or sincere. Regardless, he stayed still. Some of the locals had exited their homes, feeling somewhat safer with the presence of the National Guard. Others remained inside, fearful of retribution. Many of the guardsmen lowered their weapons, as it became clear to them that the cartel forces had moved on. Nearby the well were two fresh graves, each topped with a cross made from branches. Dager and Hernandez approached them.

"I wonder why they were buried, but not the others," said Dager.

"He wanted to send a message," said one of the civilians, an elderly priest in a white Roman collar and a black cassock.

"Father," stated Dager as a greeting.

"I came after the cartel left," he explained going over to where Dager and Hernandez were standing. "The villagers called me. They told me that the cartel permitted them to bury one of the village elders and his wife, but no one else. They said that the cartel was going to return, and they expected that Satanic display to remain, or else they would slaughter everyone here. So those poor men remain, unburied."

"Did they say when they were coming back?" asked an anxious Hernandez.

"No, señor."

"I had hoped," Hernandez said to Dager.

"Did any of the villagers tell you where they were going? The cartel soldiers?" Dager inquired.

"Try to understand, señors, the people of this village are frightened. They are saying all sorts of things. Some believe that the Devil himself was here and did this. Quite a few called him el diablo rubio."

"The blond devil," Hernandez noted. He turned to Dager. "They must mean Brennenberg."

"What do you know about Señor Brennenberg?" Dager asked.

"He is the new head of the cartel," said the aged priest. "Rumor had it that he was killed in the United States. Many of the people here believed that rumor, until they saw him. Some have gone as far as to believe that he was indeed killed, but that through some demonic power he was brought back to terrorize the country. Perhaps as some divine punishment for wickedness. Like I said, señors, there are a lot of scared people here."

"That is understandable," said Hernandez. "If there is nothing else that you can tell us, father, then you can go and minister to them."

"Gracias, señor."

"And please put in a good prayer for us, while you are at it," Hernandez added with a smile.

"I will, señor."

Hernandez turned to face Dager as the priest walked away. "I think we can agree that we need all the help we can get."

"You have a point," Dager nodded. "Where do we go next?"

"Well," he thought aloud. "Clearly, my agent and Torquemada were able to get away from here, or else they would have been on display at the plaza."

"Most likely."

"So, they must have gone somewhere else."

"Donde?"

"No sé," replied Hernandez, gritting his teeth. "Damn it, I do not know."

* * *

Compared to the village where Felipe and Maria were buried, Quetzal was a bustling metropolis. To be sure, it lacked towering skyscrapers and its population was below 20,000. However, even then, it had the trappings of a city seeking to grow. Nearly all of the streets were paved and nearly all of the buildings had wireless internet and centralized climate control. A medley of businesses existed in the town, with no one company legal or otherwise dominating the economy. Most of the employed wore suits or dresses to work, with a sizable minority wearing jumpsuits or retail uniforms.

For all of the modern progress, there was still much of Quetzal that displayed homages to its ancient roots. There were several buildings, including the office of the mayor and the largest church, which traced their origins to the colonial period, with an architecture that reflected such elegance. Many of the locals who were not part of the white-collar industries sold handcrafted jewelry or produce in a plaza square. These places featured ornately painted wagons and pushcarts. These usually came with a few coatings of white, then intricately painted designs along the wheels that were in red, blue, or green. Many an office worker patronized these places on meal breaks or after a shift ended.

On that day, there was a new presence in Quetzal, one that had only periodically appeared over the years. This presence came in the form of seven jeeps and SUVs, all black. They were filled with armed personnel, hiding their visages behind facemasks that were black with skeletal designs painted on them. Nearly all of them wore sunglasses and drab hued gloves, further obscuring their true identities. They carried assault rifles, pistols, some explosives, and a single grenade launcher. About half of them had either switchblades or pocketknives on their person. For many of the cartel soldiers who entered Quetzal, their first fights in life had involved blades instead of guns.

Local police had been warned through radio channels about the cartel force, and that it was coming their way. However, lacking the armaments necessary to fight back, they intentionally stepped aside as the motorcade entered the municipality. Some of the officers were even sympathetic to the outlaw corporation, viewing them as better organized and less corrupt than the actual government. While none of the local authorities actively helped the cartel soldiers, none of them made an effort to stop them, either. Instead, police on patrol continued to monitor the streets for other offenses, like speeding or pickpocketing. Whenever a cartel vehicle went by, they behaved as though it never happened.

The local civilian population did their best to adjust. Whenever a cartel vehicle was speeding by, they gave them the right of way. Whenever the masked men went about the sidewalks, they made room for their journey. As they pulled people aside and grilled them for information, each person, whether male or female, young or old, working class or business class, cooperated with the armed figures. Resistance was not on the agenda of any resident, neither was it viewed as necessary. After all, the typical local had no idea where the former head of the cartel was located, let alone his mysterious female company. The two had slipped into Quetzal at night, just before the first cartel soldiers arrived.

Marisol Contreras was not ignoring the thugs as they went about the town. She paid much attention to them as they went about, by foot or by wheels. She was cautious enough that the masked men did not suspect her of spying, with her keeping distance yet also tracking their movements. It was an easy task, as the cartel soldiers made no effort to cover their actions. They were audacious and believed that their willful presence was a better tool at locating their enemies than more subversive tactics.

She was waiting for a pair of masked thugs to walk away from the market square where many painted wagons were stationed. The two men casually strolled about the marketplace, looking less like they were on a desperate hunt for Torquemada and more like it was just a normal walk through the town. They were both armed with assault rifles, but neither weapon was held at the ready. Few of the people took notice of them, much less treated them differently from the potential customers. Their ambivalence was echoed, and they passed through the small crowd sans incident.

Marisol stepped away from the corner of a building, which she had been using for cover. She walked a brisk pace through the pushcarts, wagons, buyers, and sellers. As she went through the oblivious ones, she turned her head a few times to make sure no one was following her, which no one was, in fact. From there, she passed through an alleyway so narrow that she had to walk sideways to not touch the walls. From there, she turned her head in many directions, staying on the lookout for any cartel thugs. With no antagonistic persons sighted, she turned left and entered an innocuous spice store.

"Do you have any West Indies spices?" she asked the old man at the counter, not truly interested in any of his retail products.

"You will have to check in the back," he replied, then looked away, pretending to be occupied with other business.

Marisol did as she was ordered, walking around the front counter, and turning into another room connected to the front by an open archway. From there, she saw a door on the far end of the wing, which had a sign warning that only employees were allowed to enter. With no other customers present in that part of the store, Marisol went to the door, knocked on it three times, and then listened for a response. Three knocks were heard from behind the door. Remembering the instructions, she slowly knocked four more times, all while looking over her shoulder. After a brief moment of silence, Marisol saw the door swing open, with a woman in the dark speaking.

"Come in, quickly," she said.

Marisol obliged, darting through the opened door with little pause. She entered an unlit storage room, full of packaged supplies, a few filing cabinets, and a desk with computer and printer. The door was latched shut behind her by the woman who sounded very familiar. Before the eyes of Marisol could adjust to the darkness, someone flipped a switch and illumined the private room. The floors and walls were a dark gray; the shelves where the packages were stored were a shiny black. Before her was Torquemada, stern and silent, standing by two of the rows of shelves. She turned to see the woman who had beckoned her in, widely smiling as she looked into a familiar face.

"Carla!" Marisol said in a projected whisper, the two embracing. "I thought you were dead."

"Not yet, by the grace of God," Carla replied.

"You do not understand how excited I was when you answered my phone call," said Marisol with a louder voice as the two let go of each other. "Alfredo kept insisting that you might answer once you got to a place that could carry a signal."

"I was amazed that he survived," said Carla. "It seemed like no one would have been spared."

"Well, thankfully some of the wreckage covered him," Marisol explained. "By the time that he came to, they had already moved on."

"Gracias a Dios," said Carla, the two women turning to face Torquemada. "I know you two have both met."

"Yes," said Torquemada, with Marisol nodding.

"So, how bad is it out there?" Carla inquired.

"A bunch of cartel butchers. All over the place," Marisol replied. "They have been here for hours. They must be very sure that you are here."

"They probably figured out that this would be my next stop. They might even know about the mission."

"Then maybe you should turn yourself in," said Marisol. "The National Guard will be here before too long."

"How long, though?" asked Torquemada, in protest. "Brennenberg's men could come here at any minute. While you were coming here, a pair of them showed up. We were nearly found. When they come back, they will be more thorough."

"He has a point, Marisol."

"So, you are going to go to the mission instead of the airstrip?"

"It might be the best way," Carla admitted. "If nothing else, maybe we can hold out against Brennenberg long enough at the mission so that the National Guard will finally catch up."

"Quiza, es posible," Marisol conceded. "What do you need me to do?"

"Buy some wagons," said Torquemada.

* * *

"Quetzal," said Fulgencio Brennenberg, with a smile of excitement upon his face. "The name almost rolls off of the tongue, am I right?"

"Sí, Señor Brennenberg," said Pedro Aguilares, who was beside his superior in the jeep that sped toward the town. "Named for a bird."

"Yes," said Brennenberg, facing forward. "Yes, it was."

Brennenberg was standing in the rear seats for the jeep, both arms holding on to the arched bar that separated the two rows. When it was raining, a covering was put over that section of the vehicle. His blond hair waved as the speeding car produced its own wind. Aguilares was also standing up, next to Brennenberg, looking down at his shorter leader. His hood was down, and his facemask was lowered. Both men were clad in dark gray and black clothes, echoing the style of the other cartel soldiers. Brennenberg took in the breeze of the motion, as though it were revitalizing him.

"Our men keep searching the town but have found nothing," noted Pedro. "Perhaps, they have already moved on."

"No," stated Brennenberg, who stared at the ever-growing skyline of Quetzal. "No, I know he is there. I can feel it."

"With great respect, Señor Brennenberg, do you have something more than feelings?"

"I do," said the cartel leader. "That hideout of Torquemada leads to Quetzal. Our men got there before nightfall. Torquemada would not have moved from his hiding place during the day. After all, a rat runs away from a flashlight."

"I understand."

"Muy bien," said Brennenberg, with a pinch of extra enthusiasm. "We will find them when we get there. Yo te prometo."

"How do you know?"

"We will drive into the center of the town, then we will part ways. You will start searching at the west end of the town, while I will start searching at the east end. We will be more aggressive than the current presence. Any hint of doubt, any suspicion, we will act upon it in force. No more civility, Pedro. Eventually, we will meet in the middle. At that point, one of us will have captured Torquemada."

"And if we fail to find him by then?"

"We will burn down the village," said Brennenberg.

Pedro was shocked into silence.

"When I was a child growing up in the hinterlands, my grandfather had a shed full of rats. He tried and tried to get them out, but they remained. So, one day, he set the whole shed on fire. Dozens and dozens of rats loudly screeched as they were burned alive. And the few that escaped were either clubbed to death by my relatives or gored by his dogs." Brennenberg finally looked at Pedro and smiled. "He never had a rat problem ever again."

"Pero, Señor Brennenberg," Pedro replied, trying to form words. "I mean, if we, um, how can we...Can I say something, something that might offend you?"

"Go ahead," said Brennenberg as his jeep and the other vehicles in his motorcade slowed in response to the traffic conditions of the town.

"We cannot destroy an entire town and not expect some serious retribution from the government, let alone the people. I have fear that this will harm us."

"No," said Brennenberg, who took hold of Pedro's right arm. "That is how Torquemada wants you to think. He was afraid to do things like that. Pero, if we do them, if we show no fear, then the government, all of the governments in this region, they will fear us. Men fear death, men fear those who bring death. We will bring death."

"But, Señor—"

"I am a teacher as well as your boss. You will learn from me. And you will see us become the greatest force of destruction western civilization has ever seen."

Pedro decided it was prudent to halt his laments. Fortunately, Brennenberg interpreted his silence as consent. The cartel leader tightened his grip on Pedro's right arm briefly, doing so as though bestowing a fatherly affection, and then loosened his grip to again take hold of the bar between the rows of seats. He turned back to face the front, with the buildings slowly going by as the motorcade continued. The locals, ignorant of the intentions of the newly arrived Brennenberg, behaved as they had been behaving since yesterday, when the first of the cartel soldiers had come. Pedro felt like warning them of the promised doom, yet he kept quiet for fear of his leader.

"Alto aqui," Brennenberg ordered the driver, who obliged and put the vehicle into park. He then looked at Pedro. "This is where we part ways... for now."

Brennenberg jumped down from the jeep, his booted feet landing on the pavement. People paid more attention to him than the others. Several whispered, and many went out of their way to avoid eye contact. Several more ran away, fearful that being in his presence would cause some sort of misfortune to befall them. Maybe through unintended offense, maybe through some cosmic bit of bad luck. Like a black cat walking in front of them, they treated Brennenberg as a superstition. Men joined him from one of the SUVs, each armed with an assault rifle and a pistol, each masked and hooded.

Several black vehicles were driving off to the east of the town, per the orders of Brennenberg. On his hand radio, he could hear the static-laden voice of Aguilares rallying half of the cars to his lead. Meanwhile, behind the cartel leader, there were several armed pick-ups and jeeps crowding nearby him. As they clogged up the center of Quetzal, Brennenberg was around a bit, flanked by his own men. He saw the little strip of shops that was in the middle of town. Long before modern development, this stretch had been the economic center of the settlement. With recent progress, that center had actually moved to the northwest part of Quetzal. The old quarter had a certain beauty to it.

Then, looking above the roofs of the shops, Brennenberg thought he saw smoke. At first, he dismissed it as likely hailing from a chimney. However, the cloudy darkness was getting thicker, more solid. Soon, he was able to see the top licks of several flames. A dull roar was growing, like a thunderstorm trapped inside the heart of the town. A fire was stretching out, the smoke covering the heavens. People began to flee, sirens began to wail, more people panicked, more people called for help. All the while, the fire was getting louder, brighter, and the skies above it dark as night.

Emergency vehicles were blaring their sirens, honking all the louder, demanding that the cartel vehicles clear a path for them. They were the only people brave enough to challenge the army of masked men. Most of the cartel soldiers were confused; no order had been given to set the community ablaze. There was no communication from Aguilares, who was just beginning to comb the eastern half of Quetzal. Brennenberg remained in awe, distracted by the tall fires that were kicking up beyond the hiding place of the shops. Amid the uncertainties, several cartel soldiers went with their innate cooperative demeanor and bent to the wills of the firemen, moving their vehicles and themselves aside.

"What is this?" asked Brennenberg, his armed peers remaining silent. "Did Pedro decide to take the initiative?" He smiled at the thought, then sobered. "No, he would not."

"Señor Brennenberg," one of his masked guards finally spoke up. "We need to get away from the fire."

"Okay," he said, sedate. "Okay."

Soon, yellow fire trucks sped by, with first responders clad in their fireproof armor looking to do battle with the hostile conflagration. Close hydrants were tapped for water, hoses were unrolled, and, soon enough, thick streams of hard, pulsing water were shot at the growing blaze. The fires were catching on to the shops, with roofs being lit by the initial flames. Thankfully, quick work from the responders prevented these smaller ignitions from growing much larger. The main monster was still to be tamed, thought it was increasingly being contained by the many hoses shot in its direction.

Brennenberg wondered what had caused the destructive fire, which was tying up all traffic and putting his men into confusion and stagnation. The roads became parking lots, as the firetrucks cut off the various routes for the sake of preserving the community. Against the advice of his armed security, the cartel leader went closer to the fire. It was already being shrunk by the firemen, whose concentrated water was stifling the growth of the beast. Despite the thick smoke hanging above that section of town, Brennenberg was capable of seeing that which was lit. Although the items had already been heavily damaged by the flames, the point of origin for the fire was a collection of wooden pushcarts and a couple of wagons, which someone had apparently doused with gasoline and then threw a match to. Brennenberg could see like the others that it was intentional.

No sooner did he realize this than another sound caught his attention, prompting him to turn to his left. Before him, he saw a pair of people getting into an old car. One of them looked like Torquemada, while the other was most certainly female. Brennenberg gritted his teeth, but then started to laugh. He found it quite amusing when he realized what had just come to pass. And yet, even amid the laughter, his emotion was again shifted when he saw more curiosity. A young woman, black hair and light skin, looking at him. She reminded him of that wife of a governor, whom he had tried to kidnap a couple of years earlier. Yet, he was quick to figure that this woman was not her. Nevertheless, he felt something oddly familiar, as though she was somehow involved in the charade playing out before him. She walked away, then started to run, making him all the more curious.

X.

Rain fell in heavy drops that evening. It came straight down, uninfluenced by any winds. The canopy blocked many of the countless aquatic missiles from touching the ground, with them exploding on numerous leaves and branches. And yet, the descending deluge was such that the ground was soaked minutes after the watery bombardment began. Puddles stretched at every ditch and ravine along the way, dirt quickly became mud, and various underground creatures rose up to the surface for fear of drowning. There was only a little bit of thunder and some lightning; otherwise, droplets dominated.

The stormy weather impacted the beat-up car that Raul Torquemada was driving. He moved fast to put on lights and the wipers, soon adjusting them to their maximum, back and forth. The downpour was so loud as to gag the music from the radio, with only the most intense notes being audible. Torquemada grudgingly slowed down, his vehicle going half the speed it was just a minute or so previous. This was to the relief of Carla al-Hassan Sharp, who wondered if her driver was going to insist on high velocity even with the unideal conditions. Traffic began to clog up the roadway as the automobiles ahead of them likewise slowed to a crawl, with some barely moving forward.

"I hope Brennenberg's thugs are caught up in this, too," Torquemada spoke, eyes on the murky road.

"I will check with Marisol," Carla said, taking out her smart phone, entering the code to access the device and then typing up a text, which she sent mere seconds later.

"Damn it," Torquemada whispered.

"What is it?"

"I bet this means the way is blocked."

"What do you mean?"

"The way to the mission," said the driver, who briefly got to go as fast as ten miles per hour before he was again put to a near total stop. "The way there involves going through a low valley. The road always floods when it rains this hard."

Before Carla was able to respond to the information, her phone rang. "Hello?"

"Carla, it is Marisol," responded the voice on the other end.

"How is the weather where you are?" Carla asked.

"It is starting to rain," she replied. "Cars are slowing down."

"Any sign of the cartel soldiers?"

"Let me look... Yes, they are a few cars behind me."

"Are they slowing down with everyone else?"

"They are starting to... Yes, they are slowing."

"God is merciful."

"Yes, He is."

"Tell her we are taking a detour," Torquemada said, continuing to go below ten miles per hour in the thick downfall. "Tell her we are going to stop at a nearby village."

"What was that?" asked Marisol, who vaguely heard Torquemada speaking in the background.

"We need to stop at a village," said Carla, who then turned to Torquemada. "Where are we stopping?"

"A town called Veracruz," Torquemada replied, keeping both hands on the wheel and both eyes on the congested road. "It will be on the map. It has at least two thousand people."

"Veracruz," Carla conveyed to Marisol. "You should be able to find it with your GPS system." She looked at the driver. "Got a specific address?"

"I hope so," Torquemada said.

"What does *that* mean?"

"It means that this person might not be as willing to help me as the others."

"I see," said Carla.

"What is the address?" Marisol inquired.

"We will get back to you on that," Carla said. "For now, just try to get to Veracruz."

"Understood. Vaya con Dios!"

"Y tu tambien," Carla replied, hanging up the phone.

"There we go," said Torquemada, again barely above a whisper.

Carla did not need to ask what he meant, as she saw the sign for Veracruz, which was marginally visible amid the streaming rain, cloud cover, twilight hour, and hanging vines. Had they not been going so slowly on the road, they would have likely flown by it without noticing its text. Torquemada had to wait a few minutes before enough of a gap existed between the cars going the opposite way for him to turn left. Some unknown, kind commuter, a person they would never speak to in this life, kindly remained stopped and waved them permission to go in front of him and onto a less crowded route to the village.

The way got bumpier, as the minor road was in dire need of a new paving job. Carla felt like she was on some theme park ride, the contact with the potholes splashing freshly fallen water. Some of the hits felt especially brutal, with the passenger speculating that the vehicle itself was taking damage as a result. As such, Torquemada was only able to go the equivalent of residential speeds rather than the posted limit, which was about twice that. As they got to the village proper, the holes declined in frequency, allowing for more speed. The splashes got larger, as Torquemada ran across giant puddles along either side of the street. These obstructions only briefly decreased his velocity.

The rains were starting to thin out, yet they remained a persistent pounding on the ceiling of the car. There were few people out in the storm; what few there were wore long ponchos or awkwardly stood under awnings, patiently waiting for it to be less brutal for their unprotected bodies to walk back home. Main street had electric lights and working traffic signals and was flanked on either side by modern buildings. The settlement was fairly young, when compared to the communities elsewhere in the nation that were established shortly after Christopher Columbus arrived in the Caribbean.

A lone exception to this standard of recent construction was the chapel situated on an imposing hill that hugged the outskirts of the village. It was a small sanctuary, with white adobe walls that were shaped like a cross. It had a bell tower that rose forty feet into the air, which was topped with a four-foot-tall bronze crucifix. There were three other churches in the village itself: two were Catholic, while one was Pentecostal. While the two representing the Church of Rome were larger than the Pentecostal church, it was the charismatic congregation that was the fastest growing. The two Catholic congregations jointly oversaw the usage and maintenance of the chapel, oftentimes holding baptisms and weddings there. It was also used for sunrise worship services on high holidays, such as Easter.

Well below the chapel, Torquemada turned onto a narrow street that had a string of one-story homes closely packed together. They tended to appear unseemly, with poor paint jobs and bars over their windows. However poor their exteriors looked, their interiors were fairly modern, with plenty of electronic appliances and central climate control, provided the power was working. Torquemada fixed his eyes on the left side of the street, slowing down so as to better examine each house front. His eyes widened as he appeared to recognize one of them. It was easy for him to park, as the street lacked any other vehicles. He went forward, then backed up so that the car was right in front. After he turned off the automobile, he just sat there, taking deep breaths and looking down.

"Who lives here?" Carla asked.

"Maybe a friend. Maybe an enemy," he said, gritting his teeth and speaking to himself. "Why did I have to come back?"

"You said the road to the mission was flooded."

"Yes, I know," he said. "Well, let us get this over with."

Rainfall was moderate by the time that Torquemada and Carla exited the vehicle. Thunder was more persistent, yet also farther off in the distance. Droplets created little dark spots all over the clothing of both travelers as they got to the front door, which was rusted and discolored. Torquemada took another deep breath before finally knocking. The two could hear some light conversation within the one-story domicile. Then came the pronounced noise of a bolt being undone, and then the door opened. Carla beheld a young woman, about five feet tall, with tan skin and suspiciously red hair.

"Flavia," he said, grinning.

She rolled her eyes and slammed the door shut.

"She must know you better than most," Carla said, Torquemada giving her a wry smile.

Torquemada turned to the door and knocked again. "Flavia...Flavia!"

Carla spoke Spanish as a second language. Nearly all of her knowledge involved proper sentences, with some slang. She was thus less familiar with most profanity. However, she was pretty sure that was what was being uttered by the woman on the other side of the closed door. As Torquemada and Carla continued to be lightly pelted by rain, the former cartel leader again knocked on the door. Again, Carla was pretty sure that the young woman was responding with cussing. She folded her arms, wondering if they would have to find another place to wait for the waters to ebb. Then, just as Torquemada was about to knock once again, the door swung open a second time, revealing the woman yet again.

"Go away," she declared.

"Flavia, por favor, yo necescito tu apoyo."

"Quien es ella?" she asked, looking at Carla. "Is she another one of your sluts?"

"Perdonme?" Carla asked in protest.

"She is a friend, nothing more," stated Torquemada, with Carla being a little surprised by the descriptive word he used. "Please, I am in danger."

"Big deal," she said, gripping the side of the door in preparation for another slamming.

"She is in trouble, too," he insisted, pointing at Carla. "I know I was wrong, but she did nothing wrong. At least help her."

Flavia rolled her eyes and looked down. Then she looked at Carla, her glance being with more sympathy than moments earlier. "Okay, come in."

"Gracias, muchas gracias," said Torquemada as he entered the small home, with Carla following after him.

"This better be good," she said as she closed the front door and locked it. "I just put Jesús to bed, and you know how he easily wakes up when there is noise."

"I remember, I remember," he assured her.

"I told you if you ever returned, and it was not for a damn good reason, I was going to scream 'rape' at the top of my lungs so the neighbors would call the cops."

"Brennenberg is back."

Flavia was shocked by the news, taking a half step backward, leaning against a wall. She looked down and began to breathe hard, acting not unlike Torquemada had in the car a couple of minutes ago. She began to shake her head in the negative, as though trying to will the named figure out of existence. Gradually, she regained her composure, lightly nodded as though accepting some cruel fate, and approached Torquemada. Flavia attempted to form words but could not do so. Unable to make conversation with the drying guests, she ducked out of the room and went into the adjoining kitchen.

* * *

Alfredo Hernandez was craving a cigarette. In all of the hope and calamity of the past couple of days, he had not gotten the chance to indulge. At the insistence of his fiancée, he had been making a concerted effort to cut down. He was still better when compared to college years, when he was not above blowing away a whole pack a day. Semester finals were especially trying on his habit. Since then, however, he had been improving. Nevertheless, stress was a great way to make the urge stronger. When combined with a sense of stagnation, whatever resistance he held was dashed.

Hernandez was outside of the mayor's office in Quetzal. It was not far from the main street, and within a couple of miles from where a bunch of wagons had been set afire earlier that day. The sun was gone, and whatever thin black smoke persisted from the conflagration was camouflaged by the nightly heavens. Hernandez took out a newly acquired pack of cigarettes, selecting one of the thin white sticks. His lighter had gone missing since the convoy ambush, so he settled for a matchbook bought at the same store as the pack. It took a couple of tries, but the match finally lit up, giving a bit of brightness to the dark side of the building. He blew out the match once it had done its duty and tossed it to the side, the little match disappearing in the evening. Hernandez inhaled the chemicals and released a thick stream of smoke into the air, a moment of great exhale.

Shortly afterwards, a National Guardsman came by. He had his assault rifle slung against his back and took off his helmet, placing it on the ground. The young fellow leaned against the wall, standing about five feet from Hernandez. The guardsman seemed to be trying to take in the whole situation, his fingers massaging his bowed head. Hernandez studied the youthful guardsman as he puffed more smoke into the air. Eventually, the guardsman noted the presence of the agent, nodded, and took out his pack of cigarettes. Removing one from his supply, he put the rest away in a pocket. From there, the younger of the two searched for a light, his face conveying surprised frustration when it was not found.

He then looked at Hernandez, giving a tacit request. Hernandez nodded and smiled, walking over to the National Guardsman while also taking out his match book. The agent handed the young soldier the little book, with the guardsman successfully lighting a match on the first try. Hernandez was a little impressed by the success; maybe the local fellow was more used to using the subpar books of that part of the world. With his cigarette lighted, the guardsman handed back the little book to Hernandez, nodding in gratitude. Hernandez returned to his spot, enjoying the last length of his cigarette. As he flicked away the stubby remnant, Captain Enrique Dager arrived; this prompted the young soldier to stand to attention, only for the officer to wave off his act of discipline.

"We will be meeting in a few minutes," Dager told Hernandez en Español. "We will plan the operations for tomorrow."

"What is our situation?" Hernandez asked.

"No activity in the capital or other major cities. And no activity here."

"The cartel was here, though."

"Yes, they were," Dager affirmed, walking to stand beside Hernandez. "However, we do not know where the bulk of their forces are at present."

"And you will not risk looking for them at night," stated Hernanez, folding his arms.

"Correct."

Hernandez lightened up. "You know, if you all had not decided to abolish your armed forces years back, this would not be a problem."

"Really?" asked a skeptical Dager.

"If something like this had happened in my country, we would have launched a bunch of air strikes, drone attacks, and sent in the Marines, while we were at it. All before breakfast, I will add," said Hernandez, raising a finger as he made his final point.

"Quiza," Dager conceded. "Pero, your country can afford to have a large standing army and provide basic resources for your people. I think the phrase I once heard from an American historian was 'bullets and butter.'"

"Yes, 'bullets and butter.' Funny thing is, we usually talk about how you cannot do both. It is either bullets *or* butter."

"Then you can understand why we chose butter."

"Just as long as you understand why we keep choosing bullets," said Hernandez, getting a faint smile from the captain. "Do we have any idea where they are going?"

"I was going to ask you that very question," Dager said. "Your source was the one who told you that they were in Quetzal, right?"

"Right," Hernandez acknowledged. "And she was the one who told me that they were going to some mission outpost, a few miles from the border. Are you familiar with any missions out there?"

"There are a few, actually."

"A few?"

"We get many missionaries from the United States. Some of them are seasonal. The type that come for a few weeks, do some charity work, maybe preach the Gospel at street corners, but then leave by the end of the month or the end of the season. We also get some longer-term people, people who come here for a few years or more. Some of them even marry the locals and have families."

"Basically, you get the whole spectrum."

"Yes, you are able to say that."

"I assume it will take time to figure out which mission they are going to."

Dager nodded.

Hernandez sighed. "All of this is taking too long."

"Maybe you are right. Maybe we are too slow. Maybe we need to be mas rapido. Pero, caution gives life. We have yet to lose anyone since the convoy attack."

"It is easy to have no casualties when you never fight," Hernandez critically replied.

"It is about time for the meeting," said Dager, looking at a digital watch on his left wrist. "We need to leave."

"Sí, Captain Dager."

* * *

Carla al-Hassan Sharp was about to go to sleep. When Flavia offered a bed or a couch, she agreed to the latter. Flavia brought out a spare pillow and two sheets, with Carla graciously accepting the items and organizing them as best she could to be comfortable. Carla discovered that the sofa was not as pleasant to be in as previously presumed. Having laid down on it earlier, she knew that one side was a bit firmer than the other. Additionally, the seating leaned inward, meaning that, as the night progressed, she was going to have to make an extra effort to keep one arm from being smooshed.

Carla was still fully clothed, and the garments were still a little damp from the rain. Flavia was a gracious host—to Carla, at least. The young woman had offered Carla her pick of her clothes to change into, opening a closet in the lone bedroom and displaying about a dozen different outfits. However, the height difference between the two women meant that the pants were too short, the shirts were too tight, and the dresses were too revealing. Flavia did not have a dryer at her place, so there was no technologically convenient way to evaporate the vestiges of the droplets. Even so, a part of Carla was still uncomfortable with the idea of being undressed anywhere near the eyes of Raul Torquemada.

Carla was seated on the couch. She crossed herself in the Eastern manner, and silently prayed with head bowed and eyes closed. She gave thanks for the deliverance of her and Torquemada, as well as the fact that they were sheltered for the evening. She had many requests, including continued protection, a sound sleep despite the less-than-ideal accommodations, and for the operation to be worth it. She was so close to being free; she was so close to getting out of the Agency once and for all. It had to be soon. They were running out of land to run to between their current location and a mountainous border. When the flood of thoughts sent to God were concluded, she crossed herself a second time.

She removed her shoes before tucking herself in, but otherwise stayed fully clothed. The persistent water spots on her shirt and pants were bearable, and she expected no harmful consequences from them remaining. As she was drifting, she had a clear view of the combination kitchen and dining room. An uneven old wooden table was the centerpiece, with a pair of metal folding chairs for seats. There was a dark wooden crucifix in the center of the wall facing Carla, but otherwise the barrier remained undecorated. There were a couple of photos of Flavia and her son in the living room. Carla began to understand why her host acted so disturbed when she learned that Fulgencio Brennenberg was still alive, as the family photos revealed that Flavia's son had bright blue eyes.

As she got as cozy as she could, Carla saw Raul and Flavia sit at the table, each holding what appeared to be a bottle of beer. Carla knew that her host had a fair amount of alcohol in the refrigerator, with intoxicating liquids oddly placed alongside kids' juice boxes and a couple of small cartons of milk and orange juice. Earlier that evening, Flavia had expressed surprise—and even a little disappointment—when Carla informed her that she did not drink. They each opened their respective bottles, talking only a little at first. Carla was within earshot of everything, as the two either did not know or did not care that she was listening.

"You told me he was dead," she said, holding her beer bottle with both hands. She was directly facing her guest. "You said that he was shot in America."

"I thought it was true, too," said Torquemada. "As a matter of fact, I am pretty sure that Carla was the one who shot him."

"And now she is trying to get you to America?"

"It is the only way I can stop him. You know that."

"Oh, come on, Raul," said Flavia, dismissively. "You think I am going to feel sad that I might never see you again? When we hooked up, we agreed: no feelings."

"We agreed: no marriage," he corrected, taking another hefty swig of the beer. "Feelings cannot be stopped."

"Yes, they can," she stated, firmly. "I stopped feeling a long time ago. Not feeling was the only way I could handle it. If I do not feel, then he can never hurt me again. If I do not feel, you can never hurt me again, also."

"Are you kidding me?" Raul nearly shouted, his awareness of the sleeping child being the only reason he refrained from a full volume. "Brennenberg and I were nothing alike. Are nothing alike. He considered you a toy. A product. Something to play with and then throw away. That was why he… why he did what he did."

"He did what he did because of you," Flavia said, softly. She drank more of her beer before continuing. "He saw that you liked me, that you were with me. He knew that… he knew that if he wanted to be in control, he had to have everything you have."

"Flavia—"

"And you did nothing," she angrily snapped. "You left him alone. You told no one. Because you were silent, no one believed me."

"I am sorry, Flavia. I really am sorry."

"No matter," she said, becoming sedate. "If you had said something, he would have never stayed in power. He would never have gone to America with you two years ago, and he would not be here now, having kicked you out. You got yours, eventually."

"So, karma hits me."

"Karma is bull shit," she deadpanned. "Too many powerful evil men like you and Brennenberg die comfortably, while decent people like those folk who slave in your fields die poor and sad." She took another swig of her beer. "But maybe, just maybe, it was justice. Justice is the better idea."

"There is plenty of injustice in this life. We both know that."

"Yeah, but unlike karma, justice can hit after you die. I choose to believe in justice. Seeing you on your way to either being tortured to death by

Brennenberg or spending the rest of your life in an American prison looks like justice to me."

"What will become of you when I am gone?" Torquemada asked. "You know the only reason you are not on the streets like you used to be is because of me. How many times have I paid your bills, given you grocery money?"

"And I gave you me, but that was not enough," she said.

"You said no feelings."

She chortled. "Maybe I was lying. I do not know."

"Come with us," he said, bringing her to full attention. "No matter what happens, you cannot live here anymore."

"And what then? Start a 'new life' in America? The glorious El Norte?"

"Why not?" he pressed. "I am sure our American friend can help out. Maybe she is able to streamline the process. Something like that."

"Raul," Flavia said, rubbing her forehead. "Why do you keep messing with me?"

"This is not messing... this is fixing," said Raul, who briefly looked down before continuing. "You are right. I messed up. Badly. I messed up when I said no marriage. I messed up when I did nothing after Brennenberg did what he did. However, this is different. This time, I am going to fix things. This time, I am going to do right for you. You and your son. Please, Flavia... Let me finally help you."

"In return for what?"

Raul thought for a moment, took a final swig of his beer, and then looked her in the eyes with the fullest of sincerity. "Nothing. Absolutely nothing. When we get to America, you can never talk to me ever again."

"Bull shit," she said, albeit weakly.

"No, no lie. Only truth."

"Only truth?"

He nodded.

"If this is a con—"

"It is not, I promise you."

"You better do more than promise, Raul. I expect action this time."

"And you will get it."

"Ojala," she said, chugging the rest of her beer. "I better get to bed then. Jesús likes to wake me up early. I thought he would stop doing that when he stopped being a baby, but I guess little boys are always babies. Right, Raul?"

"I see what you did there."

"Yes, you did, Raul. Yes, you did."

* * *

Most of the cartel soldiers had removed their sunglasses, for the obvious reason of being able to see at night. A few who guarded the field where all of their vehicles were parked at that late hour had night vision goggles strapped to their faces. Nearly all had removed their skeletal facemasks and lowered their hoods, as the time of rest allowed it. The whole gathering appeared like the parking for a carnival or a concert, with the diverse vehicles positioned side-by-side in impromptu rows sans painted lines. Campfires were neither wanted nor needed, creating a darkness which made the encampment all the harder to behold. Only the occasional smart phone screen or the occasional car lights illumined the field. Brennenberg was leaning against one of the jeeps, using his breathing device.

"Are you all right?" asked Pedro Aguilares, who walked over to him.

"Fine," he said as he tucked the oxygen mask back into his jacket. "I think the outside air is getting to me more than usual."

"Or maybe it is stress?" Pedro suggested.

"I have no reason to be stressed," the cartel leader corrected. "Even when Torquemada has slipped away, the people we leave behind only fear us more. No matter what, we win. This is exactly what I had wanted to create."

"I see."

"Do you have anything new to tell me?"

"No, Señor Brennenberg," said Pedro, who turned his face upward to look at the network of constellations above them. "I was just walking around the cars, then I saw that you were still awake."

"I am."

"Are you sure that it is healthy for you to be up this late?"

"It was my lung that got permanently damaged, not my heart," Brennenberg replied. "I do not need to be coddled, Pedro."

"Sí, Señor Brennenberg."

"The only real change, apart from this thing I have to use from time to time, is that I have to sleep at an incline when I go to bed," he explained. "One of the positives of this little adventure has been sleeping in the cars, where I am at a sitting position when I sleep. I have slept surprisingly well."

"I am happy for you," said Pedro, who returned to looking at the stars. "They are very beautiful out here in the country."

"Yes, they are," the cartel leader said, nodding. "Death and the stars, those are constants in life. No matter what happens, they are always there. They are like old friends. The kind of friends you can call on and they always answer the phone."

"I guess so, Señor Brennenberg."

"You have known Torquemada for years, as have I. Where do you think he went to?"

"No sé, Señor."

"I know he went this way, this general way. Este manera general," he thought aloud, moving away from the jeep. "This is not a large nation. We have fewer than twenty miles between us and the border. The border is mountainous, and fairly well-guarded. He will be cornered if he keeps going that way. Plus, he has no promise that the patrolmen will allow him to enter their nation."

"They might even shoot him on the spot for trespassing," Pedro suggested.

"Sí, solamente," said Brennenberg, patting Pedro one on his broad shoulders as he paced about. "He must have a plan. In our profession, you need to have escape plans. I know that he has put some of this plan into effect. That was why we saw few weapons at that stockpile, and why so many of the young villagers are missing. They will rally at some point and then dare us to attack." He stopped his walk. "And yet, I have no idea where this last stand will take place. I have no idea." He went back to Pedro. "We need to think. We have to learn where he is going, where he is at this moment."

"Sí, Señor Brennenberg."

"Get a map, and we will put it on the jeep hood," Brennenberg ordered Pedro.

"Sure, I will find one and return."

As Pedro walked off, Brennenberg went to looking above at the eventide canopy. A well-educated man, Brennenberg knew each of the astronomical designs by name. He knew the mythology and the interpretations. Nothing was out of order in the heavens. It was the stability he hoped to bring to earth. However, rather than enforce such consistency with gravity and relative pull, his enforcement would come through violence. He heard Pedro coming, seeing the young man with a paper map under his arm. They nodded at each other, both approaching the nearest parked jeep, the hood serving a table for the unfolded map, detailing roads, city names, villages, and terrain profiles.

"We are right about here," said Brennenberg as he pointed at the cartographic illustration, an index finger suspended a few centimeters above the paper and near the name Quetzal. "The border is over there." Again, he pointed, Pedro using a flashlight to better see the map and the digits of his boss. "Somewhere in between is my former superior." He moved his index finger in a circle above that narrow space in the map when making the comment. "However, that covers many villages and towns, to say nothing of farms and jungle. Even a tiny creature like this nation can be an expansive territory."

Pedro and Brennenberg studied the map in silence for a few minutes. It was far from quiet in that field, as scores of men bantered on in mostly jovial conversations of little substance. Countless bugs and other wildlife sang in the background, providing a natural ambiance for those at rest. Some of the bug zappers brought along had a slight moan to them, which would briefly ping upward in pitch whenever a flying little one got too close to the humans. Many walked around the encampment, sometimes to exercise, sometimes just to wear down nerves, and sometimes to find a private little spot in the dark to relieve themselves. As the mild noise progressed, Brennenberg spoke up.

"A lady friend," he said. "Torquemada had his share of lady friends."

"They were more like whores."

"Yes, yes they were," said Brennenberg, laughing at the remark. "A few of them were, if I remember correctly. Still, I am starting to remember one of them. She was from some small village. Let me see..." Brennenberg started to concentrate more on the map, searching for the name. "It was a religious name...the name of the village."

"Corpus Christi? San Salvador?"

"Veracruz!" he declared, pointing at the name on the map. "I remember now. She was some young woman that Torquemada fell for. It was pitiful, believe me. It made him an even worse leader than he already was."

"Do you remember her name?"

"It began with an F, like a Florence or a...Flavia! That was it! Flavia was her name, like she was from Ancient Rome. I had her once or twice myself. My thinking was that he would not want her anymore. It was for both business *and* pleasure."

Pedro did not know how to respond, so he just stood there, exuding loyalty.

"They broke it off soon after he learned that I had her. Maybe, given all that is happening, he decided to return to her. How pathetic, how wretched."

"Sí, Señor Brennenberg."

"We will move out tomorrow morning. Sunrise."

* * *

"Que sobre mis cosas?" Jesús protested, knowing that his toys remained inside of the one-story house.

"Te compraré mas cosas en los Estados Unidos," Flavia promised. "Okay?"

"Okay," the little boy conceded.

Flavia had two suitcases beside her as she stood at the back of the compact car that Torquemada had parked in front of her place. The larger of the two cases contained her things, which included clothing, toiletries, a couple of family photos, and a rosary that had been in the family for a few generations. The smaller case had some of Jesús's clothes, a kid toothbrush with a small tube of toothpaste, and a picture Bible. With the trunk already opened, Flavia lifted both items by their handles and shoved them into the confined space. Carla and Torquemada only had bags of toiletries in the trunk, all of which had been purchased the night before by Flavia as the two hid in her place.

"Estas seguro?" Torquemada inquired over the phone. He smiled as he heard the confirmation of the earlier report. "Muy bien. Adios!"

"Well?" Carla asked.

"My friends at the mission confirmed," said Torquemada as he put his phone in his pants pocket. "The waters have gone down. We should be able to drive in today."

"Good," said Carla.

"What about Flavia and Jesús?"

"Last I checked, they were in the car."

"Then we should leave. I have this feeling that Brennenberg has figured out where we are," said Torquemada.

"That would be because he knew her, also?"

Torquemada looked down. "Yes. You are right."

"All right," said Carla. "We should leave."

The two were wearing what they had had on the previous day, as neither had a change of clothes at the house. They made no effort to double check if lights were off or if any faucets were running. If nothing else, such devices being on might help to deceive people into thinking that they were still there. No effort was made to lock the door behind them as they ventured out into the humid morning. On instinct, Carla closed the door, but then quickly moved away. As they got to the car, they saw that mother and child were actually still outside of the vehicle. Flavia simply pointed at the weapons stashed in the back as the answer. Torquemada looked at her with annoyance, wondering why she could not move them herself. Torquemada then popped the trunk, as Carla put the guns on top of the suitcases. Flavia and Jesús got into the back, fastening their seatbelts. Torquemada got into the driver's seat, turning the key to ignite the engine the moment that Carla got in.

"This might be the weirdest family road trip I have ever been on," Carla quipped to Torquemada in English, knowing that he was the only other person in the vehicle who spoke the language.

"Family," Torquemada said to Carla, continuing the conversation in English. "You know, I hate to say it, but you might not be far off."

"You mean about you and her?" Carla asked, shrewd enough to not namedrop the female passenger in the back row.

"Yes," he said, pulling into traffic.

"Why did you two agree on not getting married?"

"Do we have to talk about this?" he said, defensively. "This isn't the time or the place."

"I guess not," Carla admitted.

Carla kept quiet for the time, turning to her window and looking at the other rundown homes along the way. Many of them had kids and elderly just outside of their front doors. The children were running about, apparently street smart enough to not suddenly go in front of the moving vehicle, yet carefree enough to scream and laugh as they played. The older ones just sat there, likely just enjoying the start of the day. She did not notice any younger adults. Possibly they were still preparing things inside, or possibly they were already out of the house for work. She could only speculate.

"Have you gotten any word from Marisol yet?" Torquemada asked.

"She said she would be nearby," Carla replied. "However, she spent the night at some motel off of the main street. According to her, the National Guard will be on their way. Maybe we should wait."

"No," said Torquemada, turning right onto main street as he uttered his decision. "They will not get here in time."

Carla nodded in agreement. She had seen no evidence that they were fast enough to be relied upon for a rescue. Instead, she went back to looking outside. There was nothing in particular that caught her eye. It was simply the community of Veracruz, stretching and yawning as they began their day. She found it odd for a time, thinking about how for most all of the town, this was another regular day. One full of work, leisure, arguments and agreements, jokes and business, food and drink. Families would temporarily part ways for their shifts, only to come back again that night. None of them knew of the desperation that filled the old vehicle she was inside of. For them, it was just another automobile with a few people inside, one to be wary of when crossing the street.

Then, Carla spotted something in the passenger side rearview mirror. At first, it looked like just another pick-up truck driving through the village. Then, upon closer examination, she realized that there a few men in the back, with at least one looking to be armed. As Torquemada swerved a little to one side, her mirror view got better, and she beheld in great apprehension a figure standing in the back of the pick-up, a large machine gun at the ready. Behind that vehicle, see saw at least two others, black and bristling with weapons. She also realized that they were gaining on them.

"Raul," she cautioned.

"I know, I know," he insisted, pushing down on the gas some more. "I see them, too."

"Mama, quiénes son?" asked the curious child.

"Gente mal, mi hijo," Flavia replied, holding him close.

Suddenly, they heard gunfire. All of the people inside the car crouched down, expecting a barrage to strike them. And yet, after a few moments, they realized that nothing had struck them. Carla soon figured out that the cartel soldiers behind them had fired into the air. It was a warning for those in the way, like emergency vehicles blaring sirens. The other commuters on main street turned off to the edges of the road. Pedestrians likewise refrained from crossing the pavement, recognizing that they would be shown mercy if they stayed on the sidelines. The people of Veracruz were obedient, and thus cleared the way between the cartel soldiers and the lone car with their target at the wheel.

"It would be nice if we had those guns right about now," Torquemada muttered.

"Is there a way to access the trunk from inside the car?"

"Don't bother," he said, accelerating the vehicle to highway speeds. "It would not be much of a fight with their arms."

Even with the road cleared of neutral parties and the former cartel leader speeding up all the more, the black clad pursuers were matching his velocity. Soon, one of them fired a flurry of bullets in their general direction. Flavia and Jesús screamed and cried as some of the shots impacted the bumper and the trunk, though thankfully not the rear window. Sparks dotted the back end of the vehicle as though miniature lightning. Mother and son stayed crouched down, their bodies below the window. They expected another attack shortly. And indeed, one of the pick-ups was getting closer.

CRASH! Before the pick-up bearing a machine gun could get close enough for a second round of shooting, a civilian vehicle suddenly pulled out into traffic, getting between the fleeing car and the motorcade of masked thugs. It smashed into the side of the pick-up, which in turn shifted the vehicle enough that it hit a second cartel vehicle that was next to it. The impact threw a few men out of the vehicle, landing badly on the concrete. Others, secured by belts, hurled forward, though not with severe injuries. Three cartel jeeps that were just behind the two impacted cars slammed on their breaks, twisting and curving as they burned the pavement and narrowly avoided becoming part of a pileup. Other members of the motorcade likewise came to screeching halts behind them.

"Damn, we were lucky," Torquemada commented to Carla as Flavia led her son in prayers of thanks for deliverance, putting great distance between himself and their stopped adversaries.

"I do not believe it was luck," Carla said with confidence.

Marisol's head hurt. As she had seen the convoy as it was getting into town, she hastily prepared a plan to delay them. She prayed fervently for it to work, knowing that the odds were slim. Her original intent was to stop in front of the cartel motorcade and force them to all stop in a more peaceful manner, pleading ignorance as to their presence. However, she did not pull out as fast as she had hoped, or maybe the cartel vehicles were going faster than she had estimated. Regardless, she was breathing hard in the damaged vehicle, the passenger's side having borne the brunt of the collusion.

"Gracias a Dios, gracias a Dios," she said repeatedly, crossing herself in the Western manner as she unbuckled her seatbelt and got out of her vehicle, with the driver's side being virtually unharmed. She briefly caught a glimpse of the dark-hued vehicle that she knew her friend was in, giving a slight smile as they faded off into the jungle background. From there, she directed her emotions at the cartel soldiers. "Lo siento! Lo siento! I did not see you when I pulled out! Are you okay? Please tell me you are okay!"

At first, it seemed to be working. It was hard to read their expressions, as their faces were covered with sunglasses and mostly black facemasks that included decorative illustrations of the lower half of a skull. However, a few were nodding, while others were waving her off. Some took off their disguises, revealing young men who were affirming that they were all right. She kept up the performance, staying there lest they wonder why she would flee from the crash. "Is there anything I can do to help? I can help, I can help! Oh, I am so sorry! Please forgive me, please, please forgive me!"

Just as she got closer, seeming to get an acceptance of her assistance, one of the larger cartel soldiers confronted her. At first, Marisol believed that he was going to tell her off or maybe order her to look after one of the injured. Marisol tried to be optimistic. However, the figure grabbed her with one arm, while lowering his facemask and removing his glasses. She soon realized that it was Pedro, who pulled back his hood for good measure. Marisol kept silent, unsure of how to deal with this.

"Marisol," he said. "What are you doing here?"

"I was—I was visiting a friend," she replied, which was somewhat true. "I am sorry, Pedro, I did not see where I was going. You know me, I am a horrible driver!" Pedro remained quiet, and he would not let go. "Mira, Pedro, escuchame...Listen to me, look and listen, I am really shook up. The car of my friend is totaled, some of your men are hurt. Let me help them. I can bandage a wound. I could call their relatives. Please, let me help."

Marisol was unsure if her ploy was working. Pedro was not letting go, however, which made her all the more uncomfortable. Soon, both of them turned to look a new arrival. He was walking on foot, semi-surrounded by guards bearing assault rifles who were dressed as the men she had crashed into. The man garnered reverence and acknowledgement from all of those in his general presence. Even the people of Veracruz, who were gathering on either side of the main street to gawk over the crash, seemed to be more respectful as he came. Marisol became more frightened as he stopped within a few feet of her and Pedro. His blue eyes pierced her with the danger of recognition.

"You," Brennenberg said. "I remember you. You were in Quetzal. You were near the fire. Now you are here, by the crash."

"Señor, por favor, I have no idea what you are talking about."

"She is lying," Pedro declared. "She works for the Americans."

"Interesting," said Brennenberg, getting closer to her, but then turning his head to the side to look upward at the chapel on the hill. "Very interesting."

XI.

"**M**ama," groaned the little Jesús. "Estoy enfermo. Mi estomago."
"Yo sé, mi hijo, yo sé," Flavia assured him. "Estamos casi alli." She
then looked at the driver of the vehicle. "We are almost there, right?"

"Yes, yes, almost there," said Raul Torquemada, eyes on the poorly paved
road. "Less than a mile to go until we arrive at the mission."

"Muy bien," the mother deadpanned.

Her son was resting his head on her lap. His hands were over his stomach,
as he felt quite nauseous. They had stopped earlier because the boy had had
to use the bathroom. Given their departure from most of human habitation, he had to use the jungle as his facilities. He had been lamenting his
belly for the past thirty to forty minutes. Torquemada was convinced that
he was exaggerating his pain and felt no need to stop again until they got
to the intended destination. Flavia kept judging Torquemada with her eyes,
whispering some profanity under her breath for his apparent callousness,
yet not wanting her rhetoric to be heard by the little ears of Jesús, who took
some comfort in resting on her.

Carla al-Hassan Sharp was quietly looking out of her passenger side
window. She saw the world passing her by, the buildings giving way to the
trees and vegetation of the incomparable jungle. Fewer traces of civilization
existed in her view, with the road being the lone example by that point. It
felt as though she was going back in time, back before mankind of either
American or European heritage had discovered this part of the planet. She
wondered many things, such as how long it would take for the natural environment to conquer the villages and towns she had seen earlier if the resi-

dents left the nation. She was wondering if Torquemada was going to make it, lest her agreement with the Agency to be able to leave would fall through. She felt guilty, knowing that her efforts to keep him alive had as much to do with her own life as it did his, if not more so. She had yet to tell him this and had no plans to provide such a revelation. It was not something that mattered to her, as she knew that the issue was a moot one given their circumstances.

The old car entered a clearing and began to descend. The road itself was going down a hill into what appeared to be a long trench. There were no trees in the sunken space. It looked as though, maybe, the area had been created by some rift caused by an earthquake centuries ago. She spotted several large puddles along the way, likely holdovers from the powerful thunderstorm that forced them to stay in Veracruz overnight. The ditch looked like a space that could easily be flooded. After about a half minute of travel, the car went up onto a hill that, like the other side of the sunken stretch, was covered by thick jungle. Only the road remained clear, its pavement bearing numerous cracks.

The trees began to thin once again, the branches and the leafy canopy giving away to another, mostly cleared space. Carla saw the inhabitance from a distance. There were several white adobe structures, dotting a much steeper hill. Additionally, there were some wooden buildings as well. At the very top was what looked to be a church. It had white walls and large glass windows. It was topped by a dark brown cross, its overall designed resembling many of the Protestant sanctuaries that Carla had seen in her home state. There was a sign on the right side of the road which explained the matter:

BIENVENIDOS A LA MISION DE LA VIA DOLOROSA
UNA MISION DE LA IGLESIA LUTERANA, EEUU
EST. 1986

"The mission," Carla spoke aloud.

"The mission," confirmed Torquemada.

"Mira, Jesús, mira," Flavia ordered her son, rightfully assuming that the excitement of seeing the destination would help curb his stomach issues.

Getting closer, the driver and the passengers saw people near and around the buildings. They appeared to vary in size and age, clothing, and skin shade. As they got closer, they saw that several of them were armed. They also saw that the route to the mission property was blocked off with several dark green oil barrels, each having varying levels of bright brown rust along the sides. A pair of young men in plain clothes and bearing assault rifles approached the vehicle. Torquemada slowed to a stop as they neared. One of them pointed his weapon at the automobile, while the other went to the driver's side.

"Are you sure they want us here?" Carla asked.

Torquemada ignored the query, rolling down his car window and showing himself to the young man closest to him. The stern-faced youth, assault rifle slung along his back, immediately changed his expression upon learning the identity of the driver. He shouted at the other fellow, ordering him to lower his rifle. The other man obliged. He then shouted at a few other young men, likewise carrying arms, to remove the barrels in the way of the stopped vehicle. As they did so, he went back to the driver.

"Lo siento, Señor Torquemada, lo siento mucho," he stated, almost begging.

"It is all right, Rubio. I am happy that you are being vigilant," said Torquemada, instantly making the young man feel better. "Is Pastor Hans here?"

"Sí, Señor Torquemada, el esta aqui."

"Gracias, Rubio."

"De nada, señor, de nada," he reiterated, getting out of the way.

Torquemada nodded at the armed man, smiled, and then rolled up his car window. The way being clear, he accelerated passed the armed youths, going into the mission community itself. Behind him, the armed men went about rebuilding the barricade. Carla saw the many people going about the buildings, which were mostly domiciles. There were young and old women, more people with guns, and even several children, who were chasing each other for entertainment. As they got higher up, she saw several unarmed folks passing the time by playing soccer, using some old orange gymnasium cones to mark where the goals and out-of-bounds were located.

"Estamos aqui," Torquemada told the mother and child in the backrow.

"Gracias a Dios," she stated, her son happily rushing out of the car.

Dozens of men, women, and children approached Torquemada and his passengers. As they disembarked, they became especially gleeful at the arrival of their past benefactor. Carla watched as the toughened former cartel leader, a man known for his constant focus on business as well as survival, melted into happiness at the sight of the adoring audience. Children hugged his limbs, and he patted them on their heads. Men walked up and took turns shaking his hand, with some impatient ones gladly shaking his left one instead, or even just patting him on the arm or shoulders.

Carla was barely noticed by those who had so warmly welcomed Torquemada. It was not a matter of contempt as much as it was that the presence of him was so much more grabbing of attention. Flavia and her son blended into the crowd, with her looking for someone to help her find shelter for the evening. The crowd parted as a figure of importance entered, an older white American with a three-day beard and short, salty hair. He was wearing jeans and tennis shoes, yet from the waist up he was blatantly clerical, with a black button-up shirt and a white collar. He and Torquemada greeted each other in English, and maintained their conversation, with the general noise of the crowd making it harder for Carla to make out what exactly they were saying to one another.

She had dismissed the matter, for the time being. To her, the important goal was to find their means of aerial escape. Looking away from the impromptu gathering, Carla saw that the plateau on which they had parked had an old propeller plane off in the distance. She also saw what looked like a signal tower adjacent to the old-fashioned transport. It was yet another generic gray building. Carla walked at a decent pace toward the airstrip, resisting the urge to run. The sight was like seeing a beloved relative from afar. And yet, whatever hopes she had for the venture was dashed as she got a better look at the tarmac. It was a misshapen stretch, with potholes and sizable cracks.

"I see you found our airstrip," said an American voice.

Carla turned to see the clergyman she had just seen conversing with Torquemada walking beside the former cartel leader as they neared her.

The crowd had dispersed, with people going back to work, rest, or play. She folded her arms and looked at the man who brought her there with judgmental eyes. He merely looked down, while the American clergyman continued to exude kindness. Her gaze returned to the airstrip, with its large cracks and uneven surface, not fit for any takeoff or landing.

"We have not met," said the only other American in the vicinity. "I am Pastor Hans. I oversee the mission here."

"Pastor Hans," she stated with formality. "What happened?"

"Earthquake," he replied. "They don't happen often, but when they do, they pack a punch. That, and of course, the usual erosion of time. I keep urging our sponsor churches in the States to raise more money to fix things, but donations have been coming in slow. You know what I mean?"

"Yeah," she said, then had an idea. "You have a radio here, right? We could signal someone to come."

"I don't know, Miss…"

"Missus," Carla corrected. "Mrs. Carla Sharp."

"Well, Mrs. Sharp," the pastor began, then his eyes widened. "Hey, aren't you the wife of Governor Sharp?"

Carla was surprised. "Yes, I am."

"Oh, that's wonderful! I like Sharp. He's a good man," said Pastor Hans. "I voted for him, you know. Had to do it via absentee, but I did it."

"That is much appreciated," Carla said.

"You know, I always heard that you worked with the State Department down here. I always thought that maybe, one in a million chance, I would meet you. I guess I should become a betting man, am I right?"

"Maybe," she humored. "But going back to the radio—"

"Oh, yes, yes, that," said Pastor Hans, who shifted his posture. "Thing is, well, um, yesterday's storm knocked it out. We have a repair man, but he's not due to come back here for another two days."

"Two days?" she asked, then turned to Torquemada. "They will probably get here by then."

"What does it matter, Carla?" Torquemada asked. "As you can see, no one can land here anyway. We have to stay."

"Well, we could let the National Guard know we are here," Carla countered. "I assume your phone does not work here, either."

"That is why I chose this place," he said. "No way to track us that way."

"And no way to call for help," she noted.

"So, it is that serious, huh?" Pastor Hans inquired.

Torquemada nodded.

"I only heard rumors from the people coming in. Stuff about some blue-eyed devil who came back from the dead and was now trying to kill everyone. I had to keep assuring them that only one Man ever came back from the dead, and He's not a thug."

"I am sure you have been a great help, Hans," Torquemada told the pastor.

"I couldn't do it without you, my criminal friend," he said, lightly punching Torquemada on the shoulder before looking at Carla. "You know, there were times when this fellow personally kept this mission afloat through his donations?"

"I did not know that," said a genuinely surprised Carla.

"Someday, I might even save his soul," said the American clergyman, laughing at his comment. Torquemada seemed to interpret it as a joke. "Anyhow, I need to get back to the rest. I see that you brought Flavia and her wonderful son with you. I hope this means what I hope it means. Does it?"

"You might want to keep hoping," said Torquemada.

"Oh, Raul, I always hope for you. And I always pray for you, too," said the American pastor, who laughed as he continued. "In fact, both efforts take way more work than I thought they would."

Torquemada laughed at the remark, with Carla smiling. Hans gave one more pat to his back, and then nodded a goodbye to Carla before walking away. Carla turned back to the ruined airstrip and the useless signal station. She openly sighed, her arms folded. Torquemada approached her with caution, wondering how she would react to his presence as everyone else had gone to their own affairs in the mission. She looked back at him, still conveying a sense of betrayal in her dark eyes.

"You know, I did not promise that the airstrip was in good order."

She gritted her teeth at first. "You are right. I had a feeling it was not going to be usable."

"Besides, even if it was, I cannot leave here. Not yet."

"What do you..." Carla paused, as she had figured out the situation. "Raul Torquemada. Man of power, willing to kill to remain in power. You of all people...you actually care. You care for them."

He nodded. "If we left them, then they would never stand a chance."

"And they will stand a chance with us here?" she asked, critically.

"If you are as deadly as I think you are, then yes," he said. "With your ability and my leadership..." He grinned briefly. "...and the prayers of Pastor Hans, how can we fail?"

"We will need to plan things soon," said Carla, accepting the situation and keeping her grievances to herself.

"Yes."

"How long do you think it will take for Brennenberg to find us?"

"It depends on what happened to your friend," said Torquemada. "If she got away—"

"She didn't."

"How do you know?"

"I know."

* * *

It was dark inside, even with the front door wide open, and even with the sinking sun thrusting a few beams through the stained glass. There were many shadows; there was much shade. The candles were unlit, depriving those inside of better vision. And yet, all was seeable. This included numerous dark wooden chairs, which were normally put into two columns of rows, yet at that moment they were pushed to the sides of the sacred room. Along the broad sides of the chapel hung fourteen small paintings, each representing a station of the cross. At the front, there was a large crucifix, with the beams being made of wood while the attached Christ figure was of bronze. There were multiple statues around it, none taller than three feet, representing various saints. In front of this gathering of witnesses, there was an altar with candles on either side and a smaller crucifix in the middle.

A long rope had been tossed over one of the beams that lay above the nave, resembling a hangman's noose. At the end of it was a pair of hands, tightly tied wrist upon wrist. One man—wearing a skeletal facemask and sunglasses, clothed in shades of gray and black, head covered by a hood, feet covered by boots, and hands covered by gloves—gripped the rope to keep it steady. Two other men in nearly identical attire stood on either side, each armed with an assault rifle, a knife, and a pistol. Two more armed men, dressed as the other three, stood guard at the opened door of the chapel, facing the altar.

Marisol Contreras was breathing hard; her stomach was in knots. The rope seemed to get tighter as the minutes slowly passed. Beads of sweat slowly went down her face and back. It was a combination of the warm interior and the fear of what was to come. The others inside of the chapel may have been sweating more, however their attire and obscured faces hid any evidence of perspiration. She looked forward, seeing a still bright outdoors, including the way down the hill and several buildings. Freedom was beyond that open door. The normal world with its flaws and wonders was beyond that sanctuary.

And then her view of the outside was blocked by two new arrivals. The first to arrive was the larger and younger of the two. Pedro Aguilares wore no hood or mask and was thus identified immediately. He made eye contact with Marisol at first, but instantly looked down, an expression of pity upon his face. He was carrying with both hands a small, four-legged wooden table, no more than two feet wide. Under his left arm he had something rolled up, the exact nature of which Marisol was unable to determine at that moment. Near Pedro was a smaller man, with blond hair and blue eyes. He was breathing hard and had to take an oxygen mask from his jacket. The man inhaled and exhaled several times with the semitransparent mask covering his nose and mouth. A few moments later, he put the medical item back into his jacket and took a deep breath of relief.

Pedro got within six feet of his former girlfriend, the one who he knew had taken advantage of him on multiple occasions, and set the table down.

With the four skinny wooden legs on the stone floor, he took the rolled-up item and put it on one side of the table. He nodded at the blond man, who nodded back. Pedro took one more look at Marisol. His expression was that of pity. As the blond man rested his hands on the table, Pedro shook his head and walked away. Marisol wanted to shout, to plead with him. Yet, ultimately, she knew it would serve no purpose. The blond man, who nearly completely blocked the view of the outside from the open door, grinned.

"You know who I am, correct?"

Marisol did nothing; she said nothing.

"Oh, come on, Marisol," he said, getting closer. "This is an easy question." He closed in on her, revealing that he was four inches taller. He was sedate. "Please, say my name. Say it in the presence of the saints and the angels."

"Señor Fulgencio Brennenberg," she stated, a bit of contempt to her tone.

"Muy bien, senorita," he said, turning to walk back to the small table. "Pedro told me your name, and all that you have done to us."

Marisol went silent again.

"In a way, I should be thanking you," he said, as he rolled the item open, revealing a collection of blades and knives, which lay flat on the wooden table. "You helped cause the downfall of my predecessor. The cartel would not be as willing to appoint me king if your little intelligence gathering had not been used so effectively against us." He kept looking at the sharp objects laid out on the table, some of which glimmered thanks to the few rays of sun that struck that part of the interior. "However, since the downfall of my predecessor, you are a great hindrance to me. First, you help him and his American friend escape at Quetzal, and then again here, in the lovely village of Veracruz."

"You are making a mistake," she insisted. "It is all a coincidence. I swear!"

He looked up at the cartel soldiers standing behind her. "I would like my canvas to be unwrapped now."

Without speaking, the two soldiers who were not holding the rope slung their assault rifles upon their backs, took out their blades and approached

Marisol. She turned her head multiple times to look at each of the masked men as they got closer. Struggling with the rope did nothing, as every pull was countered by the third man holding the rope. They grabbed at her clothes, one pulling down her pants and then her panties, while the other used his blade to tear off her shirt, then her bra. She shouted in defiance, squirming a little but not too much given the close proximity of the sharp weapons. Their work was quick, and Marisol was soon left fully in the nude, one of the men going as far as to remove her shoes. She cussed at them as they backed away, before focusing back on Brennenberg.

"Much better," he commented.

He was holding one of his longer knives in his hands, studying the item as though seeing it for the first time. While his right hand gripped the handle, the fingers of his left hand rubbed his chin, in thoughtfulness. After some tacit discernment, he put the dangerous tool back among the others. Apparently, he had rejected it. At least, for the time. Marisol remained there, her bare feet feeling cold on the stone floor, but her upper body feeling hot with nerves. Her wrists were already becoming sore, as were her arms from being strung up for the past several minutes. Brennenberg, unarmed, casually walked toward Marisol, stopping mere inches away from her naked body.

"A fine canvas for which to work," he commented, his fingers moving along her upper body. "A good symmetry of the body. Like a reflection." His fingers went up her hair, brushing the long threads. "A fine mane as well. Healthy, dark, smooth." Brennenberg twirled a cluster of Marisol's black hair among his fingers. She stood as still as she could. Then, suddenly, he took a firm grip of the chunk of hair and yanked it downwards with all his might, ripping the follicles out of her head.

Marisol screamed in pain at the unexpected act of violence, her eyelids squeezed closed from the pull. The forced drove her body down, though the soldier right behind her positioned her back to an attention stance by pulling back on the rope. There were small spots of blood where the strands had once been rooted. Brennenberg was unmoved by the anguish, spending more time looking at the clump of hair in his hand. He then irreverently tossed it upon the stone and looked at the recovering Marisol. She saw him, standing there, with a look of disappointment upon his face.

"I was so stupid," he remarked, lightheartedly. "Now you have lost your balance. That blessed symmetry." He smiled. "No worries. I know how to fix the problem."

She knew what was coming and shook her head from side to side. She tried to struggle, moving a bit back and forth. Brennenberg looked at one of the men behind her, who came forward to grab her by the neck and the torso. She was forced to remain still enough that Brennenberg could take another bunch of hair on her head, again twirl it around a couple of his fingers, and then yank it off. Again, she screamed, cussing in the sanctuary, and again he showed little interest in her physical plight. More hair covered the stone. The man backed off and Marisol was back in proper posture. She now had some minor bleeding along that side of her head, as well. The removal of the two clusters made it appear as though she had more of a widow's peak than before.

"There," he said in accomplishment. "Perfect once again."

As the pain ebbed, she remained quiet.

"When I say perfect, I mean it," he said, gradually making his way back to the small table. "I really do not have to do any more to you." He went to the side of the table that was closer to the door and turned to face Marisol. "Unless, of course, you decide to remain silent and not tell me what I want to know."

Marisol kept mum.

"I am being charitable, senorita," said Brennenberg. "We will find my predecessor and your American friend. This is not a vast country. We are mere miles away from the border. And that border is barely passable. That leaves only a few little missions in the hinterlands to look into. By keeping silent, you merely delay the inevitable. However, by telling me where they are, you make my task easier...and you may even save your life." He looked down and selected a knife, one that was shorter than the piece he was investigating earlier. He gripped the item and stared into the eyes of Marisol. "You should really talk. It is the only way you leave this sanctuary as a whole person."

Marisol shed a tear. She breathed harder. Another tear fell as he awaited a response. Her heart pounded intensely, and she felt her stomach squirting acid. A third tear fell. She was breathing like she was running, yet she was remaining still in the chapel. The man holding the rope jerked on it, in an apparent effort to prompt an answer. He pulled back a little, lifting her heels off of the stone, but then moved a little more, putting her feet flat on the floor again. Marisol, fearful of moving, fearful of what was to come, mustered her might and shook her head, as one more little act of great defiance.

"A pity," Brennenberg coldly stated.

* * *

Pastor Hans unlocked the wooden trunk and lifted the top, the old lid moving upward at a ninety-degree angle. It was an old item, having been in the clergyman's family since the nineteenth century. Some of the planks looked fresher, having been gradually replaced over the decades. Indeed, it was possible that, by this point in history, none of the trunk parts were original to it, but all had been supplanted at some point. It was four feet long and two feet wide. To the surprise of Carla, it was packed full of explosives. Most of the dangerous objects were faded red sticks of dynamite, though she also saw other devices of a detonating nature. In one corner, there were dark green grenades.

"Why does a charitable mission have explosives?" she asked aloud.

"Various reasons," said the pastor in casual tone. "We're in the mountains, so sometimes we get landslides, and stuff like that. Always good to have a way to blast away a boulder or a bunch of downed trees."

"Yeah, there is that," conceded Carla.

"What do you think, Raul?" Hans asked the third person looking over the stockpile.

"It should do," said the former cartel leader, eyes still on the grenades and the sticks. "We plant things along the road, and among the outermost buildings, we can cause a lot of casualties."

"I would rather they may be used to scare them away," said Pastor Hans. "However, if the Lord wills to fight, I guess we have to fight. I mean, He did command the Ancient Israelites to wipe out the wicked nations. And I think it is easy argument to make that the cartel is not unlike a wicked nation." The pastor then smiled. "No offense, Raul."

"None taken," he said. "If anything, I think I always agreed with that idea."

"My prayers are working!" Hans declared with a smile.

The clergyman gently closed the old trunk, locking the furniture piece with a key that fit in the upper middle of the front. From there, the three exited the building that served as the parsonage for the mission. They walked past a small bedroom and a smaller kitchen. The pastor lived by humble means, having little more than those who flocked to his mission out of both spiritual and material need. They left the fairly cool habitation for a fairly warm exterior, with a sunny day before them. Instead of games and leisure, those already outside were beginning preparations for the expected conflict. This included several adults being trained on how to hold, aim, and fire a rifle.

"You know, Mrs. Sharp," began the pastor. "If you're not going to shelter with the children and the mothers, you should probably get some basic training on how to fire a gun."

"Oh, I am already very familiar with it," she assured him.

"How familiar is very familiar?" asked a skeptical Hans. "I mean, you're in a very dangerous situation. What we're expecting to come against, and all that."

"I assure you, pastor, that I am in this situation because of my ability with a gun."

"Really?" asked Hans, legitimately surprised. "You mean... Well, shoot, I always thought you were just some office worker with the State Department."

"I am a little more than that," she said. "However, if you go public with such information, I will deny it."

"Hey, no worries," he explained. "Your superhero secret is safe with me."

"Thank you."

"Any who, I have to check on some other things. See you all later!"

"Bye," said Carla.

"Adios," Torquemada said as the pastor walked off. "He is a good man, Pastor Hans."

"He deserves a better world," she concluded.

"Most likely," Torquemada agreed.

"So," Carla began. "What now?"

"Well, like I said to Hans, we should place the explosives along the road up the hill. Put some more along the houses nearest to the route as well. They have to come that way; there are no other options for them."

"No helicopters, huh?"

"Nope," said Torquemada. "We never really invested in them. After all, helicopters can be seen by overhead surveillance and easily taken out."

"Cars, on the other hand, can hide under the canopy, making it hard for satellites or drones to ever discover them."

"Now you are thinking like we do," he said, the two slowly walking about the mission.

"I am not sure if I like that."

"Me neither," he admitted. "You are pretty good with a sniper rifle, right?"

"I took out your predecessor with one," said Carla matter-of-factly.

"Well then, find a good place on one of the roofs and pick them off when you can," said Torquemada. Then, he thought some more. "So, you were the one who killed Sonoma."

"I probably should have told you sooner."

"That is okay," he said. "It would not change things here." He paused and faintly smiled. "If anything, I have to thank you. Without your help, I might not have taken over the cartel in the first place."

"Of course, because you took over, you ended up here."

"As you Americans like to say, for want of a shoe, the horse was lost."

"Yeah," Carla said, looking down.

"What is it?"

"This is not going to work," she stated, with Torquemada folding his arms in response. "Brennenberg is going to discover us, whether he gets it from Marisol or just by probing around. He is going to bring hundreds of cartel soldiers. All of them will be well-armed and trained for a fight like this. He will probably get some more firepower, too. The same bazookas and rocket-propelled grenades that he used to take out the convoy. We will be outnumbered and outgunned. And we will be facing someone who has absolutely no fear of death. He is determined, and he is driven. Meanwhile, anyone who could help us is far away." Carla sighed and looked down. "Our chance of victory is very low."

"Then why did you come along?" asked Torquemada, almost shouting. "Why did you not try to escape on your own? Brennenberg wants me, not you."

"You are my chance to escape all of this," Carla replied. "If I get you to safety, if you tell the authorities all you know about the cartel, then I get to go home. And I can stay home. I once told you how much I hate doing this, how much I hate having to kill people."

"Yes, I remember."

"You in custody means that I can finally leave this. I can finally live without it. No more scenarios where I am forced to kill people, no more long periods of time away from my daughter, missing everything she does. For the first time in my entire adult life, I can live in a normal world."

"I see," said Torquemada, calmed by her passionate counter. "Then, why did you agree with my plan to come here?"

"Because I had no choice!" she declared, and then laughed. She laughed some more, unnerving the former cartel leader. "Come to think of it, I never have a choice. It was like I was meant to be in situations like this."

"Maybe," said Torquemada. "And maybe I was meant to die here, fighting the very monster I once controlled."

"Maybe," Carla said, nodding. "Well, I guess we are both being punished."

"Yes, we are."

"I guess all we can do now is make sure that Brennenberg and his cartel friends get punished alongside us."

"Yes, they will."

* * *

175

Alfredo Hernandez could tell which of the National Guard had gone inside of the chapel and which had yet to enter. He was one of the last to get to Veracruz, being compelled to have a doctor doublecheck his wounds from the convoy attack. The medical professional had recommended bed rest of at least a few days. Alfredo politely declined. He was oblivious to the latest whereabouts of his fiancée. He had been unable to reach her but assumed that this might have had to do with the sketchy signal strength of the rural areas. He had also heard nothing from Carla but knew in advance that she was going to one of those poor communications spots in the Central American nation.

It was not until the first of the National Guardsmen entered Veracruz that the locals spoke of the nightmarish scene in the chapel on the hill. Local authorities, who had let the cartel forces go in and out of their village without a shot fired in anger, went with a pair of guardsmen to view the claims of terrified locals. Many had seen corpses deposited through violence of varying kinds, be it cartel, street crime, or car accidents. And yet, even that resolve was mightily tested when they saw her.

Alfredo looked at yet another poor wretch of a guardsman on his way to the top of the hill. He was young with a stubby beard upon his face. He was nauseous and hunched over, staring downward at nothing in particular. He was slowly breathing, trying to get his bearings as he sat on the ground, a mere twenty feet from the chapel entrance. Alfredo knew he had been inside. Nearby was another guardsman, standing firm and looking over the town from the hill. He was stern, composed, with weapon at the ready, willing and able to do what was asked of him. Alfredo knew he had not been inside.

He had to go inside; he was unable to permit himself to do otherwise. He had to see what those others had seen, yet more so. He knew her, he loved her. Alfredo felt oddly calm at the prospect, like he was somehow ignorant of what he was about to behold. He went by those who were struggling to grasp the macabre nature of the display, one of whom looked at Alfredo as he went by, trying and failing to form words of warning. Those who had not entered paid the American little heed as he went by. They knew who he was, at the least that he was on their side, and so he was not a security risk.

Hernandez walked ever closer to the open doorway, to the point where he could make out a few people going about inside the chapel. However, before he was able to enter, Captain Enrique Dager blocked his way. The National Guard officer stood in the arch of the entrance, obstructing any view of the sanctuary. Alfredo halted in his solemn walk, not particularly thrilled to see the armored law enforcer. His eyes looked sympathetic and a bit glassier than usual. During their time of planning and traveling, Alfredo had talked about his fiancée, admitting that she was performing a sort of advanced reconnaissance for him. Dager knew who it was, or at least, he was certain of her identity.

"Please step aside, Captain Dager," said Alfredo, calmly.

Dager opened his mouth but did not speak.

"I said, get out of the way."

"Hernandez," he finally replied. "Alfredo. Listen to me. You do not want to go in there."

"I have to."

"She has family nearby. We can bring them in, have them identify the body at the local morgue. You do not have to see it. You will not want to see it."

"I have to," Alfredo said. "That way, her family will not have to see her like this."

Dager paused to think about his point.

"Captain Dager, I am going to see her if I have to push you out of the way," Alfredo said, staring at the guardsman.

Dager looked down and took a breath. He nodded weakly and allowed the American agent to enter the chapel. As Alfredo looked at the captain, he saw a great deal of pity welling up from his expression. Alfredo nodded in appreciation for the sentiment. For the first time that he had known Dager, he felt some sincere concern emanating from him. Nevertheless, Alfredo was not going to be moved, regardless of the intentions that others may have for him. He was going to see what became of Marisol, no matter what.

The chapel was lit by flashlights, as the twilight fittingly made the small, sacred space like a catacomb. There were a few forensic analysts present trying their best to objectively detail the crime scene. Each of them wore business casual attire, plus a light blue bulletproof vest that covered the back and chest. They were also wearing white face masks that used two straps to be secured to their heads. One was taking the last of the photos, while another had wrapped up various pieces of evidence. Alfredo found the exercises absurd, as everyone inside the chapel and among the National Guard knew who was responsible. It was not as though the guilty party would even deny it, if asked.

Alfredo struggled to breathe as he walked into the nave, the stench of decaying flesh thick in the air. One of the forensic examiners walked up to Alfredo and handed him a spare facemask. He gave a fleeting "gracias" before putting it on. While it helped a little with the stench, the bearing significance of the tragedy was hitting him all the harder. The mask only made it harder for him to breathe, to stay steady. He nearly lost his balance at one point, but then ordered himself to have stronger bearings.

She was still suspended with rope by her wrists. When they had left, one of the cartel soldiers had secured the rope to the beam above. Many of her small body parts were gathered on the floor in a circle around her. It was a collection of fingernails, fingers, toes, and toenails. The nails had been pulled while the digits had been severed. Her severed feet and breasts were deposited on a small wooden table stationed to the left of her corpse. Her heart, liver, and both intestines were piled onto one of the chairs, stationed to the right of the corpse. There seemed to be other pieces of her scattered elsewhere, in the shadowy corners of the sanctuary. Alfredo did not go closer to look at them.

Instead, he got closer to the body, still hanging from the rope. As her feet had been chopped off, the corpse was technically suspended in the air. Her head bowed forward, the countenance hidden behind a wall of black hair. It was a particular choice on the part of the killer to leave the hair largely intact when so much else was removed. Alfredo felt an obligation, a haunting curiosity. He knew what he had to do next. Two forensic experts were still there with him. They had halted their activities to look with somber interest at the American who was beholding the dead with reserved sadness.

"Can I touch her?" Alfredo asked one of the two.

"Yes," said one of them. "We are done processing the body."

Alfredo nodded. He took hold of her hair and brushed it out of the way. What he saw would haunt him for the remainder of his days. For the first time since entering the chapel, he saw her face—what was left of it, that is. Her eyes were gouged out and her nose was cut off. The mouth was agape, with all of the teeth and the tongue removed. She did not look human. Alfredo began to feel dizzy; he had to take a few steps before he regained his solid footing. He closed his eyes, and he stroked her hair.

"You will always be beautiful to me," he said, both hands holding her bowed head. He looked passed her, beholding the crucifix that remained steadfast, and the statues of saints and martyrs on either side. Alfredo removed his facemask, no longer troubled by the thick stench of death. "Before God and these witnesses, I promise to send the devil who did this to you straight to Hell." Tears left his eyes as he spoke, the two examiners also scarred by seeing his pain. "Your suffering was brief; his will be forever."

Alfredo kissed her forehead and stormed out of the chapel.

XII.

"Una historia mas, mama," implored the little Jesús, lying in bed. "Por favor?"

"No mas historias," replied Flavia, his mother. "Tienes que dormer. Ahora."

"Okay," he relented, shifting in the small bed.

"Buenas noches, mi hijo," she said.

Jesús simply smiled and closed his eyes. After a few moments, he shifted a bit more in bed. Flavia smiled back and kissed him on the cheek. She slowly rose from the chair beside the bed, which was merely a cot with a blanket and a pillow. Flavia carefully took the skinny wooden chair and lifted it from the floor with both hands, placing it off to the side. She walked back to where her son was sleeping. His eyes remained shut, and his body was fairly still, though sometimes he shifted here and there to get more comfortable. He was a pretty decent sleeper overall, rarely waking up in the middle of the night.

As Flavia exited the impromptu bedroom, she came across a familiar man standing in the hallway. He was not wearing the usual flashy clothes that she was accustomed to seeing him adorned with. Neither did he have the swagger that had been so charming in past years. There was still the slick black hair, the small ponytail, and the mustache with a goatee. There remained the look of intensity, the eyes showing something other than sur-render. That was the man she saw that night in the short hallway at the mission near the mountains—the man who again impacted her life.

"Raul," she stated, with a twinge of formality.

"Flavia," he said, echoing the tone.

"Father Hans seems like a nice guy," she said, awkwardly changing the subject. "He let us use this place instead of putting us in a damn tent or something."

"Yes," agreed Raul. "He is a good man."

"He is," she said, then smiled. "How the hell did you two meet?"

Raul laughed at the remark as the two slowly walked down the hall, the shadows of the evening darkening their interior path. Only some dim lights were on. It was a rule at the mission, as the pastor did not want to burden the generator with too much work when so many were asleep. The hall itself had a wooden floor, but adobe brick walls. There were a few windows on one side, with doorways to small chambers on the other side. Each of the rooms had at least one person sleeping there, either on a cot or on the floor. There were only a few actual beds, and they were in the building reserved for medical cases.

"Well, how did you meet?" she asked.

"By accident," Raul explained. "When I was still a cartel thug, I was looking for a new location to set up another plantation. When I came here, I saw that there was this mission, as well as a lot of unusable land."

"And that was when you met Father Hans?"

"Yes," he said. "He was welcoming of myself and the other cartel soldiers. He even gave us a meal before we headed out."

"And you gave him money in return?"

"Later on," he recollected. "When I became more powerful. But I also wanted to keep this place a secret. I knew there may come a time when I might have to be back."

"You mean now?"

"Yes."

"He seemed grateful to see you again," Flavia observed. "You must do a lot for him."

"I would like to believe that I have," he said. "Maybe my donations are even looked upon well by the saints and angels in Heaven. Pastor Hans and them might all put in a good word for me with God."

"Bullshit," she stated, prompting Raul to stare at her. "You think feeding some poor people is going to make up for all the evil you did?"

Raul was going to argue; he was planning to shout back. He was going to list with great fury the entirety of his good works—every time he was a merciful leader, every time he approved a raise or gave a present. He was even thinking of mentioning all the financial positives he had sent to the critic before him. And yet, he was not strong enough. He was unable to shake the legitimate fear that Flavia might have been correct. As he tried to respond, only images of his criminal actions came to mind.

"I guess not," he finally stated.

"Good," she said, again surprising the former cartel leader.

"Good?"

"I think you are finally getting it."

"What do I need to get?"

"Reality," Flavia stated. "You are getting reality. It started when you lost your power, and it is getting better, every hour, I think. I mean, damn it, Raul, I am almost beginning to respect you as a human being."

"I hope so."

"You hope so," she said, then briefly chortled. "*I* hope so."

"Why do you hope so?"

She got closer to Raul, slowly and in the shadows. She looked up to him, her eyes appearing to sparkle thanks to the moonlight. Her hands slowly moved along his arms. They were alone in the hallway at that hour, standing together amid the vesper hour. The occasional rustling from one of the bedrooms and the noise of some singing bugs outside provided the calm of the moment. They were looking deep into each other's eyes, the senses of grudge and hostility melting away. She released one hand from his arm and moved her finger through his hair, slowly and with careful intent.

"I am so sorry," he said. "You were always different. Different from the others. I never saw it. Not until now."

"And I am sorry," she whispered back. "I should have made that clearer. Maybe if I had…maybe if I had…things would be different. Then and now."

"Well," he said, giving a slight smile. "At least we have now."

"Yes…now."

A door located four feet from their place suddenly opened. The two instinctively released their mutual embrace and turned to face the noise.

It was a young boy, no older than eleven or twelve, with dark tan skin and black hair. He was yawning as he walked by, barely recognizing the presence of the two grownups. Although he had yet to get his growth spurt, as he went by, it became evident that he was only a few inches shorter than Flavia. The two adults gave each other amused looks as the boy kept on walking, heading toward a bathroom across the hall. Flavia laughed a little more as he exited.

"Kids do get in the way," Raul observed.

"They have their moments," she added. "Anyway, I better get to bed."

"Buenas noches," he said to her.

"Buenas noches."

* * *

Fulgencio Brennenberg was in a clearing on that evening. He stood near a pickup full of basic supplies, including bottled water and ammunition. All of the dark-hued cars blended with the nightscape, as did the cartel soldiers who walked about or rested in similarly bleak attire. The weather was cooler than the night before, which was likely because of the higher elevation of the area. They were getting closer to the border, which was a small chain of mountains with only minor passages linking the two Central American nations. Brennenberg was able to maintain his normal breathing abilities despite the greater distance from sea level. He did not notice an increase in his usage of his apparatus. The cartel leader speculated that he had to go another thousand feet higher before it would truly influence him.

Brennenberg saw four pairs of car lights coming through the vesper and the vines. An absence of artificial illumination made them all the more obvious. The eight dots moved ever closer to the clearing, where rows of jeeps, pick-ups, and SUVs were parked. He was not concerned, as the men wearing night vision goggles who were on patrol did not sound any alarms. Indeed, the four vehicles briefly halted at the request of one of the soldiers on guard, confirming their identity and intentions before being waved into the clearing. Brennenberg watched as the vehicles emptied out, with a prominent figure walking toward him. Brennenberg likewise approached, gradually making out the countenance of Carlos Benedico, his red hair and gray mustache looking darker thanks to the evening hour.

"Señor Benedico," Brennenberg stated, formally.

"Señor Brennenberg," he replied.

"Did you bring me presents?"

"Supplies, yes," Benedico answered. "Per your request, I have given you more men, more grenades, more bazookas, more ammunition, and also some additional food and water."

"I did not request the food and water," Brennenberg corrected.

"True, but I wanted to make sure you had enough for however long this search continues."

"It will not be long," assured the cartel leader. "There are only a few little settlements left to search. We should find my predecessor very soon."

"Ojala," said Benedico, whose eyes squinted when getting a better look at the face of his superior. "Señor Brennenberg, I think you have some food on your mouth."

"Food?" asked a perplexed cartel leader, who went closer to the parked vehicle to his left to look at a rearview mirror.

"It was a smudge of some kind," said Benedico, who remained standing a few feet away. "I could not tell, but it was by your lower lip."

Brennenberg used the mirror attached to the side of the car to better examine himself. To help, he whipped out his smart phone. After pushing in the correct four-digit password, he went to a menu and selected the flashlight option. A bright beam shot out of the upper right side of the rectangular device, the little luminance being powerful amid all the darkness. As his eyes adjusted to the new light, he bent his face forward to the little mirror, seeing the mess that had gone unnoticed until the present moment. It was a reddish brown and appeared to be a bunch of little spots clustered together.

Brennenberg smiled.

"Do you see it?" Benedico inquired.

"Yes," he said, taking one of the water bottles from a stash in the parked vehicle and twisting it open. "It is not food."

"Well, what is it? Blood?"

"Yes," said the cartel leader, lightly touching the spots with wet fingers. "Are you hurt?"

"No," he assured Benedico. "I thought I had washed it all off. I guess in the excitement of the journey here, I must have not paid attention."

"So, it is not your blood?"

"It is some paint from my most recent masterpiece," Brennenberg remarked, as though he were talking about art supplies in a literal sense. "This most recent work was especially messy, yet I am very proud of it."

"I see," said Benedico, who was growing apprehensive. "Where is this, um, masterpiece?"

"I left it hanging in a church in Veracruz."

"Okay," noted a troubled cartel lieutenant. "So, um, do you need anything else from me?"

"No, I do not," Brennenberg answered. "You may return to the hacienda. Soon enough I will return with a new masterpiece, one in which my predecessor shall be the easel."

"Whatever you are going to do, you have to do it soon," said Benedico. "The other lieutenants are getting restless. And afraid. We have never concentrated this many resources into one project before. To have so many soldiers and weapons in one place, it is a point of concern. I have heard many complain about it."

"They will stop complaining when I return in victory," Brennenberg replied, unflinchingly. "They will realize how powerful I have become. As will the government of this little country. When they see how effectively I can destroy their rule, they will let me do whatever I want. With them serving as a de facto base, we can move to other nations. Guatemala, El Salvador, Nicaragua. One after the other will fall to us, as though I were Simon Bolivar, back from the dead."

"Sí, Señor Brennenberg," said Benedico, bowing his head in deference.

"I know you have doubts about what I say," he said, his eyes staring at the lieutenant. "I do not blame you. Years ago, I would have doubted everything I just said. However, this is a new night and a new man. I am that new man, and we will be that new world."

* * *

Daylight was coming over the trees and the heights. The canopy was transformed into color, the drab gray and black flowing off. A renewed chorus of bugs and birds filled the air, as did the movement of people among the mission. Young men who had been watching through the night were relieved to finally get promised rest. Many woke up feeling safer, as the enemy had not arrived at night. Assorted women prepared breakfast for most of the others, while children began to run about, beginning what was expected to be yet another day of carefree leisure at the small community.

Carla al-Hassan Sharp was awake with the dawn. Unlike the home of Flavia, she had her selection of clothes that fit. Sensing that the day may bring much conflict, she chose a darker outfit. It included dark brown pants, a thin black jacket, and a dark gray T-shirt. She also perused the available rifles. To her disliking, there were none meant for sniping. For want of a scope, she selected one of the rifles. It was not a rapid-fire weapon like the AK-47s and M-16s that were found all over the mission, but it was one that had a nice, long, smooth barrel for which a bullet could be effectively guided.

She ate alone that morning. Among those who crossed themselves before and after saying grace, she was the only one at the mission who did so in the Eastern manner. She went about the unpaved ways of the mission, noting that many of the paths were wide enough for one or two vehicles to go. With her eyes, she measured each of the buildings, thinking about which would make a good place to set up her deadly talent. The church steeple seemed like a possibility, as it did tower over most of the mission community and the valley as well. However, its exact location on the plateau was not quite right vis-à-vis the road she knew the enemy was going to take when they came.

With the rifle slung along her back, she kept looking. She went by other armed individuals, most of whom were years younger than her. It was a bit strange, seeing younger folk with assault rifles who, despite their callow appearance, were actually adults. Some nodded in respect, while a few looked lustfully at the attractive woman in their midst. Even these brave souls had their moments of moral failing. Most of those not involved in patrolling the mission went to the church. Curious, she checked her phone for more information. While the signal was still nonexistent, the device was nevertheless able to tell time. With the answer secured, she went back to looking around.

Then, she came across a two-story adobe building that looked just right. It was sandwiched between two smaller, wooden structures. The edifice served as a storehouse for supplies, namely food and medical materials. There was a pair of wide wooden doors in the middle of one side, which were locked. However, there was also a ladder along a different side of the structure, specifically one of the two broadsides. Carla scaled the metal ladder, noting that it had the additional advantage of being on the broadside that faced away from the valley where the attackers were expected to come.

She climbed over a short wall at the top and set foot on a firm roof. Carla heard a lone church bell ringing the hour for worship. She could still see a few tiny people in the distance going up to the sanctuary. Only a couple of armed individuals in basic casual attire were going about the dirt paths of the mission. Carla turned to face the great natural horizon. There was a great ocean of trees, the dark green canopy that clothed most of the world before them. Closer to the mission, the trees ebbed and there was terrain colored by varied shades of brown. Some scattered wildlife and vines were there, but nothing held dominion. Then, there was the approach to the mission, several wooden and adobe homes and other buildings, with various obstructions put up to hinder the enemy advance.

Behind her was noise. Carla did not expect a hostile party, and so the rifle remained against her back as she turned to see Torquemada ascending the ladder. He nodded in greetings, which she reciprocated. He said, "I think they are holding a mass right now."

"Well, it is Sunday morning," she said. "I had to double-check my phone."

"The days have blurred together," he observed, walking a few steps to stand beside her. He looked out beyond the mission. "This is a nice view."

"I think it will be a good place for me to situate myself when the fighting begins."

"Of course," Torquemada noted. "That is one of your talents. The long-distance kill."

"Yeah."

Torquemada paused, looked down, and then got a step closer to Carla. "She did not talk, did she?"

Carla looked back at him. "Probably not."

"We both know that it had to be a horrible death. Brennenberg has no moral scruples."

"Yeah," she said, turning to face the horizon once again.

Music was heard from the church building, which in turn was carried by the old speaker system that dotted the mission buildings. It was a guttural collective amateur singing of a hymn. Carla could make out an instrument or two among the deluge of voices, something to aid the notes of the congregation. The melody was vaguely familiar. While she normally attended St. Paul's Orthodox Cathedral back home, she sometimes went to the Methodist church that her husband's father shepherded. The lyrics were in Spanish, but the melody was coming to her. She realized that Pastor Hans likely translated it from the English, with the original lyrics having been penned in German.

"I know this one," she told Torquemada. "'Jesus, Priceless Treasure.' That is its name." She clearly impressed Torquemada. "My husband has a pastor for a father. This is his favorite hymn..." And she began to sing with her eyes closed. "'Let your arms enfold me. Those who try to wound me, cannot reach me here...Though the earth be shaking. Every heart be quaking. Jesus calms my fear.'"

"What do you think?" asked Torquemada, interrupting Carla's singing, as he wrongly assumed that the verse had concluded.

"What about?"

"Are we destined for Hell?" he asked. "Me for my sins, you for yours?"

"I happen to believe that God will forgive me."

"Can He forgive me, too?"

"Pastor Hans would be the better person to talk to."

"Pastor Hans is not here."

"But God is," said Carla. "I even believe He is with us, now."

Before Torquemada was able to reply, either in agreement or in dissent, both he and Carla heard a rumbling off in the distance. They both walked toward the edge of the building, with the former cartel leader resting his hands on the short adobe wall that kept him and Carla from simply strolling off the roof. There were a few pick-ups of dark hues, each bearing several armed men in their beds, as well as a lone standing figure manning a large machine gun bolted to the vehicle. Soon, more vehicles arrived out of the jungle, including jeeps and SUVs, also filled with belligerents. They were stopping just short of the approach to the mission, lining up as more and more came out of the growth.

"I hope you are right, Carla," said Torquemada, as people inside the mission began to react to the dreadful arrival. "I hope and pray you are right."

XIII.

Fulgencio Brennenberg surveyed the collection of adobe and wooden buildings before him. They were gathered along the side of a steep hill, which was
itself backed by ever-growing mountains. He saw the narrow road that went up
and to the side, eventually slithering along to the top of a plateau. There at the
top was the white-walled church, with what looked to be a control tower for a
small airstrip nearby. He returned his gaze to the nearest section, with obstructions like old oil drums put in the road and a couple of other pathways. His
confidence was near perfect in agreement. He just knew that Raul Torquemada
had to be there; he just knew that his adversary was trapped.

To his side, he beheld rows of various vehicles, all dark in their hues and
militarized in their purposes. There were SUVs, jeeps, and pick-up trucks.
Each was full of armed men who swore allegiance to the cartel. Most of the
pick-ups had large caliber machine guns on swinging platforms that were
bolted to the beds, with long ammunition belts attached. Some of the jeeps
also had machine guns bolted to their frames, though most were content
with using handheld firearms hanging from the sides. Many of the automobiles lacked any weaponry of their own, but nevertheless carried plenty of
armed thugs and bullets. Most of the vehicles were on, their engines creating an ominous chorus of noise that drowned out the wildlife of the jungle
behind them, as well as the church music before them.

Brennenberg was standing in the back row of one of the jeeps. Beside
him was Pedro Aguilares, standing taller than his superior. Around the
jeep were men assigned to protect the two figures. As with nearly all of the
men gathered under the leadership of Brennenberg, they wore sunglasses,

facemasks that had a black background with the lower half of a skull, black gloves, hoods, and dark clothing overall. Brennenberg removed his oxygen mask from his jacket and took several breaths. Once relieved, he put the mask back inside of his coat and then beckoned for a portable microphone. One of the masked men extended the device, which was the size of his palm and connected to the jeep via a coiled cord, so that Brennenberg could use it. He smiled, and then flipped it on.

"Bienvenidos!" he declared, his voice booming over the mission. "Y feliz domingo, tambien." He waited a few moments to see if anyone at the settlement was going to reply. Hearing nothing, he continued, "I bring you two options. Life...or death. If you want life, you will give me Señor Torquemada. If you want death, you will not give me him." He paused, waiting for a reply. Still, there was little noise. "I have checked all the other missions and villages on this side of the mountains. You have him. If you did not, you would have said so by now." Another pause, another unanswered comment. "I give you five minutes to respond. If you are quiet, I will know you chose death."

"Maybe they are unable to reply," Pedro whispered into the ear of his superior. "It is possible that they lack radio equipment."

"No, Pedro, they are able to respond," Brennenberg assured him, looking forward as he spoke. "They would have done something. Shot a flare, put up a white flag. There are many ways to speak, and they chose none of them."

"They still have time."

He looked at his lieutenant and smiled. "Yes, yes, they do."

The mission remained still as the rumbling vehicles remained in their place on the opposite side of the clearing. Brennenberg was handed a pair of binoculars. Peering through the scopes, he saw a few people walking here and there. He also saw some rustling behind a few windows. He was not entirely sure as to why there was movement, though he suspected hostility or fear to be the origin. Viewing the buildings, he saw some kids and a pair of women who looked to be their mothers, corralling them. They were rushing to one of the larger adobe structures along the hillside. Brennenberg made a mental note of their travel.

"Maybe he is not there," said Pedro.

"He is there," said the cartel leader, handing the binoculars to one of the masked men. "Otherwise, they would have surrendered upon seeing me."

"Sí, Señor Brennenberg."

"I believe five minutes have now passed," said Brennenberg, who had not been paying strict attention to the movement of time. "Send in five vehicles to my immediate right. And a bazooka team to get rid of those barrels."

"Sí, Señor Brennenberg."

Upon his affirmation, Pedro jumped down from the back row of the jeep and shouted the order to the nearest five automobiles. He also got a pair of men, one who bore the bazooka and the other who carried its rounds, to go forward. The three pick-ups and two jeeps revved up their engines, as though they were about to race. The two men with the bazooka darted about two hundred feet before stopping. One aimed the large barrel at the obstructions on the main road, while the other loaded it. When he finished his task, the loader tapped the other man on the back of the head. With a nod, he took a few more seconds to nod, and then fired the powerful weapon, which quickly blew away most of the barrier. The loud explosion ended all the music from the church, the speaker units affixed to several buildings likewise cutting off, and caused many inside the mission buildings to scream and gasp. A fair amount of dirt clouds had kicked up that quickly dispersed.

As the duo ran back to the main gathering of cartel forces, the five vehicles roared with mechanical fury and then sped forward. While they began as a row of cars, they quickly fashioned themselves into a single-file line. The motorcade got onto the narrow road that went along the mission, the front jeep easily pushing aside the remnant debris of the former primary obstruction. They went among the first several buildings with impunity, causing those who remained behind to wonder if that one show of force was enough to placate the residents. Others who had not viewed the settlement close up via binoculars momentarily wondered if anyone was even there.

Boom! A large explosion rocked the jeep at the front of the motorcade, blowing apart chunks of the vehicle and instantly killing all inside. The four vehicles behind came to abrupt stops. As they tried to figure the source of the roadside attack, another eruption came from behind, as another set of dynamite totally destroyed the pick-up truck at the very back of the halted squadron. It was then that Brennenberg and his horrified lieutenants realized that the demolitions were being actively coordinated. A couple of seconds later, several buildings let out torrents of bullets. The cartel barely fired a few shots back before they were gunned down. No one was spared.

"The bazooka team, Pedro," Brennenberg whispered in anger.

Pedro nodded and shouted at the pair of men who had earlier blown away the obstructing barrels on the road. They nodded in response and got up, running closer to the collection of buildings. They needed no further instruction, as they figured that the buildings where the gunfire had emanated from would be their target. They got within two-hundred feet of the kill zone, positioning themselves in the cleared roadway. However, no sooner did they stop to load than a lone shot rang out, hitting the loader in the forehead. The man bearing the long-barreled weapon turned in confusion, because he had heard the fall of his companion. As he stood, looking down at the body, another single shot was fired, downing the second member of the team, killing him in an instant.

"If any of you doubted their answer, you have seen it now," said Brennenberg to those around him. He then focused on Pedro. "Send in all of the first wave."

* * *

"Good shots," Raul Torquemada said to Carla.

The two were crouched down on the roof of a two-story adobe building. A short wall that lined the sides of the roof kept them hidden from the view of the cartel menace. Torquemada felt a guilty relief over the refusal of the others to not hand him over to the enemy, though it was a relief that did not come with surprise. Both of them saw the front row of vehicles that had parked across the valley push forward, coming down into the dip and then starting to rise as they accelerated toward the mission.

"Now what?" Carla asked Torquemada.

"Keep taking out any target that looks important," he said. "You know, bazooka teams, leaders, all of that."

"And what about you?"

"I need to be down there," he said. "I need to lead them."

"But Raul—"

She turned to see the former cartel leader living up to his vow, running toward the ladder in a crouched position. He swung around briefly to give a little salute before rapidly descending the rungs. Carla made no effort to cry out again, no attempt to further protest his willingness to be put in danger. In fairness, Carla wondered if there was any place at the mission that was going to truly be safe. Instead, she focused back on the approaching enemy, eyeing one of the jeep drivers who was drawing nigh. She noticed that he was a little close to one of his fellow attacking vehicles. Carla slowly moved her rifle to adapt to the motion of the target, slowed her breathing, and fired.

The shot struck the driver in the head, possibly fatally. Regardless of the lethality of the lone wound, the trauma of the impact caused him to lose control of the jeep, with the vehicle veering leftward and slamming into a pick-up truck. The crash came at such a speed as to knock the pick-up on its side, causing six men to be thrown out of the vehicle at high speed and fatally wounding another passenger. Furthermore, another vehicle that was to the right of the jeep was struck by the back end of the jeep as it turned, making that driver lose control of his car, leading it to nearly crash into yet another vehicle. That driver was able to stop his automobile, making him a perfect target.

Carla fired a new round, the shot fatally hitting the stopped driver in the side of his head. Knowing that this would, at the very least, delay several cartel soldiers from entering the fray, she turned back to the other approaching vehicles, a few of which were already engaging the armed civilians below her vantage point. Carla took aim at a machine gunner standing in the bed of a pick-up. His driver had slowed to adapt to the narrower street that they were coming upon, making him an easier target. She pulled the trigger and put a bullet in his head, causing his high-powered weapon to halt its rapid fire. One fellow, who was firing an assault rifle while crouched in the bed of the pick-up, stood to take control of the large machine gun. Carla took him out before he got a chance to open fire.

Smoke from the explosions and the many cars that had flung themselves against the mission started to obscure her vision. Nevertheless, Carla persisted in looking for any adversaries who were causing more trouble than expected for the peons trying their best to fight off a frightening army. Gunfire was the new auditory background, the wildlife of the jungle having chosen flight upon the beginning of the battle. Still, she was able to find another driver attempting to bring cartel soldiers deeper into the settlement. He was easily stopped with a single bullet, as he had already been slowed by the resistance among the structures. The two jeeps behind him came to a complete stop, their passengers getting out and firing into the walls and windows of the nearest buildings.

Carla saw another bazooka team approaching. They were trying to hide behind the pair of vehicles that crashed into each other because of her handiwork. One was loading the projectile into the long barrel. She went for the man holding the bazooka instead of the loader, putting a round through his sunglasses before he had a chance to fire. She breathed hard, as she expected to have the second man take hold of the weapon and fire it. It was an anxious moment, as her darting eyes saw other potential targets, including additional bazooka teams starting to near the mission. After mouthing the phrase "come on, come on" multiple times, the loader finally appeared, bearing the weapon. She focused on him, picking him off right before he launched the explosive into the buildings.

With that second man taken out, Carla focused in on the other bazooka teams that were getting closer. To her dismay, one of them successfully fired a shot into the mission, with an abandoned wooden building exploding into thousands of pieces. Another cloud of debris further blurred the vision of all those in the fight. While they looked for another target, Carla instead focused on another team, which was about to fire. Two good shots later and they had both perished. She returned to focusing on the team that had destroyed the wooden building. They looked to be aiming the bazooka in her general direction. She took out the man who hoisted the weapon on his shoulder, then she killed the loader before he had a chance to fire the discarded bazooka. Yet another team fired a shot, blowing up a small wooden structure that had thankfully been forsaken earlier in the day. Carla killed the loader, but the second member of the team successfully hid behind the pair of wrecked cars.

"Carla! Carla!" a puerile voice shouted behind her.

She turned to her head to see Jesús at the top of the ladder. He was smiling as she acknowledged him. As she kept her weapon pointed in the opposite direction, he jumped down from the top of the ladder. Upon hitting the roof, he stayed low, which was easy for him given his diminutive height. He was in a T-shirt and shorts, with a satchel hanging from his right shoulder. It was odd to see a kid scurrying about in a de facto warzone, running toward her with little concern about the destructive events around him.

"Jesús, por que estas aqui?" asked Carla, conveying a maternal worry about the child.

"Tiene mas balas, sí?" he asked, opening the satchel, which was filled with bullets.

"Jesús, you should be hiding with the others," Carla declared in Spanish.

"Mas balas, sí o no?" he insisted.

Carla rolled her eyes, before nodding *yes*.

Jesús smiled again and then dug his hands into the satchel. He pulled out two handfuls of rounds for the rifle. While a few of the bullets rolled along the roof, the rest were carefully placed before Carla, who took a few and loaded them into her rifle. He then dug in again and put another two handfuls of bullets before her. A nearby explosion prompted both of them to stop what they were doing and fall closer to the floor. As another smoky cloud passed by, the boy closed the satchel and Carla finished reloading her weapon. Jesús gave a thumbs up, with Carla giving a thumbs up in return. From there, he ran toward the ladder and quickly descended the rungs, disappearing amid the chaos. Carla looked again at the view of the mission, seeing more potential targets pushing against the defenders. As she picked off a few more that were overtaking a position, she saw with great frustration and dread another wave of vehicles headed in toward the mission.

* * *

Torquemada was amid the pandemonium. Around him were explosions, thickening clouds of debris and smoke, people running in various directions, gunfire and more gunfire, screams of terror and pain, the countless chippings away of adobe and wood due to constant impacts from legions of bullets, wounded and dying, and eager hearts looking to respond to the latest attack. Some were being carried, being taken to a few other buildings up the hill that were being reserved for the injured. Others were being prayed over, their ghosts having escaped their bodies amid the fight.

"Señor Torquemada!" shouted a young man, whose face was dirtied by the smoke and who carried an assault rifle at the ready.

"What is it?"

"We are going to lose the bunk room," he said. "They have almost taken it over. What do we do?"

"Blow it up," he said.

The young man nodded, and then ran back to whence he came, which was past the two-story adobe building where Carla was positioned. Going by him were a few others from that particular part of the mission, limping and covered in either blood or blackened smoke. They were weary, scared, and injured. Torquemada assumed them to have come directly from the building. As others came from either side of the former cartel leader, each with their own purpose and needed action, a great boom was heard. By this point, few fell to the ground at the tremendous sound, having been desensitized to the issue. The horizon became still darker as the thick smoke emanated from the once standing structure. Still more of that dynamite that the pastor had stored up for peaceful civilian purposes was becoming quite useful amid the battle, and quite useful in taking lives.

"Señor Torquemada," said another person, an older man who was bleeding from his arm and his side, though neither wound was particularly life-threatening.

"Yes?" he asked.

"I think they are moving more that way," the older man said, pointing to the center of the mission. "Do you think they know the road is too well-guarded?"

"I do not know," Torquemada replied. "Get some more men and go over there. I will join you soon."

"Sí, señor," said the man, who jogged past Torquemada and then started shouting at a few other armed men, urging them to follow him.

Torquemada took a deep breath and leaned against the nearest building. Yet another explosion was heard about a hundred feet in front of him. It sounded like it came from the general direction where the mildly wounded man had told him the cartel was concentrating their forces. In those fleeting moments of rest, he looked around him. Many of the faces of the determined and the terrified were familiar. They were the same people who had considered him a benevolent father figure, a patriarch who looked after his own. He recognized many of them as men and women he had known for years, who he had seen at various villages and towns, in the fields or among the loading docks. He could place first names for many of them, and some even more than that.

And then he saw a kid run by him who looked familiar. At first, he thought the child simply looked like Jesús. From behind, that boy looked like many of his peers. However, he briefly turned back, possibly because of a noise, possibly to see if Torquemada was saying something. When his face became visible again, Torquemada was quick to note the distinctive blue eyes that gazed back. He started to jog toward the familiar child, who had already returned to running the other way. Before he was able to catch up, the mother of the child emerged from a thinning cloud of debris.

"Flavia!" Torquemada shouted, the two stopping in front of each other.

"Raul, what is it?"

"I just saw Jesús running away," he explained. "He is in danger."

"Of course it was him," she said. "He and I have been making sure that everyone has enough bullets to fight those thugs."

"Flavia," Torquemada declared in disbelief. "He's your only son. You are putting him in harm's way?"

"Oh, spare me the caring bullshit," she stated. "No place is safe here. I do not want to be with all those scared old ladies and children. Jesús and I want to be useful. You need us."

"Flavia—"

"Am I wrong?"

Torquemada sighed. "I guess not."

"Well, we can't fire guns, but we make sure everyone who can is able to."

"True."

"Good," she said. "I am glad you agree."

"I love you," he said in the spur of the moment.

She simply smiled, then ran off, as she was also carrying a satchel not unlike the one that Jesús had over his shoulder. Torquemada thought of something else to say, to clarify what he meant by the simple statement of affection. However, Flavia had already sauntered off, going somewhere else in the firefight where she was needed. Torquemada spent a moment admiring her efforts, then returned to the realization that the fighting was getting worse in the center. He took up an assault rifle that was discarded on the ground, left by a badly wounded young man, and ran toward the epicenter of the gunfire.

Torquemada came upon the intense struggle soon enough, with the two sides exchanging fire over a wide dirt pathway, flanked by two adobe buildings that were being slowly eroded by the constant bullet impacts. On either side of him, Torquemada had men wearing rags or simple T-shirts and shorts or jeans. They fired shotguns and rifles, mostly just pouring out as many bullets as they could in the general direction of the hostiles. Opposite him was the enemy, donned in dark attire that covered nearly all of their bodies, with facemasks, sunglasses, and hoods worn by nearly all of them. Their fire was also more quantity than quality, but they were doing a better job of hitting people. Furthermore, they had an armored jeep that was helping them move slowly forward.

Some of the armed civilians were starting to panic; a couple of them were even turning to run when they saw Torquemada arrive. His very presence instilled some bravery, and the few planning to flee turned back to the fight. From the corner of his eye, Torquemada saw a few sticks of dynamite in an opened crate. After pouring out a clip of ammunition into the armored jeep, which was more for slowing their progress than actually stopping them, he rushed to the crate. He ignited the short fuses of the sticks and handed them out to two of the defenders. They threw up the sticks at the jeep, with them exploding overhead, causing many injuries among the driver and front passenger. Emboldened, Torquemada shouted for a charge, and the peasants followed, everyone firing at once, causing the cartel soldiers to either die or flee from the center. Another attack repulsed, and a jeep taken.

* * *

Pedro Aguilares looked on in despair. He saw the men ordered to attack the mission coming back wounded and afeard. Most straddled along the valley between the waiting vehicles and ongoing fight, with some limping along while others ran at a sprint, fearful that a single shot would take them down. Many went in a zigzag formation, in keeping with concerns over being struck from behind. One pickup came back, carrying four wounded men in the bed. Another jeep arrived, going the whole way in reverse, again laden with injured men. Many had removed their sunglasses, hoods, and facemasks, further displaying their humanity and their obvious mortality before others.

More explosions were heard off in the mission. Another building that the cartel soldiers fought long and hard to get was demolished. Tons of brick and wood collapsed on them, burying a few alive while the physical blows of the leveled structure were fatal to others. Manmade clouds continued to increase, making it a growing challenge to view the struggle from afar. Aguilares saw his superior trying to make out what was happening through a pair of binoculars, yet even he had trouble. He then looked to his right, seeing many men waiting their turn to be sent into the maelstrom. Even with the masks and shades, Pedro was able to detect the nervousness among the others.

"They are making progress," said Brennenberg, looking at the battle through the glass. "They are getting closer to nabbing him."

"Señor Brennenberg," said Aguilares, calmly. "They are putting up more of a fight than we thought. Maybe we should pull back and ask for more big guns."

"Pull back?" asked Brennenberg, turning to face the subordinate, eyes crazed with disbelief. "If we let them rest, they will only refortify. We must make an effort to push harder. They are only peons, after all. I bet most of them have not fired a gun before today."

"Con respecto, Señor, these peons are beating us back," said Pedro, fretting within over how his jefe was going to treat his audacity.

"Are we looking at the same battle, Pedro? Are we?" he asked, with hostility in his voice. "I tell you, they cannot last long. We have more men, more ammunition, and more bazookas. We will either defeat them or obliterate them. They will either break at any moment, or they will break by the evening. Either way, they will break."

"Señor Brennenberg," Aguilares began, knowing that he was not going to change the mind of his superior. "How can we make them break sooner?"

"That is a good question, Pedro," said the cartel leader. "I had assumed hitting them in the center would have broken them, because they seemed strong on the flanks. However, when I sent most of the second wave to that part of the mission, they were able to rally. So maybe they are drawing forces from the center to the flanks, and then moving them to the flanks when necessary."

Brennenberg was interrupted by an especially loud crashing noise that occurred about two hundred feet in front of him. One of the pick-up trucks had wheeled around, appearing to leave the center for the main road that went along the side of the mission. Before the driver had a chance to get onto the road, a single shot took out the driver. As he was going an especially fast speed, the turn caused the vehicle to flip over and crash into a pile of rubble. Brennenberg and Aguilares watched as a few cartel soldiers ran to the upturned car, both to protect themselves and to help the survivors out of the wreck. As one of the cartel men was trying to organize things, he was picked off by another lone bullet.

"We need to do something about that sniper," Brennenberg commented, with annoyance rather than fear. "I bet half of our losses have been from that one person."

"What do we do? The marksman is a good shot."

"Good, yes. Perfect? No," Brennenberg concluded. Again, he faced Pedro. "You will personally lead a group, consisting of both soldiers and bazooka teams. Your sole mission will be to take out that sniper once and for all. Whoever it is, they cannot hit multiple targets at once."

"Sí, Señor Brennenberg," said a solemn Aguilares.

"I will give you half of the next wave to do that little operation. The more being thrown at that side, the better."

"Sí, señor," said Pedro. "And what about the other half of the third wave? Where will they go?"

Brennenberg pondered the matter as he surveyed the destructive fighting before him. He saw the enemy successfully beating back his men at the center, though still unable to counterattack. He looked again at the left side of the mission, where a single sniper was keeping several men pinned down behind an upturned pick-up. With the aid of the binoculars, he looked again at the right side. There was little action there, yet he still saw movement. Zooming in, he saw a few more unarmed civilians. It was an older man, along with his little kids that were likely his grandchildren. They were going about from one building to another. Brennenberg felt inspired by the sight.

"I bet that is where they are," he thought aloud.

"Señor?"

"The civilians," said Brennenberg, putting away the binoculars and looking at Aguilares. "The unarmed women, children, and elderly. I bet they are held up in that part of the mission."

"Maybe."

"More than maybe," said the cartel leader, excitement growing. "We have not really gone after that part of the mission. We have yet to encounter more than minor resistance from that point. Probably because there are only a few armed men there. The people there must be the unarmed. Yes, it makes sense. I should have figured it out earlier, when I saw those kids and their mothers going off to that location." He sported a sadistic grin as he stared at Aguilares. "We will send the other half there."

"Pero, Señor Brennenberg, what good will that do? We will have fewer men to keep attacking the center and the sniper."

"They will have to move to defend them. They will have to leave their positions of protection in order to save their loved ones," said Brennenberg, facing away from Pedro. "We will have them. Finally, we will have them."

"Sí, Señor."

* * *

"Carla?" a female asked from behind the shooter.

"Sí?" asked Carla, who briefly looked to see that it was Flavia.

"Mas balas para ti," Flavia said, approaching with a satchel that included additional ammunition for the sharpshooter.

"Gracias," said Carla, who focused on keeping the cartel men below clustered behind the overturned automobile.

"Are we winning?" Flavia asked in her native tongue.

"Ojala," Carla replied.

"Adios," she said, keeping low as she went across the roof and back to the ladder.

Carla spotted the gas tank on the belly of the upturned pick-up. Knowing she needed to reload soon, she fired a shot that pierced the tank, causing some fuel to splatter. She took aim at the spot again and fired another round, this time igniting the fuel. The result was a fiery burst, which badly burned a few of the men hiding behind the vehicle and sent the rest fleeing back to their lines. With the cover of the new chaos, she ducked under the wall, which had its own bits and pieces taken out by gunfire and went about hastily reloading her rifle. Her hands were sore, and her trigger finger was starting to develop a callus. Her face was partially splotched by black smoke, while several strands of her hair had come loose from the ponytail she had tied at the onset of hostilities.

Yet, she knew she could not stop. Readying the rifle for another series of shots, she slowly rose from her crouched position behind the short wall. From there, she saw the upturn vehicle emanating a great deal of black smoke from its belly, blocking much of her view of the other side. She saw the other wrecks nearby, which had been as a result of her efficient efforts. There were many cartel personnel on foot, scrambling away from the fight. Carla decided to let them flee, as the main issue remained those who were still engaged. It was always possible that they will not fight again.

Carla went over to her right, getting up only momentarily to view things. The straightening up presented some pain, as her body had gotten used to staying in the bent position. She easily brushed off the sensations, and again went down behind the wall upon seeing hostiles along the road. From her vantage point, she saw a collection of armed peons gradually losing ground to a handful of cartel thugs. Their sporadic fire, which had claimed some casualties almost by accident, was being overpowered by the more precise fire of the enemy. A few were running away, either because they lost their nerve or were out of ammunition. They were moving up, carefully using the crashed cars for cover.

However, the smoldering shields they used to effectively stop the peons from killing them offered no protection from above. In rapid succession, Carla picked off the four cartel soldiers at the front of the advance, hitting two with head shots and the other two with body shots. The masked men halted their advance. More armed civilians came, doubling the fire of the defense. Carla picked off another cartel figure, one who looked to be in charge, before ducking behind the wall for purposes of self-preservation. She sensed several bullets lodge into the short wall, but none made it through the structure to harm her.

The gunfire was starting to die down. It seemed impossible. Screams were now outnumbering rifles. It still seemed impossible. Breathing hard, she rotated her body and slowly looked up to see what she was struggling to accept. The enemy was in retreat. As she kept peering around the area which was not blocked by plumes of smoke, she saw a cartel force that was running away from the mission. Her right hand covered her forehead as she leaned against the bullet-riddled wall. Inspired by their apparent success, she even let go of the rifle to cross herself as she kept hold of the barrier.

The rattling sound of the guns was starting to lift. It sounded farther away, more to her left. She had heard from others going by that the center had been a fierce zone of engagement. Perchance, they were starting to send even more men to that part of the mission. Or perhaps, just perhaps, even Brennenberg had finally realized his own limitations. There were some cheers nearby, apparently from the same people who helped beat back that latest incursion near the main road to the mission.

All the hopeful shouts ceased as the roaring sound of another wave was heard. With some of the smoke dispersing, Carla was able to see them coming. Believing that she had time to do so, she took some more of the bullets scattered on the roof and loaded them into her rifle. The weapon ready yet again, she peered over the wall to better examine the force that was coming. She fired a shot at one of the jeeps coming up the road but missed the driver. To her frustration, the bullet bounced off of the hood instead. Undaunted, she aimed and tried again, this time hitting the driver in the shoulder. The vehicle drove off of the road and T-boned another jeep that was coming her way.

Soon, to her unpleasant surprise, she realized that many of the mechanized enemy were coming straight for her spot in the mission. Furthermore, a few of the vehicles were carrying men with bazookas, clearly planning to get as close as possible before opening fire. Carla did what she could, given the situation. She raised up a little more, seeing faint need for the wall at that point. She fired a shot into one of the lead vehicles, killing the front passenger but leaving the driver unharmed. She fired again, wounding the driver of another vehicle. And again, killing a passenger from one vehicle that was carrying a bazooka. The figure fell out of the car as it kept moving, taking the weapon with him.

However, they went faster than before, with two of them swerving to have their broad sides facing Carla. Men got out of the vehicles and went behind the metal protection of the two parked jeeps, while three pick-up trucks sped by, raining bullets along the road and the side of the building Carla was standing atop. She tried to take them out, firing two more rounds that took out a loader from one team and a bazooka carrier in the other. However, they came with fury and fired two missiles at the building, blowing it away.

XIV.

Raul Torquemada was again leading the charge. He and about a dozen fieldhands armed with assault rifles pushed back several cartel soldiers with a cascade of bullets. Countless pieces of wood and adobe broke off from their respective structures, flying around at rapid speed, adding more ballistic danger for the masked men. A few fell, while the rest withdrew, firing their own heavy amounts of ammunition at the mission defenders. They disappeared through another cloud of smoke, which only allowed Torquemada to see the faintest traces of bodies running away from the fight.

The former cartel leader also withdrew, running back behind a collection of building rubble, a totaled jeep, and some cots taken from one of the dormitories at the mission and thrown into a pile to better provide succor to those loyal to him. There were some cheers among the victorious defenders, though they were given with less energy and less optimism. They had driven back the cartel thugs before, only to have them strike once more. Most of them were weary, many breathing hard.

Torquemada was not unscathed. He had several cuts and bruises along his upper body, courtesy of small flying debris from the intensity of the firefights. His clothes were torn in many places, the rips ranging from little holes in the fabric to gnashes around three to five inches long. Sweat and smoke caked his face and arms. His loyal followers were in similar straits, with clothes being stained with dirt, debris, and blood. Many had arms and legs wrapped in bandages or even torn shirts, usually with the crimson liquid visibly painting the cloth. And yet they stayed, nodding in approval.

Feeling that the sector was secure for the time, Torquemada walked about other paths within the settlement. He was unable to see much to his right, thanks to the two bazooka missiles that blew up the building where Carla al-Hassan Sharp had been situated. He presumed her to be dead. It was something that would have struck harder upon him had there not been so much death already on that brutal day. Despite the advances on that side of the mission, several armed peons were holding firm. It made Torquemada wonder why more cartel personnel were not being sent to that part of the mission.

"Raul! Raul!" shouted someone from behind him.

Torquemada turned to see Pastor Hans running toward him. The former cartel leader was surprised to see the peaceful cleric amid the war zone. He had ensured that Hans was hiding with the other unarmed civilians, likely helping to minister to them as that hour was especially terrifying. He was absent his usual smile, instead staring at Torquemada with a crazed look of panic. His arms were flailing, and his voice was pronounced, seeming to rise over all the shooting and screaming.

"Raul!" he declared, slowing as he got near to Torquemada. "They are attacking the women and children! They are throwing soldiers over there, where they are hiding. They must know they are there! They are attacking them!"

"I understand, Pastor Hans," said Torquemada.

"You need to go over there! You need to do something about it!"

Torquemada nodded and then rallied all the people within several feet of him to follow him. They passed the word to others, with more than twenty responding to the demand. Some reloaded as they ran, while others mouthed prayers of protection and crossed themselves. As they neared the buildings where the unarmed poor were located, the noises of motor and gun became ever louder. A few turned the corner of a building, only to be mowed down by a machine gun bolted to a pick-up truck. Others were more careful, waiting for the firing to stop before shifting ninety degrees and returning fire. The path between their present position and the densely packed buildings became a kill zone.

"Find me some dynamite," Torquemada ordered one of the other defenders.

While he waited for his command to be fulfilled, Torquemada joined four others who were using the corner of an adobe building to fire at the many cartel soldiers located roughly forty feet from them. A few others tried to cross the pathway, with varying success. A couple of them got across when the waves of gunfire were low; a couple of others were fatally riddled with bullets. After several minutes, the armed fieldhand brought Torquemada what he wanted. Torquemada lit the three sticks and, when their wicks were near the explosive contents, he tossed them at the masked men.

The explosions rocked the attackers and allowed Torquemada and his supporters to take down many with gunfire, while also safely getting across the pathway. Once there, he saw the beginnings of an evacuation, with armed peasants helping the elderly, the unarmed women, and the children to safety. Their plan was simply to move them up to the plateau, under the hopes that the few buildings up there would provide more safety. The area had initially been written off over fears that it would be the perfect place for rocket propelled grenades or bazooka salvoes to wipe out the mission inhabitants. At this point in the struggle, the defenders viewed it as the last hope for those trying to escape.

Torquemada joined those who were providing a covering fire for the fleeing civilians. The smoke was getting so thick around that part of the mission that each side basically fired at shadows in the clouds. Thus far, there were few injuries among the vulnerable that the cartel had targeted with this latest pincer. He heard screams and cries from child and adult alike as they fled to the higher ground. There were also words of assurances, from both Pastor Hans and others, encouraging them to keep moving. As more defenders ran to that part of the mission, to offer what help they could, Torquemada was feeling encouraged. Maybe, just maybe, they would successfully hold out.

And then he heard something distinct. The voice was familiar—a call of great terror. Torquemada looked to his left, near where the buildings of the settlement met a steep incline from the adjacent heights. There, where there was no escape, Torquemada saw a nightmare. It was not the masked men firing down upon a woman and her child that frightened him; it was that the woman was Flavia, and the child was Jesús. They were crouched behind an upturned pick-up truck, whose crew had been vanquished earlier in the fight. There were no trees, buildings, or other terrain to offer protection. Many sparks danced along the metal as the bullets kept drilling into the vehicle. He ran over to the sight, stopping at the end of a wall, still around thirty feet away from the cowering family.

"Flavia!" he shouted over the sporadic gunfire. "What are you doing?"

"Jesús saw some weapons here," she shouted back, pausing as more bullets struck the heavily damaged wreck. "He thought he could get them before they returned."

"Damn it!" Torquemada shouted to himself. He looked down, gritted his teeth, and then looked back at the endangered mother and child.

Torquemada asked for no help, rightly assuming that the others were too busy holding off the bulk of the force concentrated in that part of the mission. He looked up to the heavens, wondering what succor he would receive. After a couple of deep breaths, he ran toward the wrecked car. Torquemada kept his index finger firmly on the trigger, shooting over the pick-up and at the general source of the gunfire. He did not pause to aim or to see if any of his bullets were even coming close to hitting the enemy. He made it to the wreck, changing out the empty clip for a full one.

"When I count to three, we run," he said to Flavia and Jesús. "Understood?"

They nodded in the affirmative.

"Uno ... dos ... tres!"

The three got up from the wreck, with Torquemada turning to fire at the aggressors. Flavia and her son held hands as they darted for the buildings, where they were relatively safer. Torquemada was behind them, turning every moment or so to fire more rounds into the clouds, where the enemy was positioned. After emptying his clip, he ran even faster, yet was not fast enough to avoid seven shots from two different guns, which struck him in his lower back and his right leg. Blocking out the pain as best he could, he slogged the remaining few feet between himself and the buildings and fell into the arms of Flavia, as four more bullets struck him from behind.

* * *

Carla thought she was dead. She had lost all visions of the mortal world. Gone was any sense of time, and even of pain. There was only a white blank- ness, as though she was entering the very realms of glory. The last thing she recalled was being on the ladder, desperately trying to descend from the roof. Her last sight was that of the white brick wall that was in front of her, as well as the dark rungs she was holding onto as she went down. And then it all blew up, an instantaneous demise. There was no sense of present reality for those moments, those times when the consciousness was adrift and the senses muted.

Then, things began to slip back into the here and now. The whiteness that was thought to be the heavenly realms shifted around, pulsing and floating. They were as clouds, debris, and disintegrated brick in the air. A loud ringing in the ears emerged, so loud that it was to the point of hurting. Then came the sporadic gunfire, the periodic bursts of the rapid- fire weapons. Some screams and shouts, more firearms, and more rumbles of motors. Different shades were becoming clear, some darker than others. The afternoon sun was hanging over, a few beams getting through all of the thick pollution.

As the ringing started to ebb in its severity, the pain returned. Her limbs were sore, and her head ached. Littles bits of pain were felt on her arms and head, which she soon discovered were little cuts from the explosion. Her skin felt chalky, as though powdered by flour. She felt heavy weights on some of her body, her eyes adjusting enough to see that they were large chunks of wall. She started coughing excessively, nearing the point of vomiting. Instead of bile, she spewed forth dirt and dust, building pieces grounded to the level of sand pebble by the destruction, which she in her unconscious state had inhaled. Her eyes watered from the effort, some of the chalky covering nearing her lids.

Carla had been left for dead by the cartel soldiers, who did not see her amid the rubble and the thick clouds of conflict. Her coughing, while loud by most standards, was easily surpassed by the noise of assault rifles and screams. As she carefully brushed the dust away from her eyes, she saw that most of the wall facing away from the attack remained preserved. Carla knew that, had the whole structure fallen, she would likely be far more injured, or even dead. Her ribs hurt, with the coughs making them feel worse. Having injured her ribcage in the past, she did not believe them to be broken. Regardless, they hurt. Moving away the wall pieces from her body was fairly easy, though. None were heavy enough to keep her down, or even to wound her beyond bruising.

Carla saw the dark men among the thick smoke and clouds of debris. They were to her right and moving forward, apparently still facing resistance. So, the mission was not yet conquered, she realized. She moved slowly, both to not draw attention and because her body hurt so much. She looked for her rifle but did not see it. She kept searching for something to use in battle, finally finding a handgun amid the refuse. She checked the clip and saw that it still had several unfired bullets. It looked to be in working order, even though its black frame had been given a powdery layer of white.

"Vamanos!" Pedro Aguilares ordered his men. "Estamos casi alli!"

Pedro was leading his force of masked men to a gradual victory. Progress was slow, as the destruction of the building where the sniper had been caused delays for his forces as much as it caused trauma for the mission defenders. Their skeletal facemasks were proving especially useful in the chaos, as they prevented the cartel soldiers from inhaling large amounts of pollutants. The sunglasses did a fairly decent job of keeping most of the chemicals from damaging their eyes. Their opponents lacked such protections, and struggled as much to breathe as they did to hold off the enemy.

"Estan perdiendo! Estamos ganando!" he insisted, firing his share of rounds into the barely visible enemy.

Two masked men were advancing along the right flank of Pedro, trying to deliver more gunfire from the side of the road. They saw it as an opportunity, as the peons were less powerful over there. The idea held merit, as the defenders were increasingly unable to cover the full extent of the road and the remaining structures. Both men veered more to the right, getting by the bulk of the overall defensive firing line. Unbeknownst to them, however, their maneuver put them within a few feet of Carla.

Pedro quickly looked to his side to check the progress of the two masked men. It was then that he saw what appeared to be an albino woman with powdered black hair emerge by the fog of war, pointing a handgun. Before either man could respond, they were taken down, each with a shot to the side of the head. She saw Pedro and he saw her. She drew her weapon to fire, but her shots hit another cartel soldier who by chance ran between the two. Another was taken down who got between them in a failed attempt to get a shot at her. She tried to shoot Pedro dead, but her gun either jammed or ran out of bullets.

Carla saw the physically imposing cartel soldier, the one who appeared to be leading the strike force, draw his weapon toward her. She immediately dropped down for cover, painfully landing in a pile of rubble. She scratched up her arms in the process, as she heard the bullets whizzing over her. When there was a pause in the firing, she took hold of a medium-sized adobe brick and threw it at the gunman, knocking him about. Before he was able to regain his composure, she found another broken brick and hurled it at him, this time knocking him on his unprotected head.

Pedro fell to the ground, losing hold of his assault rifle. He felt the blood escaping from his forehead, where the brick had landed. It happened to be that the area of impact was with one of the jagged points of the wall piece, which further aided in wounding him. As he shook his head to make sense, he saw the ghostly woman run at him, with another chunk of adobe gripped in her hand. Her reddish eyes looked demonic, her countenance a fierce show of rage. None of the other cartel thugs were aware of her presence, as though she was a phantasm visiting only him in that wicked hour.

Carla fell upon the cartel soldier, putting her full weight upon the tackle. He grunted as he slammed back down to the broken road, debris and shell casings all over the surface like confetti from a grand party. He tried to grab her; he tried to stop the blows. However, Carla used her left arm to parry the attempts while raising the brick high above. Without any semblance of pity, she brought it down upon the already bleeding head of the foe. Then she did it again, and again, and again, crushing the face, ripping off the facemask, and destroying his once youthful features. The blows continued until his arms fell limp and his chest heaved no more. She lay on top of him, releasing her grip on the broken brick, drenched in skin and blood. She was breathing hard, sore, and coughing out more dust.

"Señor Aguilares! Señor Aguilares!"

The shouts came from the other masked men. They finally realized that the cartel lieutenant had been killed. A few of them rushed to see the woman laid over his corpse, coughing and crying. Tears came from her eyes being irritated from all the pollutants in the air. However, her body position mixed with her lachrymose appearance misled them to believe that she was a lover weeping over her fallen man. None of them had seen the sniper up close, so they were unaware that a woman had been responsible for the deaths of their comrades. For this reason alone, Carla was spared retribution. Instead, the cartel soldiers made a fighting retreat, going back to their own line of defense, which was a collection of vehicles that were either wrecked or properly parked along the road.

Carla felt hands grabbing her arms. Initially, she resisted, fearing that they were part of the cartel. Yet, when she looked up, she saw it was two men in plain clothes. Realizing they were allies, she halted her objections and allowed them to aid her travel back behind the line of defensive fire. They were also coughing and spitting, their eyes as watery as hers. One of them limped, as his left calf muscle was heavily bandaged. She was just barely able to walk with their assistance. As the guns again began to fall silent in that sector of the mission, she was put into the care of some women, who were serving as nurses.

* * *

Fulgencio Brennenberg could not believe what was happening before him. While his view of the mission was corrupted by the many thick clouds of debris and smoke, there was still enough visible to shock him. His mighty cartel army was being held at bay, with clusters of vehicles and personnel gathered at the base of the hill, exchanging fire with a persistent foe. Many of the jeeps and pick-ups that had been so successful in imposing his will on the other villages and towns were destroyed, with most of their passengers being casualties strewn along the pathways of the mission, or along the valley between the settlement and the end of the jungle, where the cartel leader stood, incredulous.

Nearer to him were more of the sour fruits wrought from his labors, as the wounded and injured trickled back to his side of the fight. Vehicles that had survived by the barrages returned full of the frightened and the hurt, the range of injury from minor to fatal. Dozens were being tended to right in front of him, with some of the cartel figures bandaging and cleaning the dark red wounds. Others gave water to those laid out along the line. Some were unharmed physically, but too scared to return to the fray.

To the right of Brennenberg was one more row of vehicles, with fresh cartel troops waiting for their turn to fight. While their countenances were obscured by the facemasks and sunglasses, many showed clear signs of angst at the possibility of going to the mission. Returning men spoke about the deadly firefights in the pathways, a sniper or two that picked off many of their number before they even had a chance at attacking the target. Rumors were already circulating that Pedro Aguilares had been killed along the main road. Trepidation was getting the better of many of them. Only the innately intimidating presence of Brennenberg prevented a full retreat from the mission.

He refused to be shaken; he refused to be moved. He was not going to let his predecessor be victorious. He had survived a wound many thought to be fatal. Months and months went by with countless figures convinced of his passing. It was as though death had vomited him out of the netherworld and returned him to the land of the living for this very purpose. His was a purpose of conquest, of spreading death and destruction to all who had wronged him and who dared to cross his way. He would be victorious, he would overcome. This was core to his drive and led him to suppress his doubts.

"They must be almost gone," he said, allowing his binoculars to fall from his hand into the jeep seat. "They cannot last much longer. They must be near death." The cartel figures around him, both healthy and beaten, turned to face their leader. He looked at them as he continued, "We almost have them. One more attack, and there will be nothing left but corpses.

One more blow, and the beast shall be felled. I know it to be true. It will happen. We will make it happen! We will!" They looked at him with dread, his confidence ever higher. He looked at the nearest cartel lieutenant. "Have the last wave go into the fight. Have them charge into the mission. Then, we shall succeed."

Grudgingly, the lieutenant nodded in submission. He rallied forth what men he could, both those who had returned and were only slightly harmed, as well as those who had yet to fire any shot in anger that day. The engines roared, the motors bellowed, and the final wave of cartel vehicles surged forward. Brennenberg breathed heavily at the wonderful sight of his dark wave pushing toward the mission. His exhaling was so intense that he had to take out his breathing mask to get his lungs back in proper working order. The noise of their prowl was such that he did not hear the compact vehicle park several feet behind him; neither did he hear the shot, though he felt a sudden jolt of pain in his right leg.

As the cartel army pushed forward, focused solely on the mission and its defenders, Brennenberg grimaced in agony and slowly fell to the ground. He turned around as he lowered himself, his back colliding with the side of his jeep, as his hand grasped the part of his right leg that was bleeding profusely. The wound was not fatal, but it did knock him down to the ground. As he recovered from the initial thrust of pain and slowly opened his eyes, there before him was an unknown man. His black hair was disheveled, as was his collared shirt and tie. He had a few small bandages on his head and hand, which had a hue that contrasted with his tan skin. His eyes were ablaze as he looked at the wounded cartel leader, keeping his pistol aimed at Brennenberg.

"Para ella," said Alfredo Hernandez. "Para Marisol."

From there, the American agent opened fire several times, walking closer to the seated Brennenberg with each shot. One bullet impacted the cartel leader's abdomen, while another punctured his chest near the healthy lung. A third hit him near the heart, while a fourth struck his damaged lung. Yet another bullet slammed into his heart, and another into his healthier lung. Each time, a thick spurt of blood jetted out of his body like a little geyser. His body gyrated with each impactful shot, like he was hooked up to an electric charger at a hospital and zapped in an effort to keep him alive.

The cartel thugs nearest to the parked jeep became aware of what was happening after the third or fourth shot, as they had been previously distracted by the powerful wave of vehicles that had passed by on their way to attack the mission. Few of them were able to lift a weapon to try and stop Hernandez, and none had the will to avenge their fallen leader. It was not that they hated him, but they no longer had the strength to keep serving him. Instead, they watched, mostly in fear, as the man who led them this far was shot to bits by the incarnation of revenge and passionate fury.

Brennenberg was still, likely dead by the time that Hernandez had gotten within two feet of him. Hernandez looked down upon the cartel leader, his pistol brought within a few inches of the bowed head of Brennenberg. Eyes still full of rage, Hernandez pressed the muzzle to the top of the hated man's head and pulled the trigger. The blast blew away most of the scalp of Brennenberg, scattering his flesh and dying most of his blond hair a bright red. Much of his cranium had been smashed by that final shot, breaking what little morale remained among those who were under his service.

"Now, you will stay dead," Hernandez declared.

With no leader to guide them and little energy to keep fighting, the criminals who watched the macabre action remained where they were, staring at Hernandez. They saw him slowly back away, vacillating between laughter and melancholy, apparently unable to choose an emotion to stick with amid the euphoria of his violent deed. After he got about seven feet from his victim, he descended to the ground, casually sitting there as he loosely held onto the pistol and kept watch over the body, like it was going to escape. There he continued to laugh and cry, to be somber and to feel triumphant.

While he struggled to decide how to handle his infliction of judgment upon the wicked, the wounded and disoriented cartel figures suddenly saw something far more dangerous to their cause emerged from the jungle growth. Scores of hummers and jeeps, nearly all of which were laden with National Guardsmen fully armed and armored, shot forth from the twisted trees and shadowy canopy. Some rang out sirens, while others immediately halted, with professional troops disembarking and quickly subduing the cartel figures who had been left behind as the last wave moved onward to the mission. What few thugs had weapons threw them to the ground and raised their hands.

Meanwhile, National Guard vehicles continued to pour out of the jungle, with the initial waves catching up to the fresh cartel soldiers who had just begun their attack. There was miniscule resistance, as they were rapidly taken from behind. Most were actually relieved to surrender, lest they be fed to the meat-grinder that was the mission defense. Those who had been fighting, stuck along the lower parts of the settlement, were quick to capitulate as well. Within minutes, nearly all of the guns were silent, as scores of masked men were rounded up, unmasked, and taken into custody.

Captain Enrique Dager stood nearby the seated agent and the fresh corpse. What blond hair remained on the shattered head was evidence enough of the identity of the man. So, he turned to Hernandez, still sitting on the ground, transfixed upon the cartel leader that he had felled. Dager did not know how to respond to the state of the American agent, knowing well what tribulation he had endured over the past few days, knowing the deep emotional pain that had come so cruelly upon him. Gradually, Hernandez turned to face the National Guard officer, giving a weak smile as a greeting.

"I did it," Hernandez said, trying to cheer himself up. "I swore to God I would do it. And I upheld my vow. While my Marisol is in Heaven, Brennenberg rots in Hell. In eternity, all has been made just and right." Dager looked on him with pity, with him suppressing tears whilst standing by the man in sorrow. For Hernandez, it came as a fusion of true happiness and absolute pain. "Justice has been served, both here and in the hereafter. That will make everything better...That will make me feel better...someday."

* * *

Carla never fully lost consciousness as she lay on the cot near the church. The moans and cries of pain were a constant noise in the foreground, while the sounds of shouts and songs of triumph were heard from a distance. Her eyes would close, time would skip ahead a couple of minutes, then her eyes would open again. They had put pillows on one end of the cot to keep her upper body partially elevated. This allowed her to breathe more easily, and to further expel more of the particles that she had inhaled during the battle. Sometimes, it was coughing that brought her back from the possibility of sleep.

Even as more people were being brought in, some so badly wounded as to be near the dominion of death, there was a newer, lighter mood. Many of the nurses were speaking happily, some even laughing in relief. A few cheered, though they seemed privy to their environment and walked away from the cots before doing so. Carla started to feel better when she saw National Guardsmen milling about. She recognized them by their body armor and helmets, bearing assault rifles in hand and pistols in holsters by their waists. A few of them wore face masks, but most lowered them when speaking to those around them. What little she caught of the conversations made it clear that victory had been won.

Carla felt at ease when the news broke, her strength renewing thanks to the rest and the intake of water courtesy those unknown kind folk who oversaw the de facto hospital. She still coughed a little as she shifted in her cot. Her eyes now stayed open, her battle with unconsciousness over. The energy of success was enough to fill her with vim. Her body was still fairly sore, especially her legs and her fingers. There was still a fair amount of dusty debris covering her clothes and some of her skin. And then, a sudden epiphany or a shock of realization; one thought dominated her.

"Raul," she said, causing two women serving as nurses to look at her. "Raul."

"Que?" the nurse closest to her inquired.

"Donde esta Raul?"

"Raul?"

"Torquemada. Raul Torquemada."

"No sé," the nurse replied, having not seen him since the fighting began. "No esta aqui."

Carla pushed herself to get up, ignoring the sore pain of her legs and the still irritated insides, which prompted her to cough some more. The two nurses started to approach, either to help her get steady or to insist that she return to the cot for more rest. Carla waved them off, eventually getting a firm stance. Still a bit wobbly, she went past the two and continued to inquire among those around her, be they other nurses, children, wounded adults, or National Guardsmen.

"Donde esta Señor Torquemada?" Carla asked a group of young people, some laying on cots, some laying on the ground, and some attending them. None knew, so none responded. She kept walking about the outdoor hospital. "Han visto Torquemada?"

"No," replied another patient leaning against an unoccupied cot, his bloodied arm in a sling. "Lo siento."

Carla walked out of the collection of wounded and started down the middle pathway of the mission, struggling to maintain her balance as the ground sloped downward. There were many people going about, including scores of National Guard units, unarmed peons who had willingly laid down their guns once their rescuers arrived, women and their children, walking wounded searching for friends and family that went missing during the chaos, and even a few unburied corpses. There was the occasional wrecked vehicle belonging to the cartel, as well as the occasional working vehicle of the guardsmen.

"Señor Torquemada? Donde esta?" she asked a group of people in ragged outfits, ranging from fairly young to middle aged. Like so many of the defenders, they were exhausted, with clothes stained by sweat, smoke, debris, and blood. "Saben donde?"

"No."

"Lo siento, no."

"No, senora. No sé."

Each of their canon of negative replies frustrated Carla. She nodded to show some respect, and then kept going on. As she continued her impromptu search, the sound speakers turned on. Somehow, some way, they had survived all of the carnage around them. Only one of the units had been taken out. Otherwise, they remained intact, the beige speakers blaring at medium volume. For some reason, whoever was in control of the system had chosen to play the Sandi Patty song for which the Via Dolorosa mission had been named after. It was a peculiar choice to Carla, but in a way, fitting.

As the lyrics described the events of Good Friday, and that dreadful walk to Calvary, she was eyeing people along the dirt path, both living and dead.

It was easier to see the paths and the buildings. Carla felt the winds as they moved in, pushing away the manmade clouds of destruction. She saw the many bullet holes along adobe walls, as well as the scant ruins of the structures that had been hit especially hard. Her limbs continued to ache as she moved on the uneven ground, her cough getting bad again. It was such that she had to stop walking, her arm touching a wall, allowing her to lean, look down, and spew out more of the particles that she was still trying to exile from her respiratory system.

"Senora, senora," said an older man, rushing to her aid. "Necesitas agua?"

She nodded between coughs. The man, who like many of his peers was dressed in an old T-shirt and blue jeans, handed her a clear, opened water bottle. After letting out a few more coughs, she tilted her head back and downed the water for several seconds, suppressing the urge to breathe let alone cough more. The nourishing liquid helped a great deal, as the cough went away with the hydration. Breathing heavily but normally, Carla returned the bottle to the stranger, who was about to leave.

"Un momento, un momento," she said, retaking his attention. "Sabes donde Señor Torquemada esta?"

"No sé. Lo siento," he stated, then kept walking.

She looked around some more; she asked some more.

"Señor Torquemada?" inquired a teenager, who was barefoot and looked to be at least four inches shorter than Carla.

"Sí, Torquemada."

"Sigueme," he said, solemnly. "Sigueme."

Carla obliged, having to walk a bit faster, as the youth was himself a quick fellow. He kept looking back from time to time, just to make sure that she was still behind him. She would smile and nod, just so she knew that she was still able to mostly keep up. Her legs seemed to have hit their peak pain minutes ago, as they felt no worse than they had before. The cough seemed to be gone, or at least, it was at a minimum. The teenager went through some rubble, going to the far end of the mission, where some sharp heights made it mostly impassable. Still, several bodies and a few wrecked automobiles were present.

And then she saw him—him and the others. Before Carla was a scene that appeared as though it was some classical masterpiece placed in the cruel modern world. There were several women and children, and a few men as well. They were found right behind him, beside him, and in the immediate background. Some were holding onto his lifeless arms; others were in prayer. A few of them had rosaries out, their fingers keeping track of which bead and which prayer was next to be made. The body was mostly undisturbed, with the departed almost looking as though he were asleep.

And yet, Carla knew that Raul Torquemada was dead. All the wounds had struck him from behind, a great deal of blood was found underneath the body. As she slowly neared the sight of much weeping and intercessory prayer, she confirmed this as there was no lift to the chest or pulsing vein in either arm. Eyelashes were still, wounds provided no more pain, and the man who was key to her operation, and had once been her great enemy, was no longer a present force on earth.

Carla's eyes glassed, and then she realized that even she was among the mourners. Wiping the tears before they could trickle down her cheeks, she saw that Flavia was beside her lover, cuddling his head and right arm in her lap. Her head had been covered and bowed, thus not revealing her countenance until that moment. Jesús was beside his mother, silently looking down at the late Torquemada. His small hands sometimes touched the chest, carefully and tenderly. Flavia saw Carla, struggled to say something, struggled to react at all, and returned to her lover like he was still alive.

Carla was struck by so much when looking at the mourners and their devotion. She was coming to terms with how she, willingly or not, was one with them in sadness. Her dolorous sentiment was not simply because her ability to lead a normal life was again dashed. She knew there was something more that grabbed at her. She truly felt heartbreak over the loss of a man who was more than she had first assumed. A villainous man whose career was one of evil, to be sure, yet a man nonetheless, who lived and loved, even if imperfectly. The wailing of the community afflicted her as much as it did themselves. The speakers sounded the bells at the end of the song, and then fell silent.

XV.

Carla al-Hassan Sharp spent the next few days in recovery. She spent the first day at a hospital located an hour and a half away from the mission. There, she received better treatment for her cuts and her cough. Most of that time passed quickly, as she was often asleep in bed. Given the sensitive nature of her identity, she was kept at a more secluded wing of the medical facility. She was neither checked in nor checked out. To the outside world, Carla had never been there. Her friends at the Agency and those in the local government collaborated on the effort, both honoring their own interests.

By the evening, Carla was well enough to travel. Alfredo Hernandez, who had occupied a different room in that one wing of the hospital, drove the car out to the airstrip in the middle of the jungle. They were seen off by a squadron of National Guardsmen, led by Captain Enrique Dager. As they boarded a single engine plane, Dager gave Hernandez a firm handshake. They were airborne by the time the stars became visible. Despite the periodic turbulence, the flight to the District of Columbia metropolitan area was successful. Hernandez returned home, while Carla was secretly checked into a local hotel. Her itinerary, mapped out by her superiors, had her in the D.C. area for another day.

It was the middle of day three that she was finally sent home. Another smaller plane was her means of travel, again keeping her from the sight of the masses. The meeting with her superiors was not scheduled until the following day, taking place in the capital of the state where her husband was governor. The days of recovery blurred together, skipping from moment to moment between rest in beds and the long flights. It was a good thing that others were overseeing her journeys, as she was barely able to keep track of each step. Thankfully, someone was always there to help.

Through all the travel, the sleeping, and the stillness, Carla was haunted. She kept thinking of the mission and what had transpired. She had failed. That was what continually came back to her, over and over. He was supposed to be with her, he was supposed to be taking these travels alongside her. He was meant to be in the hands of authorities, providing extensive information on a great criminal empire. Instead, he was buried in a simple wooden coffin in rural Central America. Carla did not expect a punishment for her failure, but she did expect things to remain the same; that was a punishment unto itself.

Everyone was happy to see her again. That, at least, was a blessing. Her grandfather and his wife greeted her at the mansion. Her husband and her daughter were thrilled as well, with the former making her feel especially welcomed that night after the little one was put to bed. When Laila awoke very early the next morning, Josiah was kind enough to wake up with her, allowing Carla more time to rest. He was doing what he could to make her start easy, from making breakfast to feeding the child. She did not talk much, yet she very much appreciated each little act of service.

Time finally slowed when she was at the office. The cuts were healed and fading from her pale skin. The ringing of her ears was almost gone, as was the soreness in her legs. That pain had been harder to beat, thanks to all of the traveling. She was well enough to dress properly, with a business casual black pantsuit and a white collared shirt. As she sat, Director Mavis Chalmers was sitting on the opposite end of the desk. It was her office, after all. Hernandez was there, as well, standing in the corner behind his boss. A few other high-ranking officials were in the room, plus others watching on a computer monitor. Some were recognizable and quite prominent public figures, while others were more shadowy yet held quite a bit of pull behind the power corridors. Carla remained sullen and detached, as Chalmers continued to explain the situation to those present in person and virtually.

"Once the assets were on location, they made contact with the target," Chalmers continued, speaking in a formal monotone. "From there, they began their plan to get the target out of the location. However, as the assets were moving the target to the point of departure, a hostile party attacked, injuring multiple assets, killing several allies, and leading our target and one of our assets to be on the run. Eventually, the asset sitting before us and the target took a last stand at a mission station. Although the asset before us tried her best to protect the target, the target was killed during the fight."

Carla felt sour over the description of her labors. The way it was coldly recited, simplified, devoid of emotion, suffering, hope, pain, and loss. She wondered about future historians who may learn of the events of the past several days, how they may likewise reutter the account with a similar detachment. Her stomach was feeling off, prompting her to cradle it with her hands, like she was expecting. She was looking down, preferring the sight of the floor and her lap to that of the major figures. Still, she kept close attention to the comments of her superior, as she continued to address the meeting.

"On paper, the mission we gave to this asset was a simple one," Chalmers continued. "It was a simple extraction of a person of interest to both our government and others. In reality, the mission experienced unexpected setbacks of a grand scale. On paper, the asset failed in her mission. This is most self-evident. Her orders were to bring one Raul Torquemada to custody, with the added benefit of his testimony bringing down the cartel that once bore his name now and forever."

A reminder, even monotonous and cold, felt hard when spoken back to her. It was an additional blow to someone already trying to recover from much tumult. Carla sighed deeply, continuing to look downward. She just wanted the meeting to be over. She already knew the end result; she already knew that her dark work was going to continue. Carla would have to again rely on constantly telling herself that her violent profession was justified, as she continued to add to her register of offenses. The sooner the meeting was over, the sooner she could get back into the ordinary cruelty.

"However," declared Chalmers, causing Carla to look up. "In reality, the events for which this asset took part in gave an unexpected series of results. Not only is Torquemada among the dead, but so is his successor, Fulgencio Brennenberg. As a result, the cartel has no central leadership. Each of the lieutenants has either lost his territory or has broken away from his peers to preserve what he has left. No one is left to lead the whole outfit. Combined with their egregious losses at the skirmish at the Via Dolorosa Lutheran Mission, the cartel has effectively ceased to exist.

"This means that we are presented with a paradox of sorts. While Torquemada was not safely brought to us, the ultimate goal we had in taking him into custody has been fulfilled. And so, in an odd way, the asset before us, Mrs. Carla Sharp, has succeeded in her duties and has been integral to restoring order and stability to an entire global region. If any one of us could put such an achievement on our resumé, we would think nothing of retiring. Indeed, we would want to, as we knew we could never best such an accomplishment."

Carla perked up, her back straightened, and her stomach settled. Suddenly she felt a well of hope within her, growing as it were when her distant hopes became reality.

"And so," concluded Chalmers. "I have decided that our asset, Mrs. Carla Sharp, shall be granted her indefinite transfer to the FBI. I believe it would behoove us to have her leave the Agency on exceptional terms."

As Carla became openly thrilled by the news, Chalmers signed the paperwork. A couple of others in the room co-signed it, then Carla happily put her name to it. From there, Chalmers scanned the document so as to create a digital copy, which was sent to the various figures virtually attending the meeting. Chalmers cracked a faint smile as she gave her former subordinate a copy of the agreement. Carla nodded in appreciation, lovingly holding the document of freedom.

"Well, um, if my husband were here, he would mention that old hymn, 'God be with you till we meet again.'" She stood up, holding the paperwork with both hands. "I guess, then, I will say the same: God be with you till we meet again."

"And with you, Carla," said Hernandez, happily shaking her hand, with others in the room following suit.

* * *

Carla struggled to believe it was real. Every time she grasped it, it became unbelievable. Then, she would look down at the paper in her hand, read the same lines, and draw the same wonderful conclusion. There was relief and there was joy; there was peace and there was comfort. Every time she relearned the good news, she was again thankful to God for her deliverance. She was also thankful for being the only person in the elevator, which slowly pulled down to the parking garage. That way, she could pace around in celebration, continuing to be openly ecstatic about what had come to pass.

The lift finally halted its descent, taking its usual long moments before finally separating its reflective silver doors. With a grunt, the way was made clear, and the heavy barrier parted before her. Carla put herself into proper order before the doors opened, lest she be too unprofessional for anyone coming into the office complex from the garage. Then again, she also wondered why that would even matter, as she was not planning to make any return. Regardless, no coworkers were waiting when the elevator allowed her to exit. She entered in a small room with glass walls, a single door, and white beams connecting the panes. Beyond this little vestibule was the parking lot.

It was there that she saw three black jeeps with tinted windows lined right by the curb leading to the small room with the elevator. Present was the usual security detail, with armed personnel present in all three vehicles. Waiting outside of the middle jeep was none other than Josiah, curious and in business casual. She smiled at him and rushed to embrace her husband. His curiosity became surprise. They kissed as well, her excitement being enough to warrant both sans explanation.

"Good news, I assume?" he asked.

"It is over," she said. "I think it is finally over."

"They are letting you go?" inquired Josiah.

She smiled in response.

"Well, then, this is a day of celebration."

"Yeah."

A gentleman, he opened the car door, allowing his happy wife to enter the vehicle. As Carla entered, she saw a little girl buckled into a car seat attached to the middle of the row. Laila saw her mother entering and gave a mostly toothless smile. Josiah went along the other side of the jeep and entered through the opposite door. With their belts fastened and safety confirmed, the security pulled out of the garage and headed at decent speed back to the mansion. Carla spent most of the ride playing with her daughter. She was so happy, so content, and so hopeful for a better future in a more peaceful world. For the first time in the storm and stress of her adult life, such a hope was actually possible.

About the Author

Michael Gryboski was born and raised in the Washington, DC metropolitan area. He graduated from George Mason University with a Bachelor of Arts and then a Master's, both in history. He previously had seven novels released by the small California-based publisher, Inknbeans Press. In addition to writing fiction, Michael also writes news articles for an online publication based in DC, as well as other works including church hymns and the occasional opinion piece. Michael would rather be correct than widely accepted.

Feel free to follow Michael on social media at the following accounts:

- www.facebook.com/MichaelCGryboski
- www.x.com/MichaelGryboski
- www.instagram.com/michaelgryboski

Coming Soon

Carla will return next year in
CARLA: THE CROSSOVER

www.ingramcontent.com/pod-product-compliance
Lightning Source LLC
Chambersburg PA
CBHW050342030726
47503CB00008B/2566